CLOSE AND DESTROY

A NOVEL BY

TOM MARSHALL

Copyright © 2024 Caribou Media Group, LLC

All rights reserved. No portion of this publication may be reproduced or transmitted in any form or by any means, electronic or mechanical, including photocopy, recording, or any information storage and retrieval system, without permission in writing from the publisher, except by a reviewer who may quote brief passages in a critical article or review to be printed in a magazine or newspaper, or electronically transmitted on radio, television or the Internet.

Characters in this book are fictional. Any resemblance to actual persons, living or dead, is coincidental.

Published by
CARIBOU

Caribou Media Group, LLC
5583 W. Waterford Ln., Suite D
Appleton, WI 54913
gundigest.com

To order books or other products call 920.471.4522
or visit us online at gundigeststore.com

ISBN: 978-1-959265-40-5

Edited by Ben Sobieck
Designed by Gene Coo

Printed in the United States of America

10 9 8 7 6 5 4 3 2 1

DEDICATION

To everyone who read chapters, argued plot points, answered technical questions, or let me fold their life experiences into this otherwise fictional work. Thank you all.

— Tom Marshall

FOREWORD

By Ric Prado

As an avid reader and now a *New York Times* Bestselling author of *Black Ops: The Life of a CIA Shadow Warrior*, I have learned to truly enjoy historical fiction. These are most often stories based on real life experiences, composed to both instruct and entertain. In many cases, these stories are altered just enough to meet the requirement many of us face of clearing our literary works through our professional overlords for the "protecting sources and methods." In my case, CIA. In Tom Marshall's case, DoD ... and many of his other experiences with USG, "3-letter agencies."

As much as I enjoy historical documents, they often delve into academic minutiae meant more to obtain three college credits than for educating while entertaining. This is why I find *Close and Destroy* such an enjoyable education of complex topics few ever analyze, much less understand. Most importantly, what is the source of the author's story? What gives him or her the insight to compose a novel? When they add feeling, atmospherics and facts that blend to transport the reader into the story, their goal is accomplished.

Great writing can be identified in several categories. For example, we have novelists who craft romance or Western novels. Then there are novels written by great researchers such as Tom Clancy. But novels written by authors who witnessed firsthand the historical facts, the story within the story, are the ones that I'm most inspired by.

It is in the latter category that Tom Marshall excels. Tom is a warrior. He's a combat veteran and one of the most respected gun gurus in the country. His service in the Merchant Marine, U.S. Army, and as a contractor in the intelligence community all provide depth and grit to his storytelling skills. And while this work is fiction, I know this story is derived from his and his teammates' experience serving overseas.

Through his prolific work at *RECOIL Magazine*, Tom has also rubbed elbows with the likes of Special Forces legend Sergeant Major Billy Waugh, Air Force Pararescue icon Chief Master Sergeant Wayne Fisk, and many others. These are all reality-based sources of special missions from diverse services in historical battle zones. Tom's sources are not found in libraries, they are acquired by direct contact with heroic figures whose trust Tom has earned, both by his own service and by documenting the stories of our heroes, lest we forget.

Another strong suit of Tom is his intellect and grasp of history. In *Close and Destroy*, Tom delivers a thrilling read that sensitizes the reader to geopolitical complications that permeate war. From radical religious zealots, many sponsored by state governments, to international powers such as the Chinese, Iranians and the Russians who utilize "militias" to carry out their wars with "plausible deniability," there are people and factions that demand our understanding. My hope is that Tom's inaugural novel helps shine a light on such complicated interactions.

Ric Prado, former CIA Senior Operations Officer
Deputy and Plank Owner of the Bin Laden Task Force
Chief of Operations in the CIA's Counterterrorism Center
(CTC) during Sept. 11, 2001

"THE MISSION...IS TO LOCATE, CLOSE WITH, AND DESTROY THE ENEMY BY FIRE AND MANEUVER, OR REPEL THE ENEMY'S ASSAULT BY FIRE AND CLOSE COMBAT."

MARINE CORPS REFERENCE PUBLICATION 3-10A.4
<u>THE RIFLE SQUAD</u>
REVISED, AUGUST 2020

PROLOGUE

HILTON PIERCE
CALLSIGN "ALLEY CAT"
RECCE TROOP – WINDSOR KRAFT STRATEGIES
TARKENT INTERNATIONAL AIRPORT
TARKENT, DARISTAN
1540 HOURS, LOCAL

Through the darkness, Hilton felt the afternoon sun against his face, bright and brutal. The sour, peaty stench of unwashed people—punctuated by the sweet chemical tinge of burnt explosives—filled the front of his skull. It wasn't until someone stepped on his ankle that his eyes snapped open in a bolt of pain. That's when he realized his ears were ringing—again—and the world was sideways. All he could see were smears of pasty gray muck and brown, sandal-clad feet.

Still in the fetal position, Hilton's hands clawed for the hem of his button-down, plaid shirt. In a motion rehearsed thousands of times over the last decade, his left hand hiked the shirt up as his right snatched a Staccato HD pistol out of the holster tucked into his jeans just behind the zipper. A chorus of screams and the intermittent popping of AK-47 fire overtook the ringing in his ears.

Holding the pistol tight to his chest, Hilton rolled to all fours, then reared back on his heels before clamoring to his feet in a low crouch. He craned his head to look over one shoulder. Behind him was the airport's pedestrian gate—an earthen wall interrupted by chain link fence, shielded by a line of American paratroopers from the 82nd Airborne. A herd of Daristani civilians crashed against their riot line like waves on the shore. Already desperate to flee their collapsing country, the explosion in the crowd rocked them forward en masse against the group of young soldiers. On the walls above them, more paratroopers huddled behind their M4 carbines and M240 machine guns. Some fired short strings over top of the crowd while others swept their muzzles frantically back and forth, unable to shoot without killing innocents.

Hilton's head whipped forward, following the gunfire. At the back edge of the crowd was a shallow, scorched crater where the suicide bomber had detonated. A macabre confetti of blood and viscera scattered around the charred cement. Further back, across the street, a squad of black-clad insurgents with AKs fired wildly toward the gate.

Hilton pushed his way through the crowd, stepping over fallen bodies shot or trampled in the panic. Once he was on the edge of the chaos, Hilton leveled the Staccato, placing its red dot sight over an insurgent fumbling to reload his AK. He let out a slow breath and pressed the trigger four times in a row. Just as the insurgent started to collapse, someone burst out of the crowd and grabbed Hilton's pistol, wrenching it out of his grip. As Hilton scrambled to put space between them, the man raised a large screwdriver, its slotted head sharpened to a crude point. Hilton shoved the man away from him and back-peddled, hands digging under his shirt once more.

The man regained his balance and charged Hilton with the screwdriver, but Hilton's hand came back up with a double-edged Contingency dagger just as the two collided like linebackers. Hilton went down on his back, and the insurgent plunged the screwdriver down into his chest. The point of the screwdriver skipped off the front plate of Hilton's body armor—hidden under his shirt—and sank an inch deep into the edge of his pectoral muscle.

Hilton rolled into the stab wound, then back the other way, burying his knife deep into the man's armpit in a backhanded stabbing motion. The angled point of Hilton's dagger severed the man's brachial artery. Hilton pulled the knife out and stabbed again, this time slamming his blade into the side of the man's neck. Instinctively, the man grabbed Hilton's forearm with both hands and pushed the blade out. A pulse of bright, red blood sprayed across Hilton's face as the man collapsed on top of him, gurgling and wheezing frantically as blood from the severed vessels poured into his lungs. Hilton bear-hugged the man and rolled them both over.

Now on top of his attacker, Hilton stabbed him directly through one eye, dropping his full bodyweight onto the pommel of the knife. The man let out a feral wet scream. Hilton heaved downward again, using his armor plate to hammer the knife through the man's orbital socket. The scream stopped short, like shutting off a light switch.

Hilton leaned back, placed a knee on the man's chest, and pried the knife free. He sheathed the blade on his belt and climbed off the corpse, scrabbling around on all fours to find his handgun as more bullets snapped overhead.

DAY ONE

SEVENTY-TWO HOURS EARLIER

**VIKTOR
PROVINCIAL POLICE STATION
HAFIZA, DARISTAN
0520 HOURS, LOCAL**

Viktor massaged the stubble on his cheeks with calloused hands that bore scarred knuckles and nails bit to the quick. He swept them up his face, then back down through stringy, shoulder-length hair. Out in the street, sporadic single gunshots pecked holes in the otherwise vacuous calm inside the police station. Flat, gray light gathered around the windows, illuminating trails of spent rifle casings fanned out across the floor and shallow puddles of congealed blood. He glanced out the window into a mountainous horizon that faded from blue-black to yellow-gray. Checking his Vostok Commander watch, he sighed as fatigue from the night assault crept into his joints. The black and red bands alternating around the bezel had seen better days, flecks of each color chipped down to the bare metal. The lens was scratched, and a little foggy from time, obscuring some of the fine hashmarks on the face. But the CCCP in tiny letters between 5 and 6 were still clearly visible. According to the mechanical hands, it was almost half past 0500.

The entire station, what was left of it, reeked of combat. The acrid, metallic residue of American incendiary grenades cut through the coppery tang of spilled blood and chalky-sweet scent of burnt gunpowder. Powdery wisps of it still hung in the air, illuminated like ghostly tendrils by the pre-dawn light. When his men had made their final charge forward, the Americans fled with their dead-or-dying local guerillas and attempted to burn the building down. Instead, the thermite grenades had only scorched furniture and floor tiles. Everything in this part of the world seemed to be built from earth or stone, which kept the fire risk relatively low.

He perched himself on the edge of one of the desks, propping one bootheel up and letting his other leg hang free. He reached down toward the propped-up boot, to a small rectangular pocket just above the hem of his pantleg. The pocket placement would be counter-intuitive to regular folk, but they were now commonplace on combat pants and battle fatigues like the ones he was wearing. The man had seen many American soldiers use this pocket to store tourniquets. He unfolded the top flap and pulled out a pack of Apollo-Soyuz cigarettes.

He heard fast footsteps as a young boy—not more than 14—rushed to cross the room, slipping on loose shells twice before he got to the long-haired man. The kid's camouflage uniform was a size too large for his malnourished frame, and the AK slung across his back looked like it might bruise his ribs if he ran too fast. He spoke a broken mix of English, Russian, and Daristani – none of them with any real competency. But as interpreters went, it was the best that Viktor was going to find.

"Mister Mustorstik—"

Viktor shook his head, lighting his cigarette with a

sour face.

"Nyet, nyet," Viktor said scornfully. "Musorshchik… Mu-sorsh-chik. No mister."

The two of them had cobbled together a system that somehow worked even as they rotated from Russian to English to Daristani without rhyme, reason, or warning. The kid repeated it slowly, still wrong, then continued in English.

"There are still prisoners left. Six of them."

"Daristani prisoners?"

"Da." The boy confirmed

"Policemen, or mercenaries for the Americans?"

"I am unsure."

The man didn't ponder.

"No prisoners," Viktor said tersely.

The boy furrowed his brow, looking into the man's eyes. Even though he'd been in several battles, he was still too young to understand the implied command. But he was also smart enough not to make the lanky, long-haired foreigner repeat himself. He turned around to walk out of the building when the man whistled to him.

"Bring me all the five-four-five," the man said.

This time, with no other option, the boy put his hands up in a shrug. The man let out a hard groan. He snatched a loaded AK magazine off his desert camo plate carrier, using his thumb to strip a single 5.45x39mm round off the top of it. He tucked the mag back into its pouch and threw the loose round at the boy, who missed the catch and chased it across the floor before crouching down to dig it out of a pile of spent brass.

The boy stood up, holding the round in front of his face. The man told him, "All the ones that look like that."

Smoke puffed out of his mouth with each word as he spoke around the Apollo-Soyuz clamped in his teeth. The boy nodded vigorously and ran out of the building, restoring quiet to the room. Viktor puffed his cigarette in silence, until six more gunshots rang out in the street.

A minute later, a much older man came in. He walked slowly, with the patience and confidence that comes from reaching old age in a war-torn world. His long white beard draped down his chest. He wore loose-fitting pants and a long button-up shirt with floppy sleeves and wide cuffs. Over his shirt, a Chinese Type-86 chest rig—heavy with AK magazines and a pair of Russian F1 grenades. Sharp blue eyes set deep into his gaunt face, skin the color of cigar leaf stretched against high cheeks and hard jaw. The long-haired man touched his chest with his right hand.

"Abu Ansar," he said.

The older man touched his own heart and gave the slightest of nods.

"Viktor. We have done a good thing here."

"We still have a lot of work to do." Viktor tucked a few strands of stringy hair behind one ear.

"This is true. But we are finally seeing the Americans face-to-face, and they are running."

Viktor knew the Americans hadn't run so much as fell back from an untenable position, but he allowed Ansar to revel in the symbolic conquest.

"You need to leave men here to hold the police station, and not just a couple. At least fifty, with trucks and heavy weapons."

Ansar shook his head.

"We have much ground to take. I cannot leave that many."

Viktor pulled the pack of Apollo-Soyuz out of his pants pocket again, shaking another one loose as he spoke. "That's exactly my point. We have much ground to take. We don't want to have to come back and take the same ground a second time."

"You think the Americans will fight for this place? It means nothing, in the end."

"I hope they do. It will tie them up as we move forward."

Ansar mulled over the points, then nodded his head in concession. "It will be as you say. I will leave the men. American soldiers are young and stupid. It is likely they will waste more lives to capture this place again. We've insulted them."

Again, Viktor understood something Ansar did not. These particular Americans were not young or stupid. They weren't even soldiers. They were contractors.

Seasoned, well-trained, well-equipped contractors with the silent backing of their government's most powerful agencies. Just like him.

"There is another thing," Ansar said.

Viktor raised his eyebrows in acknowledgement as he cupped his lighter around the end of the cigarette and puffed it to life.

"The tape. We will release it tonight," Ansar said.

"We talked about this," Viktor said in frustration.

"You said you wanted to surround the capital first. That could take another two weeks."

"I have conferred with my lieutenants."

"Lieutenants? You mean Mirwan?" Viktor struggled to conceal his contempt.

"He is my most trusted advisor."

Viktor shook his head, smoke swirling from the end of the Soyuz as he did.

"He was your advisor when the Americans came in and banished you from your own motherland. How did he help you then?"

"That was, how do you say…" Ansar stroked his beard as he searched his mind for the phrase. "…a strategic withdrawal."

Viktor took a hard drag from the cigarette and pulled it from his lips. He savored the harsh smoke in his mouth for a moment before inhaling it deeply.

Mirwan Maliki was, in Viktor's estimation, a hot-headed idealist with no knowledge of strategy beyond an intuitive penchant for bold-if-not-foolish battlefield maneuvers. While Viktor held a reputation for temper among his own men, he was also classically trained at the military academy of Frunze and believed in a rigorously methodical approach to warfare. He also understood that Al Badari's tribal upbringing relegated Viktor to a useful outsider, where Mirwan was a trusted confidant.

"Why?" Viktor asked sharply. "Why the change?"

Ansar's blue eyes narrowed sharply, offended at the prospect of being challenged—particularly by an outsider. But he conceded.

"If we focus all efforts toward a direct attack on Tarkent, we will capture everything of importance in a single strike. After this, the far provinces will fall in line. There has not been violence inside the city walls of Tarkent for several years. They are complacent. The type of siege you are suggesting is exactly what the West will expect us to do."

This time, Viktor gazed hard at the older man. They both knew that accusing Viktor of playing directly into NATO's expectation was tantamount to insult. But Viktor also appreciated the rationale behind the change. It was better thought out than most of Mirwan's previous plans.

"Cut the head off the snake," Viktor said to himself.

"As you say," Ansar agreed.

Viktor rubbed the back of his neck with one hand, cigarette pinched in the other.

"Da, I will have the tape released today. Where is Mirwan now?"

"Nhahrullah. But his fighters are already inside Tarkent, awaiting orders."

"They won't be waiting long."

CORRINE MACKENZIE
BOSTON, MASSACHUSETTS
2200 HOURS LOCAL

Corrine adjusted the weight of the messenger bag on her shoulder and glanced around anxiously. Boston-Manchester Regional Airport bustled with people. For a late arrival halfway through the work week, it seemed unusual. The unintelligible thrum of a hundred conversations reverberated through the terminal as she waited impatiently in line to sign for her rental car. A large, flat-screen TV hung from a bracket over the strip counter of rental company desks. She couldn't hear the talking head on the screen, but she was close enough to read the closed-captioning subtitles:

[The Secretary of Defense maintains that Daristan's government forces are robust and capable, and it's time for them to take the lead in the defense of their homeland. But critics are skeptical, claiming that Daristan's military is rife with corruption, incompetent, and unmotivated to fight. Some of these statements have even come from the Secretary's own leadership team at the Pentagon. Just hours ago, insurgent forces launched a massive attack against a regional police station outside the small town of Hafiza, about 200 miles west of the capitol city of Tarkent. Some US military and political leaders are advocating for continued involvement in the conflict, citing intelligence reports indicating that the Al Badari insurgency may also be receiving assistance from foreign governments, though no evidence to support this has been—]

"Ma'am!"

Corrine snapped her head away from the screen to see she was next in line. She stepped up to the counter, placing her driver's license and credit card down on the counter. The rental clerk took both and began entering information into their computer.

"You guys are really slammed today," Corrine said.

The clerk replied without looking up from their computer. "Yeah. Lot of military folks coming through this week."

Corrine leaned forward an inch as she said, "Really? Military?"

The clerk handed Corrine her license back and swiped the credit card through a payment scanner as he continued. "All coming back from Daristan, from the looks of it. I guess it's finally over."

Corrine nodded her chin toward the television. "Not quite yet."

The clerk handed her credit card back. "We're down to cargo vans and sports cars. Need a cargo van?"

"Definitely not," Corrine replied.

The clerk placed a set of keys on the counter and smiled. "I figured. Turbo-charged Mustang it is. Space

C-7, out that door and to the left."

"Thanks," she said absently. She hefted the messenger bag, shifting the weight on her shoulder again, juggled the rental keys from right hand to left, then fished her phone out of the pocket of her jeans. She dodged and squeezed her way through the crowd, face down in her phone as the automatic sliding doors opened out onto the rental lot.

Her thumb skipped hurriedly back and forth across the keypad. Corrine's mental math with time zones was clunky, but she felt pretty sure it was too early to send a text all the way to Daristan. It was not, however, too late to send one to Virginia.

JACK YOUNG
WATCH CAPTAIN
GLOBAL OPERATIONS CENTER - WINDSOR KRAFT STRATEGIES
CHESAPEAKE, VIRGINIA
2206 HOURS, LOCAL

Jack stood tense in the basement of Windsor Kraft headquarters. His eyes darted back and forth across the massive, flat-panel TV showing live video from over the city square. The video feed, courtesy of a Reaper drone doing lazy circles miles overhead, was in two-tone thermal display and had no sound.

What *did* have sound was the screen behind him locked on one of the 24-hour news networks. A female broadcaster, in her rehearsed stage voice, was saying the same shit everyone else had been saying for days.

"…The global community has been caught off guard with the speed at which Ansar Al Badari's insurgent forces have reclaimed massive swaths of the country which took NATO, and then the UN, over a decade to liberate and stabilize. Years of tense negotiations, a looming American military presence, not to mention the tens of millions of dollars spent to build up regional infrastructure, install free government, and train and equip a military to defend it, is quickly looking like a Ponzi scheme investment of money and blood for the majority of the western world. As the fundamentalist Al Badari continues to capture outlying rural provinces, the elephant in the room remains: what will become of the Daristani capital of Tarkent?"

Jack turned his head halfway over one shoulder.

"Holly," he said softly, "can we mute that?"

"Of course," the younger woman said with relief. She too was exhausted by the IV drip of apocalyptic commentary from Beltway blowhards who'd never been closer to combat than an evening drive through Prince George County.

Holly leaned back in her plush leather office chair and rubbed her temples. The windowless basement of Windsor Kraft headquarters had stopped being her office and started being her home four days ago. The Global Operations Center, abbreviated GOC but pronounced "jock," was the technical nerve center of Windsor Kraft operations worldwide. Rows of desks, banks of high-def flat screens, expensive swivel chairs, stacks of servers and hard drives looked more like ground control for a space mission than a warfighting hub. Scratchy, chocolate-brown carpet covered the floor and bottom half of all four walls, which helped soak up the harsh fluorescent lighting and the impact of Jack's constant footsteps.

Holly guessed he paced a mile or two per day, back and forth across the GOC's carpet, since Al Badari started his push to reclaim the country last week. Other support staff at the desks around her monitored smaller

Windsor Kraft missions in Africa, Eastern Europe, and Latin America. But right now, the eyes of the world—and of Windsor Kraft corporate leadership—were fixed on the disintegrating skeleton state of Daristan.

Holly's phone vibrated in her pocket. She pulled it out just far enough to glance down at the text message.

Any word?

Holly's eyes darted up to the drone feed. The Reaper's camera focused on a bustling sidewalk in Tarkent's diplomatic district. It was just past six in the morning there. Among the rising momentum of morning bustle, a single man sat at a patio table of a local café. The man looked up to the sky, seeming to stare directly into the drone's camera for a moment before dropping his head to drink from a cup on the table in front of him. Holly's thumb darted back and forth across her phone screen as she snapped out a response.

He's having breakfast.

The reply text popped up almost instantly on Holly's phone,

Smile at him for me. :-D TTYL!

Holly tucked the phone back in her pocket. She watched the man on the feed unfold a newspaper and discreetly touch his torso as he shifted in his chair. Even from across the planet, Holly knew he was adjusting the pistol under his shirt. She raised her chin ever so slightly and smiled at the screen.

HILTON PIERCE
CALLSIGN "ALLEY CAT"
RECCE TROOP - WINDSOR KRAFT STRATEGIES
TARKENT, DARISTAN
0612 HOURS, LOCAL

Hilton took another sip of tea before placing the small glass down on the table in front of him. Even the chai was shit in this country; simple green tea loaded with an ungodly amount of raw cane sugar. Not that Hilton was Epicurean out of spite—not when he tucked a $3,000 handgun into $20 jeans. No, the flavor lacked the spice and complexity of chai he'd had in Mumbai or Baghdad. It was, instead, a vehicle for sugar and caffeine. He wouldn't miss it when this was all over.

Morning prayer call blared over the public speakers hung from power poles across the city, mingled with the sounds of clanking dishes, passing motorbikes, and sidewalk chatter. In this part of the city, occupied by battalions of diplo staff, journalists, contractors, and foreign businessmen, it was no more significant—and no less irritating—than the persistent buzzing of black flies that hung over the back alleys and sidewalk drainage canals.

Hilton watched a Hilux pickup truck roll past. The bed was loaded with half-a-dozen local commandos in khaki fatigues, and a pair of Windsor Kraft contractors clad in their company-issued 5.11 uniforms. Windsor Kraft's

Combat Advisory Troop was responsible for training and directing the indigenous commando units of Daristan's mostly democratic government.

But not Hilton. As part of the company's low-visibility reconnaissance, or "Recce" troop, he wore plainclothes, with just his Staccato 9mm and a clear squiggly earbud running to an encrypted radio on his belt. In the States, his outfit would have screamed tactical wannabe, but in Tarkent's expat zone it was par for the course: trail running shoes, jeans, button-down flannel shirt, Oakley shades.

Hilton lazily turned the page of his morning paper, the American military's *Stars & Stripes*, as a belt of machine gun fire rang out in the distance. Nobody on the street so much as turned their heads toward the shots.

A teenage girl approached the edge of his table and refreshed his cup with a pour of steaming chai and two heaping spoons of sugar. She looked down at the table to avoid eye contact, as was customary in these parts.

"Thank you," Hilton said quietly. The girl nodded and scurried off.

Moments later, a young, dark-skinned man sat down across from him. He wore jet-black hair, a manicured beard, aviator sunglasses, and an outfit like he just came from a techno dance club on the southern coast of Spain. He looked up and snapped his fingers, causing the girl to materialize with another cup, which she placed in front of him and filled it as she did Hilton's. When the girl left, a big smile spread across the man's face.

"Hilton! A blessed morning to you," the man said.

Hilton couldn't help but grin. "And to you, Daoud."

Daoud leaned in close and looked around furtively, like he'd probably seen in a spy movie. "Not good news, sir. Al Badari has made great progress in the south and west."

Hilton let out an exasperated breath as he put down the newspaper and pinned it with his glass. "So I hear."

"Many generals still believe he is the rightful ruler of the country. They think if they align with him now, he will honor them when he takes over."

"If he takes over," Hilton corrected.

"I don't know, Hilton. The American military has already shut down important bases around the country. They are no longer fighting alongside us."

"The military isn't all gone away yet. And we're still here," Hilton said by way of consolation.

Daoud nodded. "I know this. But is it enough?"

Switching gears, Hilton said, "Show me."

Daoud pulled a small square of paper out of his shirt pocket, which he unfolded several times to splay a full-size map across the table.

"There was a large battle last night. Here," Daoud pointed to a spot on the western edge of the map. "In Hafiza. Do you know this area?"

Hilton knew it. It was Jameson's AO.

"How bad was it?" he asked.

JIMMY TOOMS
CALLSIGN "JAMESON"
COMBAT ADVISORY TROOP – WINDSOR KRAFT STRATEGIES
HAFIZA, DARISTAN (350KM WEST OF TARKENT)
0618 HOURS, LOCAL

Jimmy chugged half the lukewarm water bottle, then poured the rest over his head, blowing out a long breath as the water cascaded over his nose and mouth. Tossing the bottle into the dirt behind him, he picked up the garden hose draped over the Hilux's tailgate. He squeezed the pistol grip in a quick double-tap to test water pressure. Then he put one foot on the truck's back tire and hoisted himself over the sidewall into the truck bed. He squatted down on his heels and started spraying.

Swirling eddies of water, the color and consistency of grapefruit juice, sluiced back and forth across the truck bed, and the tops of Jimmy's boots. He angled the hose nozzle, using water pressure to push bits of flesh and fragments of bone off the tailgate, onto the dirt behind the truck. Several skull fragments still had hair stuck to them.

Four dead, out of his fifteen-man team of Daristani commandos. The locals called them Owls, because they were cunning, moved quietly, and hunted at night. Also, the night-vision goggles they wore gave them the appearance of unnaturally large, owl-like eyes. It didn't sound as fearsome as other indigenous guerrilla units he'd worked with in the past—who always wanted to name themselves after tigers or panthers or some other big cat. But he liked it.

Jimmy wagged the hose nozzle back and forth, using the water jet like a push broom to sweep human remains out of the truck bed. When the water in the bed finally dripped clear, he hopped off the truck, slammed the tailgate closed, and used the same wagging motion to rinse a trail of bloody handprints off the tailgate itself, as well as off the rear quarter panels and cab doors.

The trail of prints told a very clear story; a gaggle of men—bleeding and fleeing—ripping open the doors or pulling themselves over the quarters, seeking shelter from hundreds of incoming AK and PKM rounds. One side of the truck had a torso-width smear of blood where two of the survivors had pulled their comrade's corpse into the truck bed before speeding off. It was the only body of four recovered off the objective. Jimmy wouldn't be able to wash off the multiple strings of bullet holes, but those were far less shocking to the psyche than the dozens of smeared bloody handprints.

"Hey brother, I'll give you a hand with that."

Jimmy turned around to Ben Gordon, callsign "Flash." Ben was a former SARC—Special Amphibious Reconnaissance Corpsman—who ran another fifteen-man Owl team alongside Tooms the night before. He dressed identically to Jimmy: 5.11 combat pants and matching shirt, drop-leg holster slung off one hip. Streaks of dried blood, now the color of bricks, ran down both of Gordon's sleeves and one whole pantleg. As a former recon medic, he'd spent most of the night performing first-aid on wounded Owls. He'd only lost one, but nine of his fifteen had been shot over the course of the two-hour firefight with Al Badari's insurgents.

Jimmy shook his head, shrugging off the help. "I got it," he said.

One corner of Ben's mouth turned up. He understood the reluctance. But he persisted. "C'mon, Jameson. You don't clean up your own dead."

Jimmy turned back to the truck and started spraying again. Ben put a hand on his shoulder. Jimmy tensed for a moment but stopped spraying. He looked over his shoulder at Ben. "I don't need a hug, doc."

"Good, 'cause I'm out of those. What I do have is empty mags. You pull ammo out of the connex, I'll finish cleaning the trucks."

"I know what you're doing," Jimmy said.

"While you're at it, we need forty mike-mike, flashbangs, and two thermite grenades. I tossed both of mine in the police station."

"On it," Jimmy said, holding out the hose. Ben took it, and Jimmy walked away to the half-dozen shipping containers full of ordnance a hundred meters behind them.

Al Badari's forces had overrun the Hafiza regional police precinct. Ben and Jimmy, with their Owl commando teams, had helped local police officers repel the initial assault. But Al Badari returned with a larger wave of attackers, this time using trucks, RPGs, recoilless rifles, and one mortar. When it became clear they couldn't hold the ground, Ben set the precinct on fire with incendiary grenades and left the compound burning behind them as they broke contact.

When Jimmy was out of sight, Ben looked over the truck, front to back. Under the rear bumper was a mud puddle, mired with thick strings of red runoff and ivory-colored flecks. Ben clenched his teeth and punched the side of the Hilux hard enough to dent the door panel. After two deep, sucking breaths, he wiggled his fingers to check for broken bones. Then he went back to spraying.

HILTON PIERCE
CALLSIGN "ALLEY CAT"
RECCE TROOP – WINDSOR KRAFT STRATEGIES
TARKENT, DARISTAN
0642 HOURS, LOCAL

Hilton waited patiently as the local guard inspected the underside of his vehicle. The bored, disheveled guard held a small, dome-shaped mirror with wheels on the bottom of a broomstick-style handle attached to one side. He slid the mirror beneath Hilton's up-armored Land Cruiser and dragged it lazily around the undercarriage. When finished, he gave Hilton a half-hearted wave and lifted the swing-arm gate.

Hilton wove the truck slowly through a tunnel of ten-foot, concrete T-walls that dumped him into a side parking lot at the US Embassy compound. The front of the building, like any other government structure meant to project power, sported a facade of what appeared to be ten-foot plate glass panels. What looked likedIn reality, those panes were actually triple-thick, blast-rated polycarbonate. The mirror tint meant he couldn't see inside, but the guards inside could see him.

Hilton pressed the buzzer button on the speaker box by the main door. It beeped back at him. "Hilton Pierce, Windsor Kraft, for Kelly Rowland."

"Department?" a voice from the speaker asked.

"Visa services."

There was a ten-second pause, then a hydraulic *clack* as the door locks released. Hilton pulled the door open quickly and tucked himself inside before the high-pressure bolts reengaged behind him.

Two American guards—less experienced contractors from some other firm—slid a log book and visitor badge across the desk. He clipped the badge to his shirt pocket and scribbled his information into the log.

While he was writing, one of the guards asked, "Is it bad out there, yet?"

Hilton shrugged. "I had breakfast outside. Not that bad, yet."

"Windsor Kraft, huh? You guys hiring right now? I'd love to get off this chickenshit gig."

Hilton smirked. The guy was young and had the air of someone who might have needed a qualification waiver just to sit behind the front desk at the embassy. But Hilton deflected diplomatically. "I don't think anyone is hiring right now, man."

The guy leaned back in his chair with an overplayed sense of nonchalance. "I don't know, man. I think they're gonna let Al Badari get right to the edge of the city and then bomb the fuck outta him when he's got all his dudes in one place. We'll be back to normal in a week or two."

Hilton chuckled at the kid's utter confidence in this theory of grand, tide-turning deception. That kind of far-flung faith in generals and politicians was the talk of cherry privates or freshly minted lieutenants who overestimated both the capability and motivation of old men at the top to execute such battlefield audacity.

Sliding the logbook back to the young guard, Hilton said, "I hope you're right. But I'd update my resume, just in case."

He walked away as the two young guns chewed the idea quietly behind him.

Kelly's office was second from the end of the first-floor hallway. Past the elevator banks and visitor restrooms, but not a corner office. Although, in context, Hilton wasn't sure a corner office was worth it. Even the ambassador's officer on the top floor overlooked a false horizon of T-walls, concertina wire, thermal cameras and the parapets of gun towers. The door waited half open. Hilton could see Kelly behind her desk, but he knocked on the doorframe and waited.

"Hilton!" Kelly said with an unnecessary amount of excitement. She waved him in, in a big sweeping motion, and Hilton stepped into her office.

"Why'd you even knock?" she asked with a smile, amused by the idea that he be bound by social etiquette. But Hilton was sure she gave this treatment to everyone.

Kelly spoke confidently, with wide eyes and big open hand gestures, and played casually with her hair. She was liberal with high fives and pats on the back and friendly shoves when you told a funny joke. It was the kind of behavior that left every man in the embassy confused to her intentions—*is she flirting with me, or is she just like this?* Hilton had been around too many young diplomatic staffers on their first hardship posting to believe it held any significance.

"I need to check on an SIV, sponsored by Windsor Kraft," Hilton said.

The Special Immigrant Visa—SIV—program put in place by State expedited the visa issue process for locals who worked directly for the US government in Daristan. Most other NATO countries offered similar programs. Locals who worked as interpreters, intelligence assets, security guards, or other similar jobs lived in constant danger of being kidnapped and tortured by insurgents. The SIV program either rewarded them for their cooperation or whisked them away to the safety of America when the risk to their personal safety became too great. Usually, it was a little of both.

"You came all the way over to check on an SIV? Did you lose my phone number?" Kelly asked.

"I was in the area," Hilton said dismissively.

She smiled. "A likely story!"

Hilton rolled his eyes. "Had a breakfast meeting out in town, wanted to check on this before I head back to our compound."

"You guys don't have a ton of applicants under your banner, shouldn't be too hard to find. Is this for your guy Daoud?" Kelly asked and She started flipping through stacks of applications on her desk.

"Yeah."

"What's he do for y'all, anyway?"

"Local advisor."

Kelly shook her head while shuffling papers. "You Windsor Kraft guys are so cagey. I'm convinced half of you are freelance spooks."

It was more than half. But that wasn't worth telling her.

Kelly found the paper application she was looking for and flipped back and forth through it a couple of times. She blew breath out of one corner of her mouth.

"I mean, it looks like he's all in order. So…yeah…he's in process."

"In process?" Hilton asked. "Is there any kind of estimated timeline on that?"

"Is he trying to bring family with him?"

"No, it's just him."

Daoud's family had been systematically killed off over the last several years by Al Badari loyalists. Every time they popped one of his kin, he only got better at his job. But the ice was getting thin, and he needed a light at the end of the tunnel because, for Daoud, things were going to get a lot worse before they got better.

"Best case? I'll see what I can do. Four or five weeks maybe," Kelly said.

"What's worst case?" Hilton said.

"That many months."

Hilton shook his head.

Kelly put her hands up defensively. "You have no idea how many of these things I have."

"I know that. I know you're pushing as hard as you can, and you're easy to work with. Don't think I don't appreciate you. It's just…"

"Just what, Hilton?"

Hilton looked out her office window, struggling for words. Kelly was at least 10 years his junior. This was her first diplomatic post after graduating from Tufts or Vanderbilt—Hilton couldn't remember which—and she'd only been in-country six months. The embassy hadn't taken a single rocket or mortar round in years, so the *war* part of *warzone assignment* wasn't actually real to her.

But two-hundred miles west of where they stood, Jimmy Tooms used a garden hose to wash pieces of a man's skull from the bed of his pickup truck. Hilton deployed to Daristan on a revolving-door schedule since Kelly was a senior in high school. The insurgency was nothing new, and he'd been through heavy fighting seasons before. But this was different.

"I know I'm being a cagey secret squirrel contractor, but this one's important. Please, if there's anything you can do," Hilston said.

"A month isn't fast enough?" Kelly said.

"I don't think it will be."

"Are you worried about Al Badari? Look, Hilton, I don't want to tell you how to be a secret squirrel, but I think a lot of folks are blowing this out of proportion. I mean, the guy has been around since before we invaded this country. Honestly, his family is one of the oldest tribes here. Why would he tear up his whole country just to kick us out when the military is already drawing down?"

Hilton's response was a hollow hole to hide in. "Yeah, maybe you're right."

"If anything, we should be trying to arrange negotiation with him. I think we can stop a lot of the suffering these people are going through if we just sit down at the table with him," Kelly said.

A million angry thoughts flashed through Hilton's mind. Thoughts about her age and inexperience and the value of a rich, private college education and the mentality of the entire State Department. Not one was worth the breath in his lungs.

Hilton wished, deep down in his soul, that Kelly's approach would work as simply as she explained it. Then he wouldn't be in her office, trying to slick-talk Daoud's visa paperwork to the front of the line before one of Al Badari's death squads hung him upside down from a lamp post and set him on fire. Unfortunately, Hilton's shoulders carried the burden of experience—in Daristan and half-a-dozen similar shitholes around the world. He didn't believe all people were inherently bad. But it seemed like only the bad ones kept him gainfully employed.

"Alright, well, if there's anything I can do…"

"Don't worry, Hilton. I didn't lose *your* number," Kelly said with a playful jeer. "I swear I'll call you the second I get the approval on this."

**JACK YOUNG
WINDSOR KRAFT STRATEGIES
WILLIAMSBURG, VA
2346 HOURS LOCAL**

Jack hated the way he dressed. Navy blue sport coat, gray slacks, white dress shirt open at the collar. However, right down to his Marathon dive watch and VMI class ring, it provided the camouflage necessary to blend in with his environment—just like MultiCam or Tiger Stripe. Except that, in this case, the so-called terrain was an exclusive, little-known pub on the outskirts of Williamsburg with a penchant for entertaining private parties well beyond business hours.

While the location was too far off the beaten path for tourists from nearby colonial-era attractions, the pub maintained the air of a centuries-old tavern that could well have been the birthplace of revolutionary plots or a meeting place for Washington's spies. The proximity to places like Camp Peary, Fort Belvoir, Quantico, and Langley added to the air of intrigue that hung from the exposed wood beams and bare cobblestone walls.

There were a small bar at the back, a kitchen with a limited-but-elegant menu, and a rarely used patio. Several large dining tables in the main hall were sparsely populated. Most of the patrons tucked into the half-dozen "private dining coves," which were more like truncated lounges. Each was a half-moon-shaped stone alcove just large enough for four or five high-backed leather chairs, their arms and legs studded with tarnished brass carpenter's tacks. Each cove could be closed off from the rest of the patrons by a pair of dark-stained wooden doors that latched shut from the inside. Wait staff always knocked before entering and made a point not to do so too often.

Jack eased open one of the thick oak doors and smiled almost immediately. He may have hated getting dressed up, but the slender, middle-aged woman already seated with her back to the wall made it more bearable. She uncrossed her legs and unfolded herself to full five-foot-eleven height.

"Good to see you again, Jack," the woman said.

"A pleasure," Jack said. "Despite the circumstances."

Lisa Gregson was coming up on her thirty-year anniversary at the CIA's Central Asia desk, which was responsible for a whole host of nation-states largely forgotten by the average Westerner, including Daristan. Lisa spent the first part of her career as a regional political specialist. When the campaign in Daristan ramped up, she transitioned to duty as a kinetic targeting officer, mapping terrorist and insurgent networks throughout the region. She compiled lists of key players in those networks for capture/kill operations carried out by special operations or paramilitary units.

Jack took the seat next to her. They eased themselves down into the crackled leather. He reached into his blazer and pulled out a slender leather sleeve containing two cigars, which he cut before leaving the house that morning. He clamped one between his teeth and held the other one out.

"Don't threaten me with a good time," the blonde said, reaching out to pluck the cigar from its case. A Navy brat with two older brothers, Lisa had a reputation for her natural ability to "hang with the guys." She loved cigars, skeet shooting, and bourbon as a certified Bourbon Steward. It was well-known that Lisa Gregson didn't shop cheap for any of the three. Her easy-going confidence and ruthless professionalism were well-respected among her peers in both the intelligence and special operations communities.

An Elie Bleu torch lighter materialized in Jack's hand, which he only used for meetings like this, and he charred the end of Lisa's cigar before lighting his own. They both took short, quick puffs, enjoying the silence as they stoked the embers of their respective smokes. Soon, a wispy haze of rich, earthy smoke insulated the whole alcove.

"How are your boys holding?" she asked with genuine concern.

Jack blew out a long stream of smoke and cocked his head. "They're getting antsy, Leese. The basement's flooded and the water's still rising."

"Any casualties?"

"None of ours, yet. But the Combat Advisory Troop is taking heavy losses to their G's."

A former Special Forces NCO, Jack referred to host-nation commandos like the Owls simply as G's, short for "guerrillas."

Lisa's brow furrowed slightly. "When you say *losses*,

are they getting hit or are they surrendering?"

"Casualties," Jack specified. "In the dozens, last night alone. They've completely lost Hafiza. My guys are prepping to burn down the SCIF out there as we speak."

Lisa's shoulders sank a little. "Shit," was all she said.

"You've got to talk to me," Jack said. "From where I'm sitting, it looks like the whole country is gonna go under."

Lisa took a long drag off her cigar, savored the smoke, and exhaled it slowly through barely parted lips. "Do you want my personal assessment? Or the Agency's? Or the administration's?"

"All three, in reverse." Jack replied. "Administration first."

"Right now, the White House is clinging to the same old talking points. Millions of dollars, a thousand dead troops, NATO assistance, this is just Al Badari making a land grab, but Daristani military forces will hold Tarkent and the adjacent provinces without issue. At worst, it will be simmering regional conflict. But there's no reason for anyone to get worried."

"You could have just said they're sticking their heads in their asses."

"I just said it in more detail."

"Word around the office?" Jack asked.

"Mixed. There are some of us who think the core of democratic infrastructure can remain intact. That Daristan, as a republic-style nation-state, will consist of the capitol and neighboring provinces. The outlying rural areas that ring Tarkent will essentially become tribal, with a sort of constant low-intensity guerrilla war between Al Badari's fundamentalist insurgents and pro-democracy freedom fighters. Others think this will wind up looking just like Vietnam, with Americans hanging off helicopter skids."

"Which way are you leaning?"

Lisa took another long puff before answering. "Vietnam was way before my time. Yours, too. So I don't know what those last few weeks looked like. But if I had to guess…"

Jack took a long pull of his cigar, rolled the smoke around in his mouth, blew half of it out his nose, let the other half roll off his lips like morning fog. He stretched the process out over a minute. After which, he only said, "Yeah."

Lisa took a similarly long pause, puffing her cigar thoughtfully, then looking at it as she blew smoke gently through pursed lips.

"What's your exit plan look like?" she asked.

"The firm's?"

Lisa nodded.

Jack leaned back in his chair and sighed. He blew a mouthful of smoke and then casually waved it away with one hand as he spoke. "We're taking it one province at a time. Hafiza is a full-blown prairie fire. We'll shred and burn everything we can, push those guys somewhere else where they actually have a chance to do some good."

"Like where?"

"Obviously, there's a good chance they'll take what's left of their G's and consolidate in Tarkent. If Al Badari makes it to the city gates, it'll be all hands on deck to hold him back. But we've got a small outpost in Nhahrullah. We may be able to reinforce there."

Lisa raised an eyebrow. "Nhahrullah? That's Al Badari's ancestral land. It'd be like going after Saddam Hussein in Tikrit."

"Which worked out pretty well for us, as I recall," Jack said with a smirk.

"You know what I mean."

"I do. But that's the point. Maybe there's a chance for a morale victory. If we can hold it, or at least make it cost him something real, maybe he'll think twice."

"Jack, listen to me. Ansar Al Badari believes he is the rightful heir to Daristan. It's literally in his namesake. There are a lot of people in that country who agree with him, even if they hate him."

"That doesn't make them very smart."

"They're smart enough to point an AK, Jack. That's all that matters. Al Badari will not take Tarkent without taking Nhahrullah first. Which means he will expend every last bullet and RPG to get it. *If* the entirety of coalition military forces can wrap their heads around that, they might be able to use it to stall him. But the two cities are only about sixty miles apart. If he makes it all the way to his hometown, he'll already own about seventy percent of Daristan, including three of its four international borders. Two of those borders are ideologically friendly to him, which would make his supply of weapons and men essentially endless."

Jack seemed nonplussed. "Are you saying I should tell the guys to pack it in right now?"

"Right now? No. But I am saying you should be *very* wary of the totality of circumstances before you let your men start a stand-up fight in Nhahrullah and, if they do, they need to know exactly when to run. I think the writing's already on the wall here. That country isn't worth their lives anymore."

"Was it ever worth their lives?" Jack asked.

"Are any of the places we've been?" Lisa replied.

A hard silence lowered over them like a curtain. They smoked in silence, checking texts and replying to emails on their phones while attempting to savor a last bit of late night calm.

Lisa stubbed her cigar out in the large marble ash tray between them. "I'd love to stay," she said.

Jack tossed his lit cigar into the stone dish on top of hers. They stood in unison.

Lisa kissed him on the cheek and put a hand on each of his arms. "Call me if you need anything."

"Ditto."

"You've always been one of my favorites, Jack."

As she stepped away from him, he leaned out of the alcove and said, "I bet you say that to all the boys."

She looked over her shoulder and smiled.

"Some of them," she replied. "But not all."

JIMMY TOOMS AND BEN GORDON
CALLSIGNS "JAMESON" AND "FLASH"
COMBAT ADVISORY TROOP – WINDSOR KRAFT STRATEGIES
HAFIZA, DARISTAN (350KM WEST OF TARKENT)
0840 HOURS, LOCAL

Both men showered and changed into a fresh set of utilities, but neither felt clean. Standing at the edge of a towering bonfire, with the morning sun already blazing high in the sky, they sweated through their clothes.

"This is gonna take all day," Jimmy grumbled, wiping his forehead.

"It *would* take longer than that. But time is of the essence," Ben said.

"They know we're not gonna get it all, right?"

"As long as we get the important stuff."

Orders from company headquarters in Virginia said to abandon the small COP—Contingency Operating Post—in Hafiza. The two contractors and their team of Owls would be consolidating to another larger COP somewhere in the country yet to be determined.

Whatever they left behind would be confiscated by Al Badari's forces. Burning everything of importance was paramount to securing their own exit and preventing any equipment or information from being used against them in the coming weeks. Headquarters gave them six hours to do it. Computer hard drives and three-ring binders containing years' worth of information from radio frequencies to information about priority targets in the area stoked the ad hoc burn pit in front of Jimmy and Ben.

On the other side of the fire, a couple of Owls threw in uniforms, name tapes and unit patches, and spare equipment like holsters and plate carriers. Even handheld radios and spare batteries were tossed in by the shovel load. There wasn't nearly enough time to dispose of everything.

The whining of turbo-prop airplanes overhead drew their attention. Jimmy shielded his eyes against the sun as he looked skyward. Ben stared straight up, his vision protected by a pair of aviator sunglasses.

"Strike Troop?" Jimmy asked.

"Yup," Ben replied. "They're gonna be flying sorties out here until we're done."

"Keep the bad guys quiet?"

"That's the hope."

"They gonna blow the base when we leave?"

"I would."

Strike Troop was Windsor Kraft's attack aviation unit—a fleet of A-29 Super Tucanos equipped with gun pods, rockets, and laser-guided bombs. Teams of ex-Air Force JTACs—Joint Terminal Attack Controllers—were also assigned to Strike Troop to coordinate close air strikes from the ground as needed. Since there was no JTAC stationed at Hafiza, the planes would be flying force protection patrols independent of directed strike orders. Unknown to Jimmy and Ben, the pilots already had orders to conduct a full bombing run on the COP to destroy whatever buildings and equipment were left behind when the team departed to a new location.

Down at the burn pit, two more Owls walked up to Jimmy and Ben. One of them held up an AK magazine, clumsily blurting out some kind of explanation to the two Americans. The other spoke English and translated.

"We picked up this magazine off the ground at the police station, but it wouldn't load properly."

Jimmy took the magazine, examining the front and rear locking lugs. "Looks fine to me," he said dismissively.

Ben took the mag from him and stripped a round off the top of the stack. "There's your problem. Wrong bullets."

Both men looked at the cartridge.

"That's weird," Jimmy said.

The small, sleek 5.45mm bullet was well-known to both men. It was also hard to come by in this part of the world—normally found with standing militaries in Russia or former Soviet satellite states.

Ben thumbed the round back into the magazine and returned it to the Owl commando. "Get rid of it," he said casually. "None of your guns will feed this stuff."

The English-speaking Owl translated to his comrade, and the two walked off.

**HILTON PIERCE
CALLSIGN "ALLEY CAT"
RECCE TROOP – WINDSOR KRAFT STRATEGIES
TARKENT, DARISTAN
1156 HOURS, LOCAL**

High noon in a deployed chow hall is like being back in your high school cafeteria on a Tuesday afternoon. Buffet line service, sizzling flat tops, scraping chairs, the idle noise of TVs nobody is watching competing with raucous conversation. And everyone sits with their cliques.

But instead of jocks, goths, and theater kids, the lunch tables in Tarkent grouped by job function. Soldiers from the fabled 82nd Airborne pushed three tables together for a platoon-sized banquet full of high-and-tight haircuts or bobbed ponytails. Huddled at four-tops in the middle were intelligence analysts, logistics support staff, vehicle mechanics, and armorers. Two FBI liaisons occupied a two-seater under one of the flat screens, their khaki slacks and white dress shirts awkwardly pronounced in a room crowded with denim and camouflage.

Hilton placed his tray down at the last empty seat of a table in the far corner. Fellow Windsor Kraft contractors took the other three chairs.

Hugh Haughen was an ex-Special Forces Team Sergeant who, like Jimmy and Ben, ran a company of indigenous Owl commandos. His team was based out of the company's Tarkent operations center—nicknamed Clocktower—as a city-wide Quick Reaction Force. Violence inside Tarkent had been almost non-existent for a couple of years, but they recently started conducting roving patrols throughout the city as a deterrent measure in light of Ansar Al Badari's capture of several outlying provinces.

Gary Bolcewicz and Frank Releya were assigned to Windsor Kraft's Close Protection Troop – tasked with working as contract bodyguards for folks like the two FBI agents, as they traveled around the city on whatever business they had. Frank was a former Army Ranger, while Gary's background was Diplomatic Security Service.

"Gentlemen," Hilton said, pulling in his chair. They all nodded acknowledgement as they ate.

"What's the word in recon world?" Hugh asked.

"You hear about Hafiza?"

"Oh yeah."

"Talk to Jimmy or Ben?"

Mouth half-full, Hugh said, "It's fucked out there. Provincial police got totally overrun. Management told them to burn the COP."

"Are they okay?"

"It was a tough night. Couple of Owls K-I-A. Couple more wounded. But they're fine."

Everyone knew "fine" was a relative term. But it confirmed that, physically at least, neither were injured.

"Where are they displacing to?" Hilton asked.

"Not sure," Hugh replied with a shake of his head. "I heard Nhahrullah."

"Al Badari is gonna own the COP by sundown," Gary said.

"Strike Troop is supposed to level it when they leave," Hugh countered.

Quoting *Aliens*, Frank added, "I say we take off and nuke the site from orbit. It's the only way to be sure."

The table nodded and shrugged in collective agreement.

Changing subjects, Hugh nudged Hilton with an elbow and asked, "How's your shrink?"

"Still with this?" Hilton asked, clearly irritated.

"Wait, what?" Gary asked.

Hugh leaned back in his chair as Hilton rolled his eyes. "Oh, you haven't heard?"

"Fuck, Hugh…"

Haughen continued, his tone sarcastically scandalous, "Hilton met a psychiatrist on a job a few years ago. After the job was over, he started seeing her. Then he started *seeing* her."

"I heard about this!" Frank said.

"Seriously?" Gary asked.

Hilton put his hands up defensively. "First of all," he said to Hugh, "she's not a psychiatrist. She's a psychologist."

"There's a difference?"

"Secondly, this is hella old news, bro. It was like a couple years ago. Before I even started working Daristan."

"I didn't know you broke it off," Hugh said.

"Huh? No, we're still a thing, kind of."

"Guys, it's *complicated*!" Frank said to a chorus of

laughter.

"Seriously though," Gary said. "That's some real Mrs. Robinson shit."

"What? Did you even see the movie?"

"I thought it was a song," Frank said.

"It was a song written for a movie."

"What movie?"

"The Graduate, fuck stick."

"The point is," Hugh declared loudly, "Hilton is banging his therapist."

"Couldn't she get fired for that?" Frank asked.

"Forget that part," Gary interrupted. "What was the job?"

"The job?" Hilton said.

"The contract you were on, where you met her."

"*That*," Hilton answered with relief, "is classified."

"Bullshit," Gary said. "We're all cleared TS."

TS, as in Top Secret.

Hilton sighed, adding, "It was a domestic job. Operational Compliance assignment."

"Goddamn," Gary said. "*Real* cloak-and-dagger shit."

The existence of Windsor Kraft's OCP—Operational Compliance Program—was known company-wide, but rarely talked about. It was rumored to be a standalone LLC insulated from the larger corporate structure. Nobody outside the program could confirm details, but OCP was generally viewed as a clearinghouse for off-book or unofficial jobs that were not hired out by a specific government agency or private client. It was thought to be the one division of the company that operated completely unilaterally, serving only the company's own ends. Only a handful of individual contractors had worked on OCP duty, and none spoke of it afterwards.

"Just so I have this right," Frank said, "you met a chick on an OC gig, then she was your therapist, now she's your girlfriend? So, she's not still seeing you professionally."

Hilton was silent.

"I guess OCP really *doesn't* have any rules," Gary said with a smirk.

"She's *not* my therapist anymore, guys." Hilton snapped with flush cheeks. The table erupted in jeering laughter. Hugh clapped his hands at the petty exchange.

"Gentlemen, are we enjoying ourselves?" asked a new voice.

The four looked up. Standing at the edge of the table was a red-haired woman old enough to be any of their grandmothers. Fair-skinned and demure of stature, she maintained her full skin care and beauty routine—to include understated make-up and taupe-painted fingernails—even in the third-world grit that engulfed the rest of Daristan. A lifetime ago, Vivian Sackler had been a legendary Staff Operations Officer for the CIA. As a forward support coordinator for Windsor Kraft, she was affectionately revered as "Mama."

Without waiting for a response from any of the trigger pullers, Vivian said quietly, "I just thought I'd see how you all were doing and remind you that this is a public dining area, frequented by diplomatic staff and flag-rank military officers. Please consider conducting yourselves accordingly."

The four looked down at their plates and mumbled apologies.

Vivian touched Hilton's shoulder. "How's my Alley Cat?"

"Good, Mama."

"How is Corrine?"

"She's in Boston for a training conference."

"Still with the VA, I hope?"

"She is."

"When all this mess is over, you'll have to introduce us. Holly tells me she's wonderful."

Hilton smiled widely. "She is."

Vivian looked around the table and grinned. "She must be, to put up with this one. Right?"

The group chuckled.

Across the chow hall, one of the 82nd soldiers pointed at the TV.

"Hey! Turn this up!" he yelled.

One of the kitchen staff held out a remote, and volume bars zipped across the bottom of the screen. The TV showed an image of Ansar Al Badari in a clean but sterile sitting room. Steam rose from a cup of chai sitting on a coffee table in front of him. He spoke in his native tongue, and English subtitles scrolled across the screen.

[To the armies of the West, I offer five days to accelerate the ongoing removal of all forces from the lands of Al Badari. This is sovereign tribal land, and its occupation by infidels will no longer be tolerated. Many of our rural provinces have rallied to reject foreign rule, and the holy martyrs of our motherland have returned from exile to claim our destiny back from those who would pillage our state for selfish purposes. We intend to allow you to complete a hasty conclusion to your unjust war for our natural resources for the period of five days, after which all foreigners found residing inside our ancestral borders will be subject to our holy law. In the name of our Prophet, praise be unto him, we beseech you to heed his will and intent.]

The screen went black for a moment, quickly replaced with a pair of talking heads at a news desk. Whatever their commentary, it was lost in a roar of chatter across the chow hall.

"Was that supposed to be a ceasefire?" Frank asked.

"That was a declaration of war," Hugh snapped angrily.

Looking directly at him, Mama said, "I think it's time to put your Owls back on the street."

"On it, Mama."

Hugh bolted up out of his chair and walked out.

Mama gestured to his half-eaten food tray. "Could someone take that, please?"

Gary reached across the table and stacked Hugh's tray on top of his own. The remaining three stood up in unison. Frank and Gary waved a quick goodbye and left the table.

Hilton dug into his pocket for his local cell phone. "I'm gonna call a couple sources and see what I can confirm."

"Well done," Mama said. Hilton turned to leave when

she touched him on the shoulder again. "Don't let the boys get to you. We tease the ones we love."

Hilton smiled and shook his head. "I know. But thanks, Mama."

"I suspect I've got some phone calls of my own," she said.

They hugged briefly and left the chow hall in opposite directions.

Hilton's phone was already pressed to his ear when he stepped out into the afternoon sun. But Daoud's number rang straight through to voicemail.

**DAOUD
NHAHRULLAH, DARISTAN
1244 HOURS, LOCAL**

Daoud was no spy.

In fact, he'd built a modest but meaningful career for himself as a writer for a small Daristani news blog in Tarkent. Building relationships and curating information had always been a passion for him.

While he enjoyed working with the Americans to help stabilize his country and preserve the enterprise of free and open press for his people, even Daoud didn't quite grasp the immense value of his journalistic inclinations. That value was not, however, lost on Hilton Pierce—whose role in Windsor Kraft's Reconnaissance Troop, among other duties, was to maintain a network of human intelligence sources that could better inform the company's operations throughout the country.

Over the last several months, Hilton gave Daoud some rudimentary instruction in how to gather specific information that would be especially useful, and how to protect himself while doing it.

But Daoud was no spy.

So Daoud did his best to keep from sweating profusely as he sat cross-legged on a pillow in a hookah bar across the street from Nhahrullah's mosque. Four men sat around the glass pipe, two of which he did not know.

The fourth, however, was known to all. Not just to all in Nhahrullah, but across Daristan and maybe even the world. He was a decade older than he looked—his body honed to athletic precision after years training in the desert camps of Yemen and Libya. Rigorous paramilitary training, expensive physical fitness facilities, and access to Western nutrition supplements had molded the man's body into a column of lithe muscle. His beard was bushy and black, but his salt-and-pepper hair was cut closer than traditional custom would have dictated. Scars pocked his knuckles, and one ear twisted into a mushroom of cartilage. A short-barreled AK-47 laid on the floor next to the pillow he used as a seat. The rifle's triangular stock was folded along the side of the receiver.

"It's imperative," the man said in Daristani, "that we have supporters we can rely on when we wrestle our government back from the invaders."

Daoud nodded in blind agreement with the other two. For the next several minutes, the muscular man mostly rambled on about the holy blessings bestowed upon their campaign, occasionally alluding to plans to storm the capital city of Tarkent. While he provided no details, the man was adamant that martyrs laid in wait throughout the city, expecting commands to attack within the next two days. He then looked at the three men seated before him. His gaze shifted from one to the other and back again before his eyes settled on Daoud.

"You," the lean man said. "Go get my phone."

Daoud nervously replied that he didn't know where it was. The man explained it to him like he would a child, clearly exasperated. Daoud accepted the treatment and, at the end of the instructions, nodded quickly before getting up and going outside.

Across the street, behind the mosque, sat two pristine, white Toyota Land Cruisers parked in a line, their windows heavily tinted and their license plates removed. Daoud opened the passenger door of one of the SUVs. The door, lined with armor, felt heavy. Heaving the door open, he opened the console between the front seats and located the phone.

Driven by a combination of paranoia and training, the athletic man often sent lackies and supporters out for menial tasks to avoid being seen in the open. In his mind, this minimized exposure to sniper fire, street assaults, and surveillance by foreign intelligence agencies. Mosques were known to be off-limits to all coalition personnel but, all the same, an underground tunnel between the mosque and hookah bar allowed him to enter one building while conducting business in the other. This provided additional security in case the mosque was struck with an American missile, or even a suicide bombing by a rival faction.

Ironically, this hyper-vigilance put Daoud alone inside Mirwan Maliki's armored SUV.

Daoud placed Maliki's phone in his pocket. When he pulled his hand back out, he clutched a small, black rectangle in his sweaty fist. The device had not been intended for surveillance; it meant to protect Daoud in case anything happened to him. His elementary understanding of its purpose gave him the idea to repurpose it. He opened his hand, which shook as he looked down at the device. When he realized he too might be under surveillance from someone in the mosque, a jolt of panic made him drop it.

Fortunately, the truck's door was still open, and the device landed in the passenger's foot well. He leaned down into the Land Cruiser and quickly brushed the device underneath the passenger's seat. Standing back up, he pushed the heavy door closed with his whole body and walked back across the street to the hookah bar, delivering the phone into Maliki's scarred hands with measured reverence before sitting down once again.

Mirwan spoke for several more minutes about what might be expected from them. He encouraged them to continue regular contact with any coalition forces they may have relationships with. He assured them they had been chosen by fate to serve their rightful leader with courage and honor. He dismissed Daoud and one of the other two men, but the third stayed behind.

Daoud walked two blocks back to his own vehicle, his knuckles white on the steering wheel as he drove back toward Tarkent. While Daoud sped back toward the capital, Maliki conferred with the third stranger—a long-time devotee to Ansar Al Badari, and a fellow veteran of the Libyan training camp. He had posed as a green recruit in the meeting as a security measure.

"Have them both followed. I have concerns," Maliki said quietly.

"The reporter," his partner said with a nod.

Maliki shook his head. "The other one. He works on

an American military base as a cook. It will be easiest for him to betray us."

"I will focus on him."

"I said both of them," Maliki corrected. "Just to be sure."

HILTON PIERCE
CALLSIGN "ALLEY CAT"
RECCE TROOP – WINDSOR KRAFT STRATEGIES
TARKENT, DARISTAN
1510 HOURS, LOCAL

Hilton drummed the steering wheel absently as he waited for the traffic jam to gradually shake itself loose. His eyes swept methodically back and forth every couple of seconds, constantly assessing and reassessing the clogged roads and crowded sidewalks.

He hated being out in the middle of town this time of day. Early in the morning or late at night were fine, but afternoons were no good. Too many people and traffic moved too slowly. If there was a perfect time to stage an ambush against a lone American contractor in Toyota Corolla, right now was it. Windsor Kraft maintained a fleet of different vehicles for its various missions across Daristan. The small, four-door Corollas rarely got used. Most shooters preferred—and most missions demanded—the heavier armor and roomier cabs of larger vehicles like the Hilux pickup trucks or Land Cruiser SUVs. The Combat Advisory Troop sometimes used flatbed Hino trucks to haul their dozens of native Owl commandos and various heavy weapons.

His sedan wasn't completely vulnerable. It was armored thickly enough to stop handgun and AK rounds.

A burst from a PKM or a blast from an IED would punch right through, though. The suspensions and transmissions of the smaller Corolla simply couldn't handle the burden of a complete Level VII armor package like the trucks could.

The compact car did offer one distinct advantage: camouflage. Tarkent's perpetually struggling middle class relied almost exclusively on small sedans for their lower retail price and better fuel efficiency. Large, lumbering SUVs were driven almost exclusively by Daristani government employees, foreigners, or local gangsters. All offered equally appealing targets for the fundamentalist Al Badari insurgency.

Instead, Hilton sat behind the wheel of one more nondescript, beat-up Japanese sedan. From outside the vehicle, he looked like just another Daristani commuter honking and squeaky-braking their way through the incessant racket of an open-air marketplace that didn't realize it was in the 21st century. Laden donkeys pulling wooden carts full of smartphones and counterfeit luxury handbags trudged alongside the stream of cars, their owners occasionally accosted by otherwise apathetic Tarkent policemen.

Shortly after Hilton left Mama in the chow hall three hours ago, she contacted him via radio and said there was a phone call in the SCIF for him. The Sensitive Compartmentalized Information Facility was a concrete-reinforced, sound-dampened room that served as the home for any phones, computers, fax machines, or other electronic devices cleared to process classified information.

"Go for Alley Cat," Hilton had said tersely into the waiting phone after arriving at the SCIF.

"Hilton, it's Jack," said the voice from the phone.

Hilton looked up at the line of analog clocks on the wall, each one showing the time for a different key city around the world. Daristan local, Greenwich Mean, and Washington, D.C. It was early afternoon for Hilton, but after midnight in Virginia.

"Little late over there for you, sir," Hilton said.

"It's a full-time job keeping an eye on you guys right now."

"That a fact?"

Hilton and Jack had crossed paths a couple of times in the Army. Hilton, a young Sergeant in a Long-Range Surveillance Company; Jack a Special Forces Intelligence Sergeant. Their friendship ran deep, but Hilton felt wary of why he'd been requested personally by his old friend—and current supervisor—on the other side of the planet.

"Listen, Hilton, just like any good NCO, you don't like phone calls at odd hours from your superiors. I get that. You're not in trouble," Jack said.

"If I'm not in trouble, then you have some kind of priority tasking."

Jack wouldn't bother with a secure line just to shoot the shit. "Your ears only right now, Hilton."

"So it's worse than I thought."

"I need a leader's recon. You gotta scout a couple of things out for me."

"What kind of things?"

"Some place to land a small-to-medium-sized aircraft,

away from the airport. I've got a location earmarked based on drone flights and satellite overheads. But I need someone to go look at them."

"That it?"

Jack took two slow breaths into the phone. "No. I need a TRP deck for it as well."

Target Reference Points are essentially landmarks within a designated battlespace used to initiate or direct supporting fires—primarily in the form of artillery guns. If you have pilots, tank crews, or even machine gunners who share a common list of TRPs in the same battlespace, all heavy weapons fire can be coordinated simultaneously.

"Just so I understand this," Hilton said. "You want me to locate and designate an emergency airstrip away from the city's actual airport and establish suitable landmarks for pre-programmed heavy fires to defend said airstrip."

"Yes, to all."

"Any TRPs I establish will be *inside* the city. If we use them, there will be substantial civilian casualties and infrastructure damage."

"Understood," came Jack's clipped response.

"Jack, this sounds an awful lot like you want me to set up an Alamo plan. Things are definitely getting dicey here, but if you know something I don't, now is the time to share."

"I don't know anything, per se. But I am starting to trade Beltway gossip with a couple of friends, and it's not good."

"Time to pack my bags already? I heard we still have

five days. Four now, I guess."

"Plan for the worst, hope for the best. We're just planning right now, Hilton. That's all. This is so we have a safety net independent of DoD or State Department."

Hilton didn't buy it, but he wasn't going to push any harder. "Copy all, sir," he said.

"Close hold on this op. Anything you produce on this comes directly back to me, through secure comms. If you work up range cards, GRGs, whatever, email it to me from the SCIF," Jack said.

"Anything else?" Hilton asked.

On the other end, Jack shook his head even though Hilton couldn't see it. "Get to work."

Hilton hung up without saying anything else.

He replayed the terse and cryptic conversation in his mind as he inched the Corolla forward another half car-length through midday traffic. Hilton rolled his shoulders and shifted in his seat. Underneath his button-up work shirt was a Haley Strategic INCOG plate carrier, astripped down slick with no pouches or attachments, carrying lightweight ballistic plates. To maintain a lower profile during prime ambush hours, he wedged his carbine between the driver's door and seat cushion—readily accessible but below the window line. He also stashed a micro chest rig and small bailout bag in the passenger-side footwell next to him. His Staccato, knife, radio, and cell phone were either tucked in his belt or spread throughout the pockets of his street clothes—also below the car's window line.

Hilton breathed a sigh of relief as he entered the traffic

circle. He left it on the first exit. The road he turned into was empty, save for a couple of donkey-drawn carts and less than a dozen cars. Hilton eased the gas pedal further down and felt the Corolla's modified drivetrain kick into the next gear. He handily passed the other vehicles, weaving deftly between them on the cobblestone road. His eyes darted back-and-forth quicker from one edge of the road to the other, looking for classic tells of an IED—freshly churned dirt or newly-laid pavement, wires, large boxes, or trash bags in the road, or even bloated animal carcasses which were sometimes cut open and stuffed with explosives.

The area he headed toward was on the very western edge of Tarkent, which was largely abandoned, even by locals. Westerners and coalition military forces had not patrolled the area in four or five years, which made the likelihood of hitting a pre-positioned IED pretty slim, especially rolling solo in a local vehicle. The same factors that made an ambush unlikely also made the possibility so dangerous.

The overweight sedan thumped on its shocks as the cobblestone abruptly ended, dumping Hilton onto an unimproved dirt road that ran a couple hundred meters through big, blocky warehouses, and parking lots full of rusty tractor-trailers and flatbed trucks. At the end of warehouse row, the city just stopped. At its edge was a large, flat, dirt floor.

From where Hilton stopped the car, a section of ancient stone wall that still ringed most of Tarkent sat a hundred meters ahead. Left and right of where Hilton's

Corolla sat idling, the open dirt area extended for at least a quarter mile in each direction.

In the mid-1990s, Tarkent made a bid to host the Olympics. Hilton couldn't remember who they lost out to—he thought maybe Lillehammer—but the neighborhoods had already been bulldozed and graded for an athletes' village that never came to be. Coalition forces used it as an ad hoc landing zone when they first seized control of the city more than a decade ago, but the location was quickly abandoned by Western militaries on account of being too far away from the rest of the city infrastructure.

Besides, a joint force of Army Rangers and British Pathfinders had seized Tarkent Airport proper with little resistance. It made far more sense as a logistics hub than trying to build up a dirt patch from nothing. The would-be village's largely forgotten location on the ragged outskirt of Tarkent's western industrial district made it a prime location for an improvised airfield. While the dirt strip wouldn't accommodate commercial airliners, you could fit dozens of helicopters on it, or a private jet rated for primitive strips. A C-130 could make it work if the pilot was rated for assault landings.

Hilton checked his mirrors for people watching him. Then he clicked a button on his wrist-mounted GPS to mark his current position, as the entryway to the so-called airstrip. He pulled his vehicle out into the middle of the dirt flat and raced to one end, dropping another GPS waypoint before spinning the vehicle around and racing to the opposite end to drop another pin to mark either end of what would become a runway if Jack's concerns were spot-on. Since the vehicle was also equipped with a dashcam, he would have video footage of the entire strip and surrounding area.

Finally, Hilton got out of the vehicle, opened his trunk, and popped open the ring of latches on a small, black Pelican case. Inside the case were a small, quad-copter drone and control unit. He got the drone airborne and did several slow, sweeping passes of the dirt flat before passing the drone over adjacent rooftops and alleyways, and even over the head-height stone wall that was Tarkent's ancient western boundary. The drone created a small puff of dust as it landed at Hilton's feet. He quickly packed it back up into the Pelican case and slammed the trunk. The vehicle was already rolling when he keyed his radio.

"Clocktower, Alley Cat," Hilton said.

"Go for Clocktower," came the response.

"I'm R-T-B time now, E-T-A five-zero mikes."

Hilton checked his watch and did the math. He'd be losing daylight about twenty minutes before he got back to Windsor Kraft's operations base on the outskirts of Tarkent Airport. Getting back after dark wasn't a big deal to him—he often conducted meetings with intelligence sources well after dark or before first light. But the night life in Tarkent had become noticeably quieter over the last couple of weeks as Al Badari loyalists started to occupy some of the outlying provinces.

Hilton merged back into the traffic circle closer to the heart of town, did two complete laps to look around before pulling out, and grinding to a halt—yet again—behind a truck that looked all too familiar to him: the

M1224 MaxxPro MRAP, or Mine Resistant Ambush Protected vehicle.

The MaxxPros were massive, rolling bank vaults with armor-slatted windows and a gun turret up top. They looked like someone bolted an oversized lock box to the back of a tractor-trailer cab. These armored taxi cabs moved squads of infantry from point A to B. They could withstand the blasts of increasingly large and sophisticated roadside bombs. The daunting armor suite and accompanying drivetrain made them tall, ungainly targets that lumbered through the narrow streets of Tarkent. These particular MaxxPros bore the widely recognized "double-A" insignia of the 82nd Airborne Division, stenciled on the back of each truck with black spray paint.

On either side of the MaxxPro were four young soldiers in MultiCam uniforms with bulky armor vests, heavy helmets, and M4 carbines decked out with all manner of lights, lasers, and optics. The grunts trudged slowly along, heads swiveling left and right, occasionally waving at shop-keeps or handing fistfuls of candy to children passing by.

This formed a so-called "presence patrol"—something conventional Army leaders required to keep their soldiers busy and remind the bad guys they were still here. Hilton only ever did a few of them, as that type of mission rarely got assigned to the small, aggressive LRS Companies he'd served in. He hated them all the same. Knowing he was in a local vehicle with no NATO markings, Hilton kept at least twenty-five yards back to avoid spooking the junior enlisted trigger-pullers walking the gauntlet in front of him.

Block by block, the MRAPs crept forward at walking speed while Hilton grew increasingly impatient behind the wheel. Once the MRAP cleared the next major intersection, Hilton banked his sedan hard right down the side street, hoping he could move a block over and pass them on a parallel thoroughfare.

Hilton was two car-lengths down the side street, threading his small car between Dumpsters and empty wooden carts, when the side door of one building opened up. Six locals with AKs and a PKM machine gun poured out. Every one of them walked right past Hilton's ratty Corolla, their attention laser-focused on the intersection he just turned off of. His stomach dropped.

"Clocktower, Alley Cat, mil convoy half-a-block west of my current grid, imminent contact," Hilton said into his radio.

"Alley Cat, Clocktower, confirm."

"I have eyes on six armed locals, maneuvering on convoy time now."

"Alley Cat, what is *your* status?"

Hilton shook his head. He knew what was coming. "They don't know I'm here."

"Roger. Proceed with R-T-B. Clocktower will relay."

The explosion erupted behind him, but it was large enough to rock the Corolla on its shocks. He saw black smoke in his rearview mirror as he reached down and grabbed the micro rig off the floor next to him, slipping it over his head and buckling it on. He quickly slid the driver's seat back two notches to make room between his kit and the steering wheel.

"Clocktower, Alley Cat, audible contact, explosion half-block west my grid," Hilton said.

Hilton heard no gunfire from the intersection behind him. The explosion left an uncomfortable silence in its wake.

They were waiting.

That was worse.

Hilton pushed the gas pedal halfway down and zipped to the next intersection, turning onto the nearest parallel street. The half-dozen cars on the street around him were up on the sidewalk, not moving. Many sat empty, with doors still hanging open. Not a soul stood in the open. The locals had lived like this for years. They knew the drill.

Hilton sped up to another intersection and skidded to a halt as four more black-clad insurgents sprinted in front of him. Three held AKs and one carried an RPG-7 across his shoulder. Two of them wore large, green satchels with bundles of pointy RPG warheads sticking out of them. They glanced at the idling Corolla but, like the others, assumed him to be a local and simply ran past his front bumper.

Hilton waited until the last one was past his grill before raising his carbine. With his left hand, he unbuckled his seatbelt, then reached back across and popped the driver's door latch. He pushed the armored door open with his left foot and leaned out, dropping the Cobalt's stubby suppressor into the V-notch between the driver's door and the vehicle's frame.

The last insurgent in the line turned around first, just as Hilton fired his first three rounds into their point man. The leader collapsed onto the sidewalk, and Hilton put two bullets into each of the other three before any could return fire. He pulled his carbine back into the vehicle and slammed the driver's door, throwing the car into reverse as he keyed his mic.

"Clocktower, Alley Cat, Barn Fire! I say again, Barn Fire!" Hilton said.

"Barn fire" meant Windsor Kraft's pro-word for direct enemy contact, which doubled as a trigger to activate Hugh's strike force of Owls based at the airport.

"Clocktower copies Barn Fire, SITREP."

"Four enemy K-I-A. Friendly forces in contact immediately west. Moving to engage. Alley Cat, out!"

HUGH HAUGHEN AND SCOTT BOOTH
CALLSIGNS "ROOK" AND "SINATRA"
COMBAT ADVISORY TROOP – WINDSOR KRAFT STRATEGIES
TARKENT INTERNATIONAL AIRPORT, DARISTAN

Hugh plucked a dry-erase marker out of the pen pocket on the sleeve of his combat shirt and quickly scribbled the ten-digit GPS grid onto his "leader's board"—an elastic armband around his left forearm with a clear plastic window on it. Underneath the plastic window was a small sheaf of 3x5 index cards with short-hand notes of his need-to-know information: radio frequencies, a roster of his Owl commandos, pre-designated key landmarks around the city, and some quick reference cards for things like 9-Line medevac reports.

As Hugh stood up, Gary Bolcewicz stepped into the SCIF. A 7.62mm B&T marksman's rifle was already slung across his back.

"You get the call?" Hugh asked.

Gary nodded. "You have the grid?"

Hugh held out his arm with the leader's board strapped to it.

Gary pulled a small notebook out of his pants pocket, flicked it open, and pulled a pen out of the spiral binding. Jotting the sequence of numbers, he said, "Bird is already warming up. We'll be airborne in five once I'm out the door. Where you at?"

"Trucks and guns are hot, Owls on board," Hugh said. "We'll be out the gate in three."

Gary stuffed the pen back into his notebook and said, "Be right behind you."

They exited the SCIF in unison. Once outside, Gary took off in a jog, heavy rifle shuffling on his shoulders. Hugh broke in the other direction toward a line of armored Hilux pickup trucks. A PKM topped each one, with a fire team of Owls sitting in the bed. His deputy team commander, Scott Booth, already sat in the driver's seat of the lead truck.

Hugh vaulted into the bed of the last truck. A dismounted Owl pushed open the heavy, steel blast gate separating Clocktower base from the airport access road. Hugh keyed his radio and read off the GPS coordinates to Hilton's location.

"Copy all, rolling," was Scott's reply.

The trucks eased slowly onto the access road and halted. The lone Owl hauled the blast door closed behind the last truck and then scrambled into one of the other pickup beds. The Owl slapped the side of the truck twice. The convoy lurched forward, quickly building speed as a cloud of dust rose behind them on the gravel road.

A minute later, Hugh could hear the buzzing whine of the Little Bird as it passed overhead.

HILTON PIERCE
CALLSIGN "ALLEY CAT"
RECCE TROOP – WINDSOR KRAFT STRATEGIES
TARKENT, DARISTAN

The Corolla sped in reverse toward the side street he'd just come out of. Hilton knew that two of his co-workers and a dozen of their local Owl commandos would already be starting the engines of their armored Hilux pickups. He also knew it would be ten to twenty minutes before they'd get to his position. But the Windsor Kraft Little Bird helo, with a shooter hanging out one side, would be there in half that time—less if he was lucky.

Hilton cranked the wheel hard to initiate a J-turn, spinning the car 180 degrees and pointing it back down the alleyway. He stomped the gas, juking the car harshly between the same Dumpsters and carts, until he could see a cluster of US Army uniforms crouched at the end of the alley. One of them spun toward him, and Hilton took two M4 rounds in the armored windshield before skidding the car to a halt behind a heavy metal Dumpster.

He kicked the driver's door open and, still sitting behind the wheel, yelled out, "Friendly! Friendly!"

Hilton stuck both arms out of the driver's door and held them high, palms up and fingers spread. Almost immediately, two GIs came around the Dumpster, rifles raised.

In his best command voice, Hilton yelled, "Check fire check fire! Friendly!"

The "check fire" command was programmed into every grunt worth his salt, and they lowered their M4s instantly. A soldier with corporal stripes and "Martinez" on his name tape gave him a bewildered look.

"Who the fuck are you?!?" he asked between heaving breaths.

"Windsor Kraft," Hilton said.

The two soldiers traded confused glances.

"Where's your fuckin' team?" Martinez asked.

"My QRF is en route. We already called yours."

"You're out here alone?" his buddy, whose uniform identified him as Private Stimson, asked in shock.

"Not anymore," Hilton said with a smirk. He looked at Martinez. "On you, corporal."

Martinez understood in a second, head nodding underneath his helmet.

"Keep up," Martinez said. He turned and took off, junior soldier a step behind him.

Hilton grabbed his carbine, kicked the Corolla's door closed, and took off down the alley behind them. At the corner of the intersection, their machine gunner ripped off two long bursts from his M240 machine gun. Stimson took a knee next to him, looking down his optic before tapping off a string of shots from his M4.

Hilton peered around the corner, peering through the Vudu 1-6x scope atop his carbine. The cab of the lead MRAP was completely crumpled from the IED blast. Four soldiers laid on the ground behind it. Two weren't moving. One was dragging himself around the truck. The fourth looked bloodied up but returned fire. The rest of the platoon spread out among the three trucks, standing or crouching while shooting into storefronts on Hilton's side of the street, a half-block or so in front of him.

Two of the first six insurgents he'd seen were also dead in the street. The rest holed up in one of the buildings, taking fire. The center of the gunfight was maybe fifteen yards, muzzle-to-muzzle, but the 82nd troopers continued to take sporadic fire from the line of store fronts.

Hilton pulled back into the alleyway. He knew enough about Daristani architecture to know the entire row of store fronts were built as one long building, with interior divider walls to partition off each individual shop. The same was true front-to-back. Meaning if they moved one block back, where Hilton had reversed in from, they could ambush the remaining insurgents from behind, entering through an adjacent shop. Knowing which shop to enter from would be guesswork, at best.

He looked down at the Army fireteam crouched next to him. Private Stimson and Corporal Martinez both wore Ranger tabs on their left shoulders.

Hilton took a knee and squeezed Martinez's shoulder, leaning in close to his ear. "Give me one!"

"One what?" Martinez said.

"Shooter."

Martinez pulled his face off the M4's butt stock and looked at him. "*What*?"

Hilton pointed down the alley. "We can get these guys from behind!"

"We need more guys!"

Hilton looked him in the eye. "I don't."

Martinez shook his head. He squeezed the mic clipped to his left shoulder. "One-six, Martinez. Myself plus one, moving one block east to suppress from the rear."

One-six would be Martinez's platoon leader. A junior lieutenant, no doubt.

"Negative, Martinez. We don't have a fire team," the platoon leader said.

Hilton leaned in and grabbed the microphone off Martinez's vest. "One-six, this is callsign Alley Cat. I'm an independent tiered asset at Martinez's location. We're moving to close, one block east. Hold security and keep the heat on these fuckers. Alley Cat, out."

He handed the mic back to Martinez.

"He's gonna have my ass," Martinez said.

"Send me the bill," Hilton replied.

Martinez rolled his eyes and said, "On *you*, sir."

Hilton took off down the alley, Martinez in lockstep. Hilton stopped at the Corolla and ripped the door open. Martinez followed suit, dropping into the seat behind Hilton, who threw the car into reverse and sped backwards down the alley, onto the next street. Hilton could hear Martinez slam a fresh magazine into his M4 as they sped halfway to the next intersection, still littered with the fighters Hilton had ambushed.

The car slammed to a halt in front of the storefront Hilton hoped would connect directly to where the last insurgents held out. He left the car running in the middle of the street and bailed out. Hilton picked an entryway and stacked up on it. Martinez took the opposite side of the door and nodded at Hilton, who pushed the door open and disappeared inside.

From inside the store, they heard the unmistakable *whoosh* of an RPG round going off one street over. A woman in traditional hijab and her three children crouched against one wall. Hilton looked at her, took one hand off his gun, and held a finger to his lips. The woman nodded and pulled the children tighter to her body. He looked at Martinez and motioned toward a cheap plywood door at the back of the shop.

"Cease fire," Hilton whispered.

Martinez keyed his mic and whispered, "One-six, Martinez. Cease fire. Cease fire."

They stacked up again, opposite each other. Hilton held up his balled fist as a "hold" command. Martinez nodded.

Hilton let his carbine hang on the sling and plucked a flashbang grenade off his chest rig. He held it tight to his chest and ripped the safety pin out. The chatter of gunfire from the street ceased all at once. Hilton cracked the plywood door open and tossed the grenade through. He saw the flash under the door as the grenade went off and shouldered the door fully open. Hilton and Martinez fired in unison. The soldier's M4 cracked loudly next to the quiet chugging of Hilton's suppressed Cobalt. Hilton turned to engage a second insurgent, skylighted by the window he stood in front of, but the fighter pitched forward in a limp heap before Hilton could squeeze the trigger.

Almost on cue, the earpiece in Hilton's ear crackled to life. "Alley Cat, Cossack, over."

Hilton could hear the rotor wash of the Little Bird behind Cossack's voice on the radio. He looked at Martinez. "You got these guys?"

"Roger," Martinez said.

Hilton let his carbine hang and keyed his radio. "Alley Cat, send it."

"We're on station, engaged one. SITREP?" Cossack said.

"I'm internal, plus one US. All threats neutralized, this location. All friendlies up. Nice shot, brother," Hilton said.

Cossack, who Hilton knew as Gary Bolcewicz, came back over the chopping blades of the Little Bird. "Copy all. Exterior looks secure from up here. QRF is four mikes out."

Hilton nodded. "Understood." He looked at Martinez. "I think that's it. Good work."

Martinez took a deep breath and nodded his head.

"Call your P-L. Tell him we're coming out," Hilton said.

Martinez squeezed his shoulder mic. "One-Six, Martinez. Two friendlies, coming out of the target building."

"One-Six copies. Holding fire. Come out," came the reply.

Martinez went to the door and looked back to see Hilton turned away from him, heading out the back. "Sir?"

"Go ahead, corporal. I'm good," Hilton said.

Martinez looked puzzled for a moment.

"Pleasure doing business with you, Alley Cat."

"Likewise."

Martinez turned and stepped out into the street.

Hilton hit his radio. "Cossack, Alley Cat, exiting target building to the rear, one block east."

"Copy."

Hilton walked through the building, passing the family still crouched on the floor and out into the street. He swept his carbine up and down the block before walking up to the Corolla. He dropped into the driver's seat, opened the glove box, and took out the single thermite incendiary grenade before tearing off the GPS tracker Velcroed to the dashboard. He got out of the vehicle and looked up at the Little Bird circling overhead. He waved to it. Gary gave him a lazy salute back as they buzzed over the rooftops.

Hilton dropped the GPS tracker on the ground and shot it twice with his rifle before picking it back up and stuffing it behind his chest rig. Then he turned off the engine and popped the Corolla's hood. Propping the hood open, he pulled the pin on the incendiary canister and set it atop the engine block. As he turned to walk away from the vehicle, the grenade made a popping sound, followed by a long hiss, as a pool of molten slag seeped through the engine compartment, hollowing out the front of the vehicle and rendering it inoperable.

The roaring of diesel engines grew louder as a column of tan and gray Hilux pickups rounded the corner. They pulled up in front of him. Two Owl commandos hopped off the back of the lead truck as it ground to a halt. Hilton recognized the senior man, Jazeeri—or Jazz—as the QRF team leader for Windsor Kraft's Tarkent base.

"Mister Hilton," he said with a curt nod.

Hilton nodded back and they shook hands. "Thanks for coming out, Jazeeri."

The commando squad leader pointed to the line of dead insurgents in the street behind Hilton."You get them?"

Without looking, Hilton said, "Yes, sir, I did."

"I'm glad you're okay. This is…not good. Tarkent has been safe for years."

"I know, Jazz. Times are changing."

Hilton heard another round of diesel engines. A column of up-armored US Army Humvees chugged down the street behind him.

"Time to go," Hilton said.

The two Owls climbed back into the lead Hilux and pulled Hilton up behind them. Hilton looked up and saw two black specks on the horizon—Army medevac Blackhawks, no doubt. He flopped down in the bed of the Hilux as it started rolling toward Tarkent airport, the Little Bird flying low over top of them.

**CORRINE MACKENZIE
BOSTON, MASSACHUSETTS
1148 HOURS LOCAL**

Corrine used one foot to push the door closed behind her, swearing under her breath as hot coffee sloshed out of the paper cup down the back of her hand. A sandwich in the other hand, hotel key card clenched in her teeth, she shuffled quickly across the room, kicking off her heels as she crossed the hotel room. She placed her lunch down on the desk, threw the curtains open, and nestled into the plush roller chair. Her fingers moved so quickly across the keys of her laptop that it took her three tries to get her password right to unlock the computer.

In person, being three minutes late for a lunch date would have meant nothing. But with Hilton half a world away and every news outlet regurgitating footage of firefights erupting across Daristan, getting stuck in line at the lobby café had almost driven her to tears in the elevator ride back to her room.

She swiped back and forth on the laptop's touchpad, trying to find the shortcut icon for their video chat app. With her cursor over the icon, she double-tapped just in time to see an incoming call. A wave of relief washed over her as she accepted the call. She took in the familiar backdrop of his room—a converted shipping container—before she saw his face.

"Are you okay?" Hilton asked.

Corrine sniffed defensively. "Yeah, why?"

"You look frazzled."

"Oh," she said with a dismissive wave of one hand. "Got stuck in line for breakfast."

"No worries," he said nonchalantly. "I just got back anyway."

"How are you?" she asked.

It was quick, but she saw the answer form in Hilton's mind before the words came out.

"I'm fine," he replied, stuffing down flashbacks to his firefight on the opposite end of the city a few hours ago. "How's your room?"

She looked around the room, then out the window over her view of downtown Boston.

"It's good," she said with a nod. "They put me up in downtown. It's fancy."

"How's the coffee?"

"You would approve," Corrine replied with a smile. Hilton was snobby about coffee, and he rarely drank coffee on deployment unless she mailed it to him. But, downrange, caffeine functioned as a tool, just like boots or bullets. He'd pop a couple of caffeine pills or chug one of the military's famed Rip It energy drinks before he'd accept a substandard cup of joe.

"So, it looks like work is…busy," she said cautiously.

He rolled his eyes. "You watching the news again?"

"Kind of hard not to, Hilton."

"I warned you about that," he said sternly.

"It's all they play at the airports."

"Well, it's quiet here," he lied. "Try not to watch too closely. I'm okay."

"You sure?"

"You're looking at me."

She wasn't going to address how well he concealed his emotions when it came to work. His lack of reaction to questions told more than he would ever say out loud. She decided she didn't want to sacrifice their time together probing the matter.

"You look good," she said.

"You always say that," he answered.

"Because I always think it."

He grinned. "Is that so?"

She giggled, "Yes!"

"Are you thinking about how good I look now?"

She looked at the dirt on his face and the dampness at the collar of his T-shirt, thinking it must not be as quiet in Tarkent as Hilton was letting on.

"Maybe," she said, stretching the word out with a coy smile.

Winking into the camera, he told her, "Show me."

Corrine felt her neck flush. "I have to be downstairs in like twenty minutes."

"You know I only need five, baby."

"I *know* you only need two. But if calling it five makes you feel better."

Hilton laughed but, at the end of it, his shoulders fell, and he sighed. "It's…going to be a long week, but I think it'll be the last week."

"Hilton Pierce! Are you bartering emotional vulnerability for physical stimulus?"

"You know I love it when you talk clinical."

She covered her giggle with the back of one hand. "You're incorrigible."

"It's fine," he said, smirking. "Maybe next time."

She groaned, the flush rising from neck to cheeks.

"Hang on," Corrine said with feigned exasperation. She saw the smile spread across his face before looking away from the screen to adjust in her chair. Dutifully hiking her skirt up over both hips, Corrine placed one foot up on the desk to give him a proper view. From the other side of the planet, she could hear the ripping of his Velcro battle belt off camera. She leaned back in her chair, two fingers hooked inside her black lace underwear, when the door burst open over Hilton's shoulder.

Alone in her hotel room, Corrine shrieked and bolted forward in her roller chair. Hilton spun his chair around, putting his back to the camera and blocking his screen from the man leaning halfway into his room. Even though she couldn't see the other person, they must have seen Hilton's belt hanging open, because she heard a knowing laugh on the other end.

"I should have waited two minutes," the voice said.

"I swear to God, if this isn't…," Hilton started to say.

"Phone call, lover boy."

"Can it wait two minutes?"

"It's your source hotline."

"God damn it. Tell them to call my cell."

"They tried that, but you didn't answer."

"Tell them to try again. I'll answer this time."

"Sorry man."

"Yeah."

Corrine didn't know what a source hotline was, but the rest of the conversation made it sound important. She heard the door slam shut. Hilton spun back around to face her. She was still hunched over, legs tightly crossed and face hot with embarrassment.

"You don't have five minutes, do you?" she asked, crestfallen.

"I don't even have two," Hilton said, the defeat clear in his voice.

"It's alright."

"Not really," he muttered.

"I'll take some pictures for you later."

He nodded in concession and said, "Thank you."

"Hey, it's fine, baby. We'll make it up. Just be safe, okay?"

She heard a cell phone chirping off screen. Hilton looked away, his face hardening.

"Go to work," she told him. "I've got a full afternoon here."

"I'll talk to you soon," he said, already gone. "Take care, darlin'."

"Take care."

The screen went black in front of her. Skirt still high around her waist, Corrine leaned forward and propped her elbows on the desk, resting her head in both hands.

"Fuck," she whispered.

HILTON PIERCE
CALLSIGN "ALLEY CAT"
RECCE TROOP – WINDSOR KRAFT STRATEGIES
TARKENT, DARISTAN
2022 HOURS LOCAL

It was dark and quiet when Hilton returned to downtown Tarkent. The afternoon traffic had all melted away. Shops were closed, save for a few late-night cafes and hookah bars. Most of their customers were foreign journalists up late tapping out drafts on laptops, or pairs of local police officers milling around on their beats.

Hilton pulled his truck into a traffic circle, going around it for two laps before continuing. A hundred yards past the circle, he hooked a U-turn in the middle of the empty street and doubled back to the circle. This time, a lone man stood on the sidewalk right at the edge of the road. Hilton turned into the circle once more, tapping his brakes just long enough for the man to climb into his passenger seat.

Hilton took the next turn out of the circle and took what might appear to be a rambling truck tour of the city. In reality, he used a carefully planned route that kept him close to medical clinics, coalition security checkpoints, and large hotels frequented by expats—all of which had their own armed security teams.

Back at the Clocktower, a watch desk with several direct phone lines was manned 24/7. It received calls and emails from company headquarters back in Virginia, eleven time zones behind. But there was also a dedicated line for Windsor Kraft's local intelligence sources. After being vetted and recruited, sources received the number to call in case of emergency or to deliver urgent information.

Moments before Corrine had lifted her skirt in her Boston hotel room, Daoud had called the line in a panic, saying he had important information that he could only deliver directly to Hilton, and only in person. They hastily agreed upon one of their pre-set pickup locations before Hilton hung up the phone and ran to find Frank and Gary from Close Protection. That pair now rode in a second Hilux, trailing a steady hundred meters behind Hilton's own truck as a rolling overwatch in case the emergency meeting turned out to be a double-cross, or there was another attack along their route.

Back at Clocktower, Rook and Sinatra sat in lawn chairs next to a four-truck chalk of armored pickups with their Owl team, in case of a full-scale ambush.

After checking all his mirrors again, Hilton swung the truck onto a dirt side street between city blocks. Finally, he said to Daoud, "Are you okay?"

"Yes," the man answered, though he still breathed heavier than normal.

"You don't look fine. What's going on?"

"I saw him, Hilton. Today."

"Saw who? Start from the beginning."

"This afternoon. After prayer, I was chosen. I think

they want me to martyr."

"*Who* wants you to martyr?"

"Maliki."

"*Mirwan* Maliki? You talked to him? Daoud, what the fuck!?"

Speaking in short, choppy sentences—his English broken by panic—Daoud recounted his meeting with Maliki across from the mosque in Nhahrullah. Hilton's pulse spiked by the end of it.

"Do you know where he's staying?" Hilton asked.

"No. But you do," Daoud replied. His face widened with excitement.

"That doesn't make any sense. How would I know where he's staying?"

"My tracker."

"Your wha…?" Hilton hadn't even gotten the thought out when he realized what Daoud was saying. "What did you do?"

"The tracker you gave me. I put it in Maliki's car. Under the seat."

"Did anyone see you?"

"I don't think so. I was alone."

Hilton almost yelled at him. "If you were alone, then it had to be you! If they find it, I don't know if I can protect you, Daoud!"

"If you find him, you don't have to protect me. Right? Besides, I was careful. I did everything you taught me," Daoud said.

Behind the wheel, Hilton shook his head.

"We can stop them! *You* can stop them!" Daoud said,

his voice rising.

"If Maliki talked to you, you're already being followed."

"So go get him. If you get him, Al Badari will drop what he's doing to find Maliki."

"Okay. You're coming back with me. I'll get you cleared to stay on base tonight. You'll be there until after someone picks up Maliki."

"You said I'm already being followed. If they see me go onto your base, they'll know something is wrong."

"You said you were careful."

"What if they're watching my home, and I don't return."

"It won't matter. We'll get you on a flight out of the country."

"What about my visa?"

Hilton's stomach churned. That visa paperwork sat in a stack somewhere in Kelly's office at the embassy. They wouldn't let him in at this hour, especially not with an unvetted local civilian. Hilton smacked the steering wheel with both hands.

"Shit," he muttered.

"I will be okay if you move quickly, Hilton. I trust you," Daoud said.

They drove in silence while Hilton weaved the truck street to street.

"Okay," Hilton said. "You ready?"

"Yes."

They looped around another traffic circle, more than a mile from their pickup point, before pulling into a narrow alleyway between storefronts.

"See you soon," Hilton said.

Just before they exited the end of the alley, Daoud pushed his door open and rolled out of the truck. Hilton gunned the engine and turned hard, using momentum to close the passenger door. He immediately checked his rearview mirror and tapped his brakes twice. A hundred meters back, a pair of headlights flickered.

Hilton pressed down hard on the accelerator, the diesel engine whining against the weight of the truck's armor package. The two trucks raced back to Clocktower, blowing every red light that hung over an empty intersection. Hilton was out of his truck by the time Frank and Gary pulled into the parking space next to his.

"Thanks, guys!" Hilton called, jogging toward the operations center. He dropped into a chair at an empty desk and snatched up the phone, dialing quickly with one hand as the other dug a small notebook out of the cargo pocket of his khaki utility pants. Holly answered on the second ring.

"Operations," she said politely.

"Holly, it's Hilton. Put Jack on."

"He stepped out."

"Find him."

"Hang on."

The line clicked. Hilton spun back and forth in the chair while he waited. He glanced up at the multi-zone LED clock on the wall. It was approaching 11 a.m. on the East Coast. The line clicked again, and Jack's voice greeted him.

"Working late?" Jack said.

"Night's just getting started," Hilton said.

"What's up?"

"I have a source who made direct contact with Mirwan Maliki. He removed the GPS tracker off his own vehicle and dropped it in Maliki's. I need you to ping it."

"What's the number?"

Hilton flipped through his notebook and found the ID number for Daoud's tracking device. He read it out to Jack, one digit at a time.

"Wait one."

Hilton could hear the keyboard clicking on the other end of the line. Then, trying to contain his excitement, Jack said, "I think we got him, Hilton. It's sitting at a remote compound outside of Nhahrullah. Signal is fixed, and it's inside the compound walls."

"Now what?"

"Jameson and Flash moved their Owls to the Nhahrullah COP a few hours ago."

"What if we just spin up Strike Troop from here? Once the props are turning, it's fifteen mikes time on target, tops."

"Negative," Jack said. "Langley will want him alive, and they'll want whatever intel is on site. If we take him, and they get anything out of the compound, we may be able to stop Al Badari in his tracks."

"What do I do, boss?" Hilton said.

"Where's your source?"

"Out in the cold. Maliki may have people sitting on his house. If he doesn't go home, it's a red flag."

"He agreed to go back?"

"It was his idea. And I have no way to track him now."

"Shit."

"My thoughts exactly."

"Well done. You're finished. Get some sleep and try to track him down in the morning. I've got work to do."

"Get after it," Hilton said.

"Out here," Jack replied. The line went dead.

In Virginia, Jack dialed another number on his phone. He covered the end of the phone with his hand, telling Holly, "Keep a screen on that tracker. If it moves one foot, yell at me. Get a Predator in the air and route it to that location. Maximum offset, no direct overflight." His hand uncovered the phone. "Lisa! Drop everything you're doing."

On the other end, Lisa rebuffed immediately, "Jack, I can't do lunch today I'm…"

"We found Mirwan Maliki."

"Hang on," she snapped.

Jack heard rustling in her office at Langley. She came back quickly and said, "Say that slowly."

"We found Maliki," Jack repeated. "One of my guys has a source that met with him face to face today and tagged his truck. I'm looking at his real-time location right now."

"You're looking at a *truck's* real-time location, Jack. Don't get excited."

"The truck is in a walled compound outside of Nhahrullah."

"Is the source reliable?"

"Best estimate."

"Can you do better?"

"Can *you*?"

"Don't fuck with me, Jack."

"I'm spinning up a company Pred right now, and we've got an Owl strike force with advisors already at the Nhahrullah COP. It's gonna take us about an hour to get the bird in range."

"Have you WARNO'ed the Owls yet?"

A "WARNing Order" is a rough outline of a mission that's unconfirmed but expected to be greenlit by higher command shortly. It allows the ground troops to start building a complete tactical plan while waiting for approval.

"The intel is less than five minutes old. You were my first call," Jack said.

Lisa drummed her fingernails on her desk.

Jack pressed harder. "Lisa, we've got the assets to do this. If we snatch Maliki, it's our best chance to flush out Al Badari. We might be able to stop this shit storm dead in its tracks."

"How far is your COP from this compound?" Lisa asked.

Jack turned to Holly and relayed the question. She looked at the GPS coordinates reading off the tracker and scrolled across a digital map on her computer screen, spitting out her calculation without looking up from the monitor.

"About fifteen klicks," Jack said into the phone.

"Jesus, he's right under your noses."

"Say the word."

"I'll call you right back," Lisa said.

"Shit."

The line went dead in Jack's ear. It took 40 minutes before the phone rang in Windsor Kraft's GOC. Jack snatched the handset off its cradle, placed it to his ear, and said nothing.

"Jack?" Lisa said.

"I'm here," Jack said.

"How much longer until your bird can get eyes on?"

"Ten more minutes, give or take."

"I'll be there in three hours."

"What about the Owls?"

"Wait the ten minutes. If it looks like a dry hole, call my cell."

"And if it looks good?"

"Stand up the assault force."

"Roger that."

"See you soon, Jack."

He placed the handset down and looked over to Holly. She stared at him intently.

"She wants us to look at it first," Jack said.

Holly blew out an impatient breath and glanced at the large flat screen on the wall showing the drone's camera feed. It would take twelve more minutes, not ten, until the Predator got close enough to see the compound with its camera set to maximum zoom. High walls. Multiple buildings. A row of parked SUVs. The largest building sported a machine gun team on the roof. Men with rifles slung across their back sat outside one of the smaller out-buildings.

Jack reached for the handset on his desk.

It was thirty minutes before midnight in Daristan when a phone rang at COP Nhahrullah.

DAY TWO

**JIMMY TOOMS AND BEN GORDON
CALLSIGNS "JAMESON" AND "FLASH"
COMBAT ADVISORY TROOP – WINDSOR KRAFT STRATEGIES
NHAHRULLAH, DARISTAN (100KM NORTH OF TARKENT)
0214 HOURS, LOCAL**

The buckle on Jimmy's battle belt clicked shut. He tugged on the back and sides of the belt to double check fit. Then he grabbed his Staccato off the plywood table, glancing through the red dot to verify the brightness setting. Finally, he tapped the switch on his pistol-mounted light and pulled the slide back half an inch to confirm a round in the chamber before jabbing the handgun into its holster. He draped a fully loaded plate carrier over his head, cinched the cummerbund around his torso, and slung his carbine across his chest—performing all the same checks on it that he had on his pistol: red dot, weapon light, laser, round in the chamber. It was half-conscious at this point, but those little checks embodied the rigor and ritual of every mission. It was the same as an accountant double-checking their math, or a doctor tapping their stethoscope before listening to your heartbeat.

"You ready?"

It was Ben, leaning halfway in the door.

Jimmy turned to face him and stepped forward. Ben held the door, and they crossed the portal together. Even at 2 a.m., it was still almost 90 degrees and unseasonably humid. A column of trucks sat idling on the road in front of them. Ubiquitous armored Hilux pickups predominantly made up the line, each topped with pintle mounts sporting an array of Soviet-era heavy weapons—PKM machine guns, AGS grenade launchers, and SPG-9 recoilless rifles. Two Hino dump trucks joined them, their buckets removed and replaced with ZPU-2 anti-aircraft cannons. An Owl sat atop each cannon, flanked on either side by a massive barrel and twelve hundred rounds of 14.5mm tungsten-cored ammunition. Individual slugs weighed over two ounces apiece and left the ZPU travelling 1,000 meters per second.

Jimmy felt his shoulders tense as he eyed the line of trucks. Their objective was to capture Mirwan Maliki alive, not kill him, but it was open season on everyone and everything who stood in their way.

"See you port side, sailor," Ben said.

Jimmy looked over to see Ben holding up one clenched fist. Jimmy bumped fists with him, and the two parted. Ben rode in the rearmost Hilux, a designated casualty pickup vehicle loaded with extra stretchers and trauma bags. Jimmy went in the second pickup, just behind the point truck, running command-and-control with the Owls' Daristani Lieutenant.

**JACK YOUNG
WATCH CAPTAIN
GLOBAL OPERATIONS CENTER - WINDSOR KRAFT STRATEGIES
CHESAPEAKE, VA
1620 HOURS, LOCAL**

Jack let out a quiet breath as he watched the line of trucks leave the front gate of Contingency Operating Post Nhahrullah. Live thermal video feed piped into the GOC via the Predator drone circling overhead half-the-world away. Lisa Gregson rode shotgun as liaison, since Mirwan was a priority target for the Agency.

Both felt cautiously optimistic that Mirwan could provide insight into where Al Badari holed up inside Daristan. The chances he directed this campaign remotely from outside the country were, by all estimates, incredibly slim. He wanted to walk into Daristani Parliament and sit in the president's chair personally, and there was nowhere outside of Daristan close enough for him to make the trip without being spotted or captured. Odds were he'd been inside the country for several months, hiding in Daristan's mountainous hinterlands while his army did the fighting for him.

"What's their time to target?" Lisa asked.

"Sub thirty minutes," Jack replied.

"Who's running this op?"

"Two of my guys, and a forty-five-man platoon of

Owls."

"Right. But *who*?" she asked again.

Jack glanced over at her, then back to the screen as he told her. "Jimmy Tooms and Ben Gordon. Jimmy is a former Dev Group assaulter. Ben's a SARC."

"A what?"

"Force Recon medic," he clarified.

"How long have they been in-country?"

"They ran the Combat Advisory Troop in Hafiza for three years before collapsing the COP and displacing to Nhahrullah a few days ago. Spent their careers as East Coast guys, the whole way. Little Creek, then Dam Neck for Jimmy. Parris Island, then Lejeune for Ben. Crossed paths a few times in the mil, I believe. Either way, they're close. And two of our best."

"Families?"

"Jimmy had a rough divorce about 18 months ago. They've got a little girl. Ben's engaged. She's a pro bodybuilder, or fitness competitor, something like that. She's a good woman."

"You've met her?" Lisa asked.

"Twice," Jack said.

"Hope I don't have to," Lisa said grimly.

"They'll do fine," Jack said, keeping his voice steady, knowing no such thing was guaranteed.

"Fresh pot, if anyone needs it?"

Jack and Lisa both looked behind them. The industrial coffee machine at the back of the GOC bubbled as it spit the last droplets of coffee into the fishbowl pot.

**JIMMY TOOMS AND BEN GORDON
CALLSIGNS "JAMESON" AND "FLASH"
COMBAT ADVISORY TROOP – WINDSOR KRAFT STRATEGIES
NHAHRULLAH, DARISTAN (100KM NORTH OF TARKENT)
0252 HOURS, LOCAL**

The two dump trucks, with their ZPU cannons, took up positions at the northwest and eastern sides of the walled-in compound – each offset by about a hundred yards outside the gate. The trucks received support from ten-man Owl squads holding outer cordon around the perimeter to protect the assault squad from attacks that could come from nearby villages.

Ben pulled his two-truck chalk of armored Hiluxes alongside Jimmy's. Their vehicles would move the assault squad—themselves plus the last 10 Owls—up to the compound to breach. Not knowing which building Mirwan would be in, they would have to clear the entire compound. Using maps and satellite imagery, they knew there were two houses and three small outlying buildings that appeared to be either storage sheds or small, one-room guard quarters.

The plan called for sending half the assault element through the front gate. The other half would blow a "mouse hole" through the mud-brick wall on the eastern side of the compound and make entry that way. The eastern element would take two of the small buildings and the main house at the back of the compound. The main gate element would clear a small building near the gate as well as the two smaller guest houses.

Jimmy flashed the IR headlights on his truck. Ben saw the signal through his night vision goggles, and his trucks charged forward, quickly gaining speed. They raced directly toward the front of the compound before peeling around the outer wall to set up for the east side breach.

Jimmy counted off in his head, giving Ben's truck a thirty-second head start. When the clock in his head ran out, he looked at his driver and tapped on the dashboard. The Owl behind the wheel jammed the clutch, threw their truck into gear, and took off, with its buddy truck close behind. Halfway to the gate, Jimmy's earmuffs crackled as Ben keyed his radio.

"Setting breach," Ben said.

"Roger. En route," Jimmy said.

Just as Jimmy's truck skidded to a halt at the front gate, Ben's voice came over the radio again. "We're set."

As soon as Jimmy's truck stopped, four Owls leapt out of the truck bed and unhooked a heavy metal chain from the front bumper. Two Owls aimed their AKs into the compound as the other two looped the chain around the gate.

Jimmy squeezed the PTT button on his plate carrier. "Breach, breach, breach!"

He slapped his driver on the leg, and the commando shifted the truck into reverse. Just as the engine revved up, a massive explosion erupted at the east wall. Ignoring the blast, Jimmy's driver stomped the gas pedal, and the

Hilux engine roared against the chain's tension before the front gates ripped out of the wall.

Jimmy bailed out of the passenger seat. He could already hear dogs barking and gunfire inside the compound as his four-man Owl team made entry. The two lead commandos stacked up on the small outlier building. Jimmy sprinted to catch up to them. By the time he reached the building, one man had kicked the door open while his partner threw a flashbang inside. The grenade went off with a lightning flash and a loud concussion. Both men entered the dark room and almost immediately came back out, each hauling a prisoner by the backs of their robes.

Before the dust settled from the breaching charge, Ben's four Owls were through the mouse hole. The men paired off, and each two-man team stacked up on the pair of small out-buildings. A flashbang into each room detonated almost simultaneously. The Owls brought one man out of the first building, and three out of the second. They threw all four insurgents to the ground, cinching zip-cuffs around their wrists and ankles.

Ben rolled each insurgent over onto their backs and shined an infrared flashlight on their faces to check if any were Mirwan Maliki. Over the radio, he said, "Guard shacks clear, four PUCs. Moving to main house. Flash, out."

Ben glanced over his shoulder to see another team of Owls coming through the mouse hole. They were the designated PUC—Persons Under Control—handlers. They hauled all four insurgents to their feet, cut the zip-cuffs on their ankles, and walked them out of the compound to one of the trucks outside.

Ben pinched the carabiner hooked to his battle belt and pulled off two duct-taped bundles of IR chem lights. He bent each bundle, cracking the chem lights. Shaking them to activate the plastic light sticks—which would only be visible through their night vision—he tossed a bundle into each of the small buildings. AKs at the ready, his assault team formed a loose column and approached the main residence. Ben fell in at the back of the line.

Meanwhile, Jimmy's assault team stacked up at the front door of the guest house. One of the Owls stood in front of the door and gave it a hard kick. The door didn't move. The commando grabbed the doorknob and pulled hard, then threw his shoulder into the door. It still wouldn't budge.

Jimmy ran up to the door from behind the assault team, pushed the kick man aside, and pulled a small strip of explosive breaching charge out of his cargo pocket. The charge was pre-primed, with a looped zip-tie around the top of it. He hung the charge on the door and un-spooled the length of shock tube wrapped around it, backing up as he let slack out. The Owl team backed away from the door as Jimmy turned away and jerked the pull-ring out of the detonator. The charge exploded with a harsh *crack*.

As the door swung inward, a burst of AK fire sprayed out. Jimmy pitched forward into the dirt, two rounds hitting his back armor plate. One of the Owls pulled a frag grenade off his belt, popped the safety spoon and tossed it into the building. The grenade went off, and the Owls made entry.

Jimmy rolled out of the doorway and scrambled to all fours, wheezing from the blunt force of the rounds against his rib cage. Another volley of AK fire spit out from inside the building, then another grenade explosion. By the time Jimmy was on his feet, the Owls exited the building, dragging one of their own behind. The wounded Owl left a trail of blood in the dirt from a bullet hole in his leg.

Jimmy keyed his radio. "Flash, Jameson. Guest house clear. One Owl down. Bring up the ambulance."

Puffs of dirt kicked up around them as a burst of machine gun fire came at them from the roof of the main house. Two of the Owls returned fire as Jimmy and the third commando pulled their wounded behind the guest house. One Hilux rolled through the front gate, its gunner returning fire to the main house with the truck's bed-mounted PKM. The truck swerved around Jimmy and came to a stop at the corner of the guest house. Under the staccato thumping of belt-fed return fire, he heard empty casings clattering into the truck bed.

Jimmy took a knee. He plucked a tourniquet off his kit and looped it around the wounded Owl's shredded thigh. He cinched the tourniquet as tight as he could, pressing the Velcro strap down before cranking the windlass to staunch the flow of blood from the commando's femoral artery.

Ben saw the muzzle flashes from the rooftop of the main house as they made their approach. Part of his brain registered the sound of Alpha Squad's evac truck pulling into the compound, before he saw the streak of incoming green tracers from an Owl machine gun chewing into the roof of the house in front of them.

"Shift to the rear," Ben ordered. Each Owl passed the command to the man in front of them. The point man pivoted and circled around the back of the house. "Jameson, Flash. Moving to breach from the rear."

Jimmy had just finished applying the tourniquet when he keyed his radio with a bloody hand. "Roger, copy secondary breach."

Ben took his team to the back of the house. They stacked on the back door.

"Standby," Ben whispered. He pulled a frag grenade and tossed it over his head onto the roof. It detonated, and the machine gun fire stopped.

Jimmy's voice came through Ben's headset. "Rooftop clear. Move."

"Roger."

Ben squeezed the shoulder of the Owl in front of him—the command to make entry. The Owl team smashed a small square window next to the back door, which they kicked in simultaneously. The team threw flashbangs into each opening. Following the twin blasts, all four of them flowed through the doorway, with Ben immediately behind.

Inside were two rooms near the door in a hallway, both on the right side. Two Owls peeled off and entered the first two, with the second two moving around them to clear the second room. Ben moved past both rooms and held his position in the hallway, carbine pointed toward the main living area. Two gunshots rang out from one of the rooms, followed by a rapid string of commands shouted in angry Daristani.

One of the Owls came up behind Ben and touched his arm. "Mister Ben. First room."

"Hold the hall," Ben replied.

The Owl stepped in front of Ben and pointed his AK down the hallway. Ben turned around and went into the first room. A man clad in black robes laid face down on the bed, bound in zip cuffs. Ben rolled him over and shined the IR flashlight in his face. The man spit at him, blurring one tube of his NVGs with a gob of saliva. Ben laid into him with a hard right cross that sent blood spraying from the corner of the man's mouth. Ben grabbed the man by his chest-length beard and turned his head back toward him, shining the IR flashlight on him again. Even through spit-blurred night vision, Ben could make out the face he'd memorized hours before.

"Jameson, Flash. Payday. I say again, Payday," Ben said.

"Jameson copies," came the reply.

Ben heard gunfire out in the hallway. He turned away from Mirwan and jammed his carbine through the door. He saw muzzle flashes from the living room. Two insurgents had flipped a heavy wooden table and were shooting at them from behind it. The Owl holding the hallway fired back. The quiet chugging of Ben's suppressed rifle joined the clatter of gunfire. He put half-a-dozen rounds through the table and watched both insurgents roll out from behind it. One wasn't moving, but the other dragged himself toward them, pistol in hand. Ben fired two rounds into him, and he stopped moving. The team of Owls swirled around him and made their way into the living room.

"Clear!" one of them called.

"Check the roof," Ben said.

Two Owls walked out of the back of the house and climbed up a ladder propped against the side of the building. They found two machine gunners on the roof, but both were already dead, their bodies mangled by a combination of PKM fire from Jimmy's evac truck and fragmentation from Ben's hand grenade.

**JACK YOUNG
WATCH CAPTAIN
GLOBAL OPERATIONS CENTER - WINDSOR KRAFT STRATEGIES
CHESAPEAKE, VA
1707 HOURS, LOCAL**

"Jameson, Flash. Payday. I say again, Payday."

Jack blew out a long breath, the corners of his mouth tugged up in a grin.

Lisa smiled, full on, and rubbed the middle of Jack's back before patting it roughly. A moment of affection, sealed off by the locker-room style "attaboy" back slap. The duality of the gesture captured both Lisa's personality and their relationship—far less than romantic, but a little more than strictly colleagues. Jack looked sideways at her, his smile widening to match hers. The smile left his face as soon as he turned his attention back to the screen.

"It's not over yet," he said, rubbing the bristly salt-and-pepper stubble on his jawline.

They watched quietly as the two Owls climbed the roof of the main house. Jimmy's team moved slowly around the inside perimeter, checking their work. The rest of Ben's team was not visible inside the house. Jack knew they were tossing every closet and cabinet, smashing dishes and knocking over end tables and armoires, looking for documents, computers, or portable hard drives—anything that might contain usable intelligence.

The buzz-phrase was SSE, or Sensitive Site Exploitation. The reality was closer to methodical ransacking.

After some time, both teams exited the compound, and the Hilux pickup trucks maneuvered back into a single staggered column. The cannon-bearing Hinos inserted themselves throughout as the entire unit began their halted, lumbering movement off the objective.

While they did have a desk-mounted speaker to monitor the team's radio traffic, the black-and-white thermal drone feed didn't carry live audio. As the last vehicle in the column rolled away from Maliki's compound, two dogs materialized out of nowhere, running at full gallop behind them.

Jack shook his head. "Even the dogs want to get out of Daristan."

"Do you blame them?" Lisa asked.

"Too bad you guys can't give us a contract to extract *them*."

Lisa scoffed, her eyes narrow and fixed on the monitor. "Jack, I bet your boys would burn that country down to fill a C-17 with rescue dogs."

"Just say the word."

She sighed, and said, "If they could talk to us, I'd get you that contract tonight."

Jack grinned. "Imagine that? Couple gallons of fresh water and two bags of kibble, they'd tell you everything."

"It'd be the biggest mass defection we've ever seen."

Jack nudged her with an elbow. "They might even give you a medal."

Straight-faced, she replied, "I'd have to sell it to pay for all the dog food."

Jack was still chuckling when the entire screen flashed white. Behind them, Holly drew a sharp breath. The image refreshed in a second, just in time for them to see the white streak of an RPG flying in from off screen, followed by the chalky flecks of inbound machine-gun tracers. The second and last pickups in the column billowed smoke. The radio speaker on the desk in front of them hissed for half a second before Ben's voice ripped through the stillness in the GOC.

"Contact right!"

JIMMY TOOMS AND BEN GORDON
CALLSIGNS "JAMESON" AND "FLASH"
COMBAT ADVISORY TROOP – WINDSOR KRAFT STRATEGIES
NHAHRULLAH, DARISTAN (100KM NORTH OF TARKENT)
0310 HOURS, LOCAL

Jimmy flinched as the truck in front of him rocked over onto two wheels before smashing back down on all four. Almost simultaneously, he heard the RPG detonate somewhere behind him, and the hard *thwacks* of bullets hitting his armored door. The bulletproof passenger side window, only inches from his head, became spider-webbed but continued to absorb incoming rounds. His driver had already pushed his door open and bailed out, taking up a firing position behind the front bumper.

Jimmy hauled himself over the console, the small of his back tingling as he felt the vibrations of incoming rounds hitting the window behind him, and tumbled out of the truck behind his driver, scrambling to a position at the back bumper. He knew all the other trucks would execute the same maneuver, setting up to return fire.

Just as he raised his carbine, one of the ZPUs came to life. He felt the concussion in his chest as the massive, twin-barrel auto-cannon chugged hundreds of slugs into the night air. Up and down the line of trucks, Owls laid on heavy volleys of crackling fire from their AKs and PKMs, completely drowning out the suppressed shots from Jimmy's carbine. He ducked behind the back of his truck to reload when his radio earpiece crackled with a woman's distinct west Texas twang.

"Jameson, Mongoose," the woman said.

Mongoose was the drone pilot's callsign.

"Go for Jameson," Jimmy said.

"Nine hostiles, two hundred meters west, your position, over."

Ben cut in. "Flash copies. Moving to flank. Lay it on thick."

"Jameson copies."

Ben ran up to the cab of the second Hino truck, the second-to-last vehicle in the column. He banged on the door with a closed fist, and the driver opened it.

"Follow us! *That* way!" he said, gesturing with his whole arm. The driver nodded and slammed the door closed.

Ben ran back to his Hilux, pocked with bullet impacts but still running. He pulled a single-shot 40mm grenade launcher and bandolier of shells out of the truck bed, and climbed back into the passenger seat. His driver hopped in behind him and shut the door. Ben gave him quick directions on which way to go. The driver nodded frantically, and their truck peeled away from the column and took off, bouncing hard over the rutted, rocky terrain. The Hino gun truck was ten yards behind them.

Ben glanced out the driver's side window to see a wall of ZPU and PKM tracers streaming from the rest of the column toward the attackers. A couple of incoming rounds skipped off the side of their truck, but Jimmy kept sustained fire to keep them from turning on Ben's small team. Ben groped each individual grenade on the cloth bandolier until he felt the distinct shape and raised markings on the specific round he wanted. He pulled that one round, then draped the belt around his neck. The launcher's stubby barrel popped open with a soft *clunk*.

"Flash, Mongoose, you're on their flank, seven-five meters south your position, over."

"Flash copies." He turned to his driver. "Right here."

Ben threw his door open and rolled out before the truck came to a full stop. As soon as both feet hit the ground, he palmed the grenade into the launcher, aimed high over the truck, and crushed the launcher's heavy trigger with his finger. The grenade launcher kicked into his shoulder as the round sailed high into the night.

Three seconds later, the infrared flare ignited, almost directly over the cluster of bad guys hunkered down in their ambush position. With the naked eye, the insurgents wouldn't see anything. But for Jimmy and the Owls, all wearing night vision goggles, the IR flare would hang like a spotlight over the insurgents for the next 30 to 40 seconds.

The Hino truck gunner behind him—also wearing NVGs—swiveled his massive anti-aircraft cannons to line up directly under the flare's glow. The big truck rocked on its shocks as a blistering hail of ZPU rounds went right into the ambush nest.

Ben opened the launcher and plucked the empty case out of the pipe. Pinching a high-explosive grenade off the belt, he fed it into the breach, slammed the weapon closed, and laid his arms across the hood of the Hilux. The HE grenade went downrange with a hollow *thunk*. Not waiting for the impact, Ben emptied and reloaded with another HE round. Just as he slammed the breach closed again, he saw a flash through his NVGs and heard the crunching explosion from his first shot. He shouldered the launcher and fired again.

When the second grenade detonated, the drone pilot called back, "Flash, Mongoose. All hostiles neutralized or immobile, over."

"Flash copies."

"Jameson copies."

Moments later, all the Owls ceased fire. Ben still leaned over the hood of his truck, the grenade launcher's sights lined up over the insurgents' position. After another ten seconds, he keyed his mic. "Mongoose, Flash. SITREP, over."

**JACK YOUNG
WATCH CAPTAIN
GLOBAL OPERATIONS CENTER - WINDSOR KRAFT
STRATEGIES
CHESAPEAKE, VA
1716 HOURS, LOCAL**

Jack and Lisa stared intently at the monitor. They had pulled up chairs to sit right in front of the radio speaker.

"Mongoose, Flash. SITREP, over."

"Mongoose has no hostile movement, over."

"Flash copies, break, Jameson, Flash."

"Go for Jameson."

"We're holding. What's your status?"

"Two vics down hard. Three Owls K-I-A, four Owls wounded. Six PUCs K-I-A. How copy, over?"

"Flash copies. What about Payday?"

Jameson took several seconds to come back on the radio. "He's fine. Payday intact."

Lisa leaned back in her chair and exhaled.

"At least there's that," Jack said.

"Jameson, what's your status?" Ben said over the radio.

Jimmy came back instantly this time. "I'm good."

"Copy. Can you push a fireteam up to clear the nest? We'll hold the flank."

"Affirmative. Two mikes."

"Roger."

Two minutes later, a Hilux separated from the column in a slow roll head-on toward where the attack originated.

Jack's eyes drew to the bottom corner of the screen. Two small forms ran in a circle around each other, then bolted off screen in the opposite direction from the ambush.

"Was that the dogs?" Lisa asked.

Jack just grinned and nodded his head.

"Christ on a cracker," she said in disbelief. "Your guys, Maliki, *and* the dogs all made it out of that clean?"

"Yes, ma'am."

"Fuckin' A."

"Yes, ma'am," he said again.

The radio chatter continued.

"Dustoff, Dustoff, this is Jameson."

"Go for Dustoff."

"Dustoff, nine-line request, prepare to copy."

"Send it, Jameson."

"Line 1…"

BEN GORDON
CALLSIGN "FLASH"
COMBAT ADVISORY TROOP – WINDSOR KRAFT STRATEGIES
NHAHRULLAH, DARISTAN (100KM NORTH OF TARKENT)
0325 HOURS, LOCAL

While Jimmy called in the nine-line MEDEVAC and prepped an LZ with infrared chem lights, Ben took a team of Owls to clear the ambush nest. All the attackers had, indeed, been neutralized. But as he stepped from body to body, using a red-lens penlight to quickly check each one, his brow crinkled beneath his Ops Core helmet.

Clicking on his radio mic, Ben said, "Hey Jimmy, you got a sec?"

"Wait one," Jimmy replied.

While he waited, Ben turned to one of the Owls, pointing at three corpses. "These here. Search them. Take everything in their pockets. Pull all the patches off their uniforms."

The commando nodded, relaying the orders to his teammates in Daristani. Moments later, one of the Owls stood up over a body, pointed to it, and said something in his native tongue.

Ben turned to the one English-speaking commando, who told him, "There are no name tapes, and the patches are stitched on."

"Cut them off," Ben said tersely.

The order was translated, and in the darkness, Ben heard the mechanical *snick* of a pocketknife flipped open. Shortly after, the crunching sound of Jimmy's footsteps echoed from behind him.

"What'cha got?" Jimmy asked.

Ben said nothing, but clicked his flashlight back on, shining it down. An Owl bent over the body, sawing a cloth patch off the camouflage uniform sleeve. Ben waved his light over the face. Even under the red hue, the complexion was clearly Caucasian. The dead man's hair was buzzed clean on the sides, with a ragged mohawk-style swath running down the middle of his scalp to the nape of his neck. His beard looked thick, but meticulously trimmed, and glistened against the crimson light from a heavy coat of oil.

"He's not Daristani," Jimmy said flatly. He leaned down and pulled the fighter's rifle off his chest, running his hands over it.

Unlike the rickety AKs used by Al Badari's insurgents, this particular Kalashnikov sported a long-railed forend, holographic sight, and an adjustable AR-style buttstock. It was most definitely not the rifle of a third-world peasant guerilla.

Jimmy held the rifle out. Ben examined it closely with his flashlight. With his free hand, Ben peeled the half-empty magazine out of the gun and looked down into the top of it. The bullets looked long and skinny, almost dart-like.

"Five-four-five," Ben said.

Later-generation 5.45x39mm ammunition was more

advanced, and harder to come by, than the older 7.62mm ammunition found in AK-47s the world over—the Soviet Union's chief export for decades.

Jimmy tossed the rifle on the ground. Ben dropped the magazine at his feet. The Owl commando hunched over the body finished his work and held up a dark oval of cloth that he'd cut from the dead man's arm. Jimmy took it from him, holding it under Ben's light. A skeletal angel, bone wings flared out from its body, clutched an AK in a crude embroidering on the patch.

"Fuck," Jimmy whispered.

"Yeah," Ben added. "We're dumping all their pocket litter. Let's hope one of them was dumb enough to carry a wallet."

The beating rotors of an incoming MEDEVAC helicopter ended their conversation.

**HILTON PIERCE
CALLSIGN "ALLEY CAT"
RECCE TROOP - WINDSOR KRAFT STRATEGIES
TARKENT, DARISTAN
0628 HOURS, LOCAL**

Hilton glanced at his watch. Again. It was almost half past, later than Daoud normally showed up, but not much later. Considering the simmering instability, and the utter lack of urgency that pervaded Daristani culture, fifteen minutes fell well within the margins of normal. It shouldn't have bothered Hilton at all.

But it did.

Hilton nudged his elbow against the Staccato HD, which he now wore uncovered on his hip instead of concealed under his shirt in an appendix holster. He'd seen more of that in the expat district over the last couple of days; bodyguards and contractors carrying weapons in the open, instead of concealed under flannel shirts or photographer's vests. Several NATO armies now required their personnel to move around the city in "battle rattle"—camouflage plate carriers laden with mags, med kits, radios, and grenade pouches.

Hilton knew how much colonels and generals hated wearing their kit. Seeing it signaled growing discomfort over the non-stop stream of intelligence about Al Badari forces capturing larger swaths of the countryside and a possible takeover of Tarkent.

His eyes darted around the café as the girl approached his table to refill his glass with a steaming pour of green tea. It was possible, if not likely, Al Badari already had scouts inside the city walls, if not inside the expat district specifically. Al Badari was a lot of things, but ignorant wasn't one of them. He knew light-skinned foreigners sobbing with snotty noses in front of a shaky camera made great propaganda. Kidnapping proved a successful business model in most of the countries Hilton had worked in.

The Staccato's grip clicked softly against the arm of his wrought-iron chair as he shifted his weight. The IFAK remained in his back pocket. The small, plastic radio earpiece planted firmly in his left ear. Hilton glanced skyward. A thick blanket of clouds the shade of ice cubes draped across the sky. Even though he couldn't see the drone, he knew the drone could see him.

JACK YOUNG
WATCH CAPTAIN
GLOBAL OPERATIONS CENTER - WINDSOR KRAFT
STRATEGIES
CHESAPEAKE, VA
0230 HOURS, LOCAL

Jack heard the GOC door open behind him but didn't bother looking. Holly came up next to him, holding out a grease-stained paper sack with his dinner in it. Eyes still fixed on the monitors, he took the bag. Holly had gone home, caught a couple hours of sleep, and come back with a late dinner—or early breakfast—from an all-night fast food joint on her way back to the GOC. Jack had slept in his office.

"Thanks, Holly."

"I miss anything?" she asked, following his gaze toward the bank of flat screens.

"Not yet."

"You expecting something?"

"Any day now," he replied.

"You should get out of here for a little bit."

"I'm fine."

"I didn't say you weren't. But still."

"Hilton's contact is late."

Holly looked up at the multi-zone LED clock over the TVs.

"Not by Daristani standards."

"By his standards."

"Could be stuck. Al Badari's men are probably throwing up roadblocks all over the place."

Jack sat down at the nearest empty desk with his food. He removed the paper-wrapped burger, then the carton of fries. Holly had already placed his drink cup down, knowing where he'd most likely sit.

"Nothing I say is gonna change your mind, huh?" Holly said.

"Not tonight," he said, unwrapping the burger halfway and taking a bite. He still ate like a career soldier—that is to say, aggressively. "Eat when you can, sleep when you can" was a mantra among warfighters perhaps as old as organized warfare itself. The burger disappeared in a half-dozen bites with little space for breathing and chewing.

While he ate, Holly seated herself behind her desk. She placed her food, then her cell phone, on the desk next to her keyboard. She ate much slower and more casually than her boss, taking a couple of small bites between checking emails, news websites, and secure cables from their staff at Tarkent airport. She kept a stack of napkins next to her keyboard, and she wiped her hands after every bite to keep her workstation clean.

They were already moving non-essential personal out of Daristan, squeezing them onto the shrinking number of available commercial flights to Jordan or eastern Europe. Military flights presented an option but, as of now, contractors were low priority on those. Some of the

Windsor Kraft staffers who were still Reservists or National Guardsmen were able to use their military IDs to get on C-17s headed to Rammstein or Incirlik.

Keeping track of who headed where, on which birds, formed a frantic task Holly could barely keep a handle on. She kept regular emails going to other PMCs from Britain, France, and Australia to cross-coordinate flight options.

The café Hilton liked trailed out of the edge of the main flat screen as the drone continued its slow loop around the city. She watched the screen change as the drone banked toward the massive, Biblical-era earthen gates into the heart of Tarkent.

Holly looked away to stuff a few French fries in her mouth and into a stomach that had already folded in half. She looked back up while chewing.

"Jack," she said, hurriedly licking her lips as she pointed. "What's that?"

HILTON PIERCE
CALLSIGN "ALLEY CAT"
RECCE TROOP - WINDSOR KRAFT STRATEGIES
TARKENT, DARISTAN
0632 HOURS, LOCAL

Hilton felt the eruption before he heard it. Something akin to the first big drop in a roller coaster, or maybe standing on the deck of a boat that just crested a big swell. But a split-second before he heard the first gunshots, he just *knew*. A long rip of PKM machine gun fire—almost half of a 100-round belt—overlapped the snappy blast of a suicide vest detonating.

Somewhere deep in the archives of his mind, Hilton knew it was a high-brisance explosive like PETN—a popular choice for suicide bombers—that created the short cracking explosion, as opposed to low-order mixtures like black powder or ANFO.

Not that it mattered in the moment.

About two-thirds of the people around him curled up under tables in a mimicry of shelter-in-place drills for mortar rounds, or —for the older crowd—the duck-and-cover drills of the Cold War.

But this was not incoming artillery, and it certainly was not a nuclear warhead. Crew-served machine guns and explosive vests required insurgents to get much closer to their targets. Al Badari's men weren't breaching the gates of Tarkent.

They were already inside.

Hilston supposed they probably came in days ago, if not longer, waiting like Greeks inside the proverbial wooden horse.

And he felt as exposed as a sleeping Trojan. Hilton's armored Hilux pickup sat parked almost a block away. He liked walking that last block to survey the street before sitting down for his meet with Daoud. This represented perhaps a degree of complacency, considering a direct attack in the diplomatic district hadn't occurred in almost three years.

Those expats, humanitarians, and diplomatic staff who weren't cowering under tables ran frantically in every direction possible. Some criss-crossed the street, hoping to avoid bullets or mortar shells. Others sprinted in a straight line down the sidewalk. Still others hunched against the doors of their armored SUVs, pulling frantically on locked handles while their car keys jingled uselessly in their pockets.

Hilton threaded himself between the pockets of panicked civilians as they jinked and twirled past him in sheer terror. He came within ten yards from his truck when two Al Badari insurgents, dressed like modern-day ninjas in black robes with drab green chest rigs, burst from the alleyway to his right. They almost knocked him over as they blew past, both of them spraying wildly into the street with tattered AK-47 rifles.

The automatic gunfire four feet away from him seemed distant and muffled, but the sound of his Staccato scraping against its Kydex holster sounded loud and sharp. Hilton drew instinctively and shot both insurgents in the back.

Two rounds between the shoulder blades on the first guy.

One round in the back of the head on the second.

Back to the first, for three more rounds through the neck.

Both fighters pitched forward into the middle of the street. Neither got up.

Hilton punched the handgun back into its holster, then pulled the truck keys out of his pocket. With the driver's door open, he reached in and ripped his chest rig out of the passenger foot well. He cinched it around his torso as he dropped behind the wheel. With the rig's harness secure, Hilton slammed the door closed behind him. Checking the rearview mirror as he twisted the key in the ignition, he caught a flutter of movement across the oblong reflection.

A man seemed to float across the street behind him, like Christ walking on water. He wore white robes and a black sash draped across his shoulders with a matching turban over his head. The tip of his snow-white beard touched his sternum. An AK slung across his chest, but the man seemed to have no interest in shooting.

As the Hilux's diesel engine grumbled to life, the man turned his head slightly toward the sound. Hilton caught two pinpricks of bright blue eyes in the rearview, before the man disappeared down a side street.

Hilton keyed the radio on his belt. "Clocktower, Alley

Cat. I am in heavy contact inside the diplomatic district. Say again, heavy direct contact."

A woman's voice came through the radio, from her desk back at Tarkent airport. "This is Clocktower, shelter in place or break contact. Return to base. How copy?"

Hilton shook his head, as he pulled his truck away from the curb and into the street. "Negative, Clocktower! I have eyes on Ansar Al Badari. Moving to engage."

"Alley Cat, confirm direct sighting of Ansar…"

Hilton cut her off as he stomped the gas pedal. "Confirm! It's Ansar. On foot, headed toward the Presidential Palace. Moving to intercept."

By the time Hilton got his response, the Hilux was already halfway through its tire-screeching U-turn.

"Clocktower copies. Out."

**VIKTOR
TARKENT, DARISTAN
0635 HOURS LOCAL**

"What the fuck is he doing?" Viktor spat.

The men standing with him shrugged and traded nervous glances.

Viktor had specifically told Ansar to stay with him until the fighting was over. A nondescript Hino cargo truck, parked a block from the palace, served as their command post and transport. The high-walled, open top truck would keep them hidden from view while still allowing some short-range radio communication.

Viktor and Ansar had argued vehemently about the latter's place in the assault. Ever the self-proclaimed warrior prince, Al Badari insisted on leading the charge into the most pivotal battle of his entire campaign. Wrapped up in ill-conceived notions of nobility and kingship, he felt the most important thing was for his men to see him walk through the palace gates before anyone else. Viktor, biased toward the practical and clandestine, tried to convince him that the battle in question would be for naught if Al Badari was killed in the melee.

A failed attack on the Presidential Palace resulting in Al Badari's death might be the one thing able to embolden the West to redouble its stake in Daristan's future as a potentially successful democratic state. That kind of defeat would be twofold: a permanent failure for Al Badari's cause, and a strategic loss for Viktor's employers that might prove to be equally permanent for Viktor himself.

Against Viktor's warning, Al Badari nearly toppled out of his chair to leap dashingly off the back of the Hino less than a minute after the first explosions.

Viktor's body tensed with rage. With the central district full of diplomats and military officers, shaky cell phone footage of the attack would be smeared across global television in a matter of minutes. If he or his men were caught in any of those recordings, his fate might still be sealed when he returned home—regardless of the tactical victory.

Viktor grabbed a radio off a card table in the back of the truck, clipping it to his belt. Then he reached under the table and hauled up a backpack with a much larger communications handset in it. Turning to the second-in-command, he slammed the backpack into the man's chest.

"Keep this. If you leave this truck before I call for you, I'll shoot you on sight," Viktor said.

The man bear-hugged the backpack and nodded rapidly.

Viktor grabbed his stubby AK carbine and hopped out of the truck. The chaos on the street felt oddly comforting to him. After years of guerilla warfare, Viktor's ability to process death and destruction became so refined as to be almost superhuman. Limp bodies on the sidewalk, broken glass, ball bearings under his feet, and bloody scorch marks against the sides of buildings. These things held only one value for him: the ballooning warmth of success that uncoiled his insides like the first swig of vodka on a snowy morning.

Among the flocks of people huddled and crouched under withering violence, Viktor strode purposefully but unrushed toward the palace. Flattened into the alcove of a storefront, two Swedish cameramen panned expensive cell phones in gimbal mounts back and forth across the mayhem.

Viktor passed by them before his mind registered the cameras. He pivoted and raised his AK in one smooth motion, dumping half a magazine of 5.45mm slugs into the journalists. Stepping into the alcove, he kicked the recording equipment away from their shuddering bodies, firing a round into each cell phone. Lowering the AK, he stepped back out onto the sidewalk and continued toward the palace.

Viktor fired sporadically as he moved, killing anyone with a phone in their hands. He reloaded as he walked. At the end of the next block, he saw a flutter of white robes as Al Badari disappeared down a side street. Viktor yelled for him, but the man was already gone. Viktor picked up his pace, jogging to catch him. Viktor was about to make the turn when the screech of skidding tires stopped him just steps away from the curb. A Hilux pickup truck flailed into a hasty turn, engine revving hard as it passed feet in front of Viktor, speeding down the side street after Al Badari. He caught only a glimpse of the man behind the wheel, but the driver's expression was unmistakable.

Straining forward against the seatbelt. Eyes fixed forward. Mouth clenched.

That truck wasn't fleeing. It was chasing.

Viktor cursed in Russian as he broke into a full sprint. He knew better than to follow an armored truck on foot. Instead, he kept running and button-hooked down the next alley, hoping to intercept Ansar at the palace gates.

HILTON PIERCE
CALLSIGN "ALLEY CAT"
RECCE TROOP - WINDSOR KRAFT STRATEGIES
TARKENT, DARISTAN
0637 HOURS, LOCAL

The heavy, armored truck fish-tailed as it made a hard-left down the side street Al Badari had disappeared into. Hilton glanced straight out and up through the windshield. Four pristine white minarets pierced the horizon a quarter mile in front of him. The Presidential Palace served as home to both Daristan's NATO-allied leader and the seat of its national Parliament.

Sporadic gunfire continued in the alleys and cross-streets on either side of him, stray bullets bursting against the truck's armor like hail in a hurricane. But the man in the white robes was nowhere in sight. Hilton's radio earpiece crackled again.

"Alley Cat, Clocktower. SITREP."

"Moving east toward the palace. Negative contact Al Badari. Out," Hilton replied.

A flurry of gunfire erupted three blocks ahead. Two insurgents opened fire on the front gate of the palace. A squad of royal guards—trained by US special forces—held their own, returning fire with machine guns and tossing hand grenades over the gate into the street.

The middle of Hilton's windshield burst into snowy

spiderwebs as stray machine gun rounds chugged across the bulletproof glass. Hilton cranked the steering wheel hard left. His Hilux jumped the curb and bucked up onto the sidewalk. Slamming the truck into park, he kicked the driver's door open with one leg, while pulling his Cobalt up from the passenger side footwell. Hilton steadied his aim against the side of the truck, centering a black-clad machine gunner in his crosshairs. He tapped the trigger four times. The insurgent crumpled in the street.

Hilton pulled back from the scope to survey his handiwork, but just as he raised his head over the rifle, a flood of black robes mobbed the palace gate. They poured in from both ends of the street, fifteen or twenty of them. Two ran right up to the palace gates and grabbed onto the bars. An instant later both men detonated their explosive vests in unison.

The wrought-iron bars tore off their hinges. The remaining mob of insurgents poured through the gate before the smoke cleared, several of them slipping and sliding on the blood smears that used to be their comrades.

Hilton put his eye back on the scope, calculating how many he could kill before they turned on him and opened fire. A flurry of white passed across the scope hairs. Hilton's finger touched the match-grade trigger as he shifted his rifle back and forth across the sea of black robes, looking for Al Badari's white garb. That's when Hilton saw him: the last man to enter the palace gates, and the tail end of the insurgents' entry team.

Hilton physically recoiled from his scope at the sight of the man, who was such a contrast to the others. The robed insurgents bunched up tightly as they poured into the palace courtyard. This man walked leisurely through the blast hole. His plate carrier, bristling with pouches and grenades, heaved slightly with each deliberate step. Once inside the palace walls, the man glanced over his shoulder, seeming to stare directly into Hilton's crosshairs. Hilton could clearly see the man's wavy, shoulder-length hair, thin moustache, and the deep scar running down the left side of his jawline.

Hilton pulled the rifle hard into his shoulder and pressed the trigger, just as a rocket-propelled grenade sailed over his head toward the palace. He tumbled off balance and fell onto the sidewalk, sending his shot high and wide into the afternoon sky.

Hilton rolled onto his back, snapped the carbine back up, and dumped a half-dozen rounds into the two-man RPG team in a truck at the intersection behind him. Hilton clamored to his feet, tossed his rifle into the cab of his truck, and jumped in behind it. He slammed the door shut, twisting his body to look out the back window as he shifted into reverse, and stomped the gas pedal hard again. Hilton cranked the wheel at the last second, angling his rear bumper toward the other truck's front bumper. He tapped the brakes to load weight onto the rear shocks, then stomped the gas again just as the truck made contact, spinning the other truck almost a full ninety degrees as he rammed through the intersection.

Hilton jerked the shifter into gear and sped away, passing the café table he'd sat at less than ten minutes ago. He keyed his radio.

"Clocktower, Alley Cat. Unable to intercept Al Badari. Palace gates have been breached. Oscar Mike to your location."

JACK YOUNG
WATCH CAPTAIN
GLOBAL OPERATIONS CENTER - WINDSOR KRAFT STRATEGIES
CHESAPEAKE, VA
0238 HOURS, LOCAL

Jack and Holly watched in silence as Hilton reversed his truck directly into the front of the technical, pushing the vehicle ninety degrees as if opening a door. Jack felt his feet and hands twitch as Hilton smashed the clutch, jerked the shifter from reverse to second gear in a U-shaped stroke, revved the engine to 2,500 RPM, and dumped the clutch to bolt the truck forward out of the kill zone. While the drone camera couldn't see inside Hilton's Hilux, it was a maneuver Jack trained and executed hundreds, if not thousands, of times himself.

Hilton's radio transmission crackled from the radio-monitoring station across the GOC.

"Clocktower, Alley Cat. Unable to intercept Al Badari. Palace gates have been breached. Oscar Mike to your location. Out."

The camera on the drone clicked to wide view. The rest of the city appeared quiet. Scattered heat signatures of people ran into buildings. Vehicles sped away from the city center, where the Palace complex was located. But there were no other attacks.

Al Badari's men were not ransacking the city. They

cut the head off the Daristan snake. Once they seized the Presidential Palace, Hall of Government, and National Court building—all located inside the Palace Compound—it would be over. Badari only needed to seize the seat of power, and the people would fall in line—their trust in a dysfunctional, NATO-chaperoned democracy shattered like so much broken glass across the sidewalk.

From his basement bunker in southern Virginia, Jack watched more than a decade of combined Western influence crumble in real time. Within ten minutes, the stuttered flashes of small arms fire inside the Palace compound ceased.

A dozen bodies scattered around the Palace courtyards faded from white to gray as they cooled. Other bodies, bright white and ambulatory, milled about in the uncertainty of swift victory and unchallenged occupation.

The drone camera, controlled by a pilot at Clocktower headquarters in Tarkent, zoomed back in on the Palace compound. All three buildings—Palace, Parliament, and National Court—were being systematically evacuated. A single file of people streamed out the front entrance of each building, shepherded on either side by other men who stood several feet to each flank of the main columns.

"Jack?"

Jack turned. Holly unconsciously wrung a paper napkin in both hands. She finally tore her gaze from the screen to look her boss in the eye.

"What do we do?" Holly said.

Jack glanced back at the screen. Files of people goaded at gunpoint merged into a single crowd at the front steps of the Palace.

"Take a bathroom break," Jack said, just above a whisper.

"What?"

Holly raised her eyebrows.

"*Now,* Holly!" Jack said.

Holly's chair rolled back five feet as she shot up and hurried out of the GOC, heels tapping on the scratchy carpet, before the door clicked shut behind her.

Jack turned back to the flat screen just in time to watch the white blob of massed people collapse in a hail of executioners' bullets. Al Badari's men turned their rifles skyward, loosing a cloud of celebratory gunfire into the sky. Gravity would stop those bullets miles below the drone, but the rapid-pulsing muzzle flashes and white streaks of hot bullets appeared to be only feet from the camera lens. Just as fast, the gunfire ceased once more.

Three of the insurgents laid their rifles down and pulled large machetes from under their robes. They stepped into the mass of corpses and began swinging.

In the sterile hallway outside the GOC, Holly sat alone on a cold cement floor, sobbing into her crumpled fast-food napkin.

HILTON PIERCE
CALLSIGN "ALLEY CAT"
RECCE TROOP – WINDSOR KRAFT STRATEGIES
TARKENT, DARISTAN
0651 HOURS, LOCAL

Hilton stormed into the Clocktower ops center, carbine still slung across his back. A young, male support staffer greeted him. Hilton looked past the man, and loudly said,

"Would anybody like to tell me what the fuck is going on?"

The staffer in front of him held out a paper towel. "You're bleeding."

Hilton snatched the towel from his hand, dabbed the corner of his forehead and looked at it. A muck of dirt, sweat, and dark blood sat in the middle of the paper. He had no idea when that happened and didn't particularly care.

"I'm fine," Hilton said.

Not missing a beat, the staffer told him, "The president, all seven National Court judges and most of Parliament have just been executed. Cell phone videos are already running on social media. Badari's men decapitated all of them and lined up the heads on the sidewalk in front of the Palace Compound."

"When's the airstrike?" Hilton asked.

"What airstrike?"

"If NATO levels the compound now, they can kill Al Badari and send Rangers in to seize what's left."

The younger man stared at him blankly.

"What is it?" Hilton asked.

"I…I don't think they're gonna do that," the staffer said.

"What do you mean?"

"Air Traffic Control is quiet. No jets scrambling, sir."

"Fuck," Hilton muttered. "Call CJ-SOTF and see what they're doing."

The staffer nodded but didn't move.

Hilton grabbed him firmly by the shoulders. "Hey. Hey! Look at me!"

The man blinked.

"This is happening," Hilton said quietly. "Every minute we sit is a minute closer to this entire country being overrun. If we don't keep our finger on the pulse, we're going to be trapped here, surrounded by an army that will put *all* our heads out on the sidewalk. Do you understand?"

"Yes."

"Call *cee-jay-sotiff*. Get me a handle on this thing."

"Yeah…yeah, roger. I'm on it."

The young man spun on his heels and sunk back into his workstation.

The Combined Joint Special Operations Task Force— CJ-SOTF— was the American-led hub for all allied special operations working in-country. If they were going to retake the palace, the mission needed to mount up now. If they weren't, the news would be much worse.

Hilton walked up behind Mama's workstation. He took a breath before leaning down and speaking gently. "Ma'am, who do we have left outside the city?"

Without looking up, she replied, "Nhahrullah. They're drawn down to a skeleton Pro Det and the Combat Advisory Team."

"Jimmy and Ben," Hilton said.

"That's right."

"Do they have attack air assets?" he asked.

"Negative. They're only a hundred klicks north, so we support them from here."

"Is anyone from Strike Troop on site?"

Mama nodded.

"King is out there," Hilton said.

"If the mil isn't going to put birds in the air, we need to cover that COP."

Hilton glanced at his Suunto watch. "It's early in the day. Al Badari isn't done yet."

BILL WILLIAMS
CALLSIGN "SQUARE"
FORCE PROTECTION TROOP – WINDSOR KRAFT STRATEGIES
NHAHRULLAH, DARISTAN (100KM NORTH OF TARKENT)
0658 HOURS, LOCAL

Bill walked into the briefing room with a paper cup of Earl Grey in one hand and his plate carrier draped over the other arm. He laid the carrier on the floor before sitting down on the end of the cracked leather couch and blowing the steam off the top of his breakfast tea. He was the last man from day shift to make it to the briefing room, but the Team Lead for night shift hadn't yet arrived, so his tardiness was immaterial.

COP Nhahrullah wasn't a massive base, but it was large enough to require a dedicated force protection detachment—Windsor Kraft contractors solely responsible for security of the base itself. This allowed the Combat Advisory Troop to focus on recruiting, training, and leading its Owl unit. The protection detachment, or "Pro Det," for Nhahrullah was only fourteen-men strong: three teams of four shooters—who rotated eight-hour shifts—plus a site supervisor and deputy site supe.

Bill worked as a day shift shooter. He slept when Flash and Jameson had returned several hours ago with Mirwan Maliki and a badly beat-up convoy of Owls. But he'd already bumped into one of the night shift guys in the chow hall when he went to fix his tea. When the night shift TL walked in, the surprise was already spoiled.

"Big news last night. The Owls scooped up Mirwan Maliki. He's one of Al Badari's top lieutenants. Word is Maliki and Al Badari rode together for a decade, and Maliki takes guidance directly from Al Badari himself."

"What's that mean for us?" Bill asked.

"Two things," the TL replied. "CIA is sending a team from Tarkent to pick him up. No clue when. Sometime today. They're supposed to let us know when they go wheels-up, but you know how it goes with those guys."

"Yeah, rog."

The night Team Lead continued, "If Maliki really is that high up the food chain, word is gonna travel fast. I'd expect they hit us directly in the next twelve to eighteen hours to try and get him back."

Bill's forehead crinkled as he took a slow pull of his tea. When he finished, he said, "We should tell the Agency team to make a big show of picking him up. Multiple helos, maybe have a fixed-wing buzz the COP or drop some JDAMs into an open field. Try and send the message he's been transferred. Could take the heat off us, if they think he's already been moved elsewhere."

"It's a good thought. I don't know if they can pull those assets together fast enough, or if they'd even want to. I'll let the Site Supe know, see if he can run it up the flagpole."

Bill nodded and took another drink of tea.

The overnight Team Lead asked for questions. Bill and his shift mates stayed silent.

"Alright," the night Lead said with a shrug. "Keep our seats warm."

Everyone chuckled or grumbled as they gathered their gear and filed out to their posts.

The COP was built with a north-south orientation, with the main entrance on the south side. Bill's first post of the day put him on a parapet on the east wall, overlooking several hundred yards of rocky open field. He hated getting this seat first thing in the morning, because it put the rising sun directly in his eyes. He tipped his Oakley shades down over his eyes and checked the gear pre-staged at his parapet.

A U-shaped notch in the concrete wall served as a reinforced gun port, with an FN Evolys machine gun filling the notch. Unlike the military's 7.62mm machine guns, Windsor Kraft issued their belt-feds in 6.5mm Creedmoor for extended range and better accuracy against point targets. On the ground next to the Evolys sat a larger footlocker filled with first aid supplies, spare ammunition for the machine gun, and a single-shot 40mm grenade launcher with bandoleer of gold-tipped, high-explosive rounds.

With all equipment accounted for, Bill perched himself on the high-top swivel chair next to the machine gun. The chair was tall and narrow, like you'd find at a sports bar or diner, vinyl cushion cracked and metal legs rusted from years in the elements. It wobbled a little and squeaked when swiveled, but it let Bill stay off his feet for part of his time on the wall, and he was thankful for it.

About a hundred yards away, half-a-dozen locals meandered back and forth across the field. It wasn't unusual. They scavenged or foraged for all kinds of supplies, or grazed goats, outside the base regularly. Unlike Tarkent, Nhahrullah was a rural backwater with homes scattered across a jagged countryside that served as the base for some of Daristan's highest mountain peaks. Most of the locals worked as herders or farmers, although Bill had never seen any of the land tall with crops.

Bill panned the landscape with binoculars. He saw small fig or date orchards on a couple of plots, and makeshift pens full of goats and chickens. Still, he knew the mountains hid spider-webbed networks of tunnels inside used to move men and stockpile supplies for Al Badari loyalists.

Nhahrullah was quiet, but dangerous.

That's what gave him pause when his binoculars landed on a convoy of pickup trucks. Just like in the US, rural areas of Daristan were rife with the ubiquitous Toyota workhorse. Seeing two or three of them was common, as families moved crops to market or hauled in supplies from larger villages. But six of them, evenly spaced and moving slow along the dirt road four hundred yards directly east of the base, looked out of place for any farm town.

Bill picked up his radio. "Homebase, Square."

Homebase meant the small office at the center of the COP that served as a rickety, scaled-down version of the GOC back in Virginia.

"Send it, Square," came the reply.

"Six trucks, moving north-to-south along the service road, four-zero-zero east my position," Bill said.

"I have them on camera. What are they hauling?"

"Beds look empty from here. Can you see anything?"

High-resolution security cameras dotted the outer perimeter, including some on fifty-foot-tall pole arms to give a panoramic view of the surrounding terrain.

"Too much glare from the sun to get a good look right now."

"Yeah, that's what I was worri—looks like they're turning."

"Say again, Square."

Bill's voice went up slightly. "They're turning off the service road. All six of them."

The voice over the radio also went up in pitch. "What direction?"

Bill dropped the binoculars and crouched down behind the machine gun. Bill nestled the stock into his shoulder, craning his neck down to the machine gun's optic. Since the trucks turned simultaneously, lining up side-to-side, instead of nose-to-tail. The front bumpers of all six pointed right at him.

"Square, Homebase, *what direction*?" the voice over the radio repeated.

"Inbound! Six trucks, line formation, picking up speed!" Bill said.

Homebase said something back, but Bill couldn't hear it over the sound of the explosion behind him. He snapped the machine gun's safety selector to full-auto and opened fire on the two middle trucks.

JESSE SOLOMON
CALLSIGN "KING"
STRIKE TROOP - WINDSOR KRAFT STRATEGIES
NHAHRULLAH, DARISTAN (100KM NORTH OF TARKENT)
0708 HOURS, LOCAL

Jesse Solomon sat in the chow hall, mixing powdered creamer into his morning cup of coffee, when he heard the explosion. The radio on his belt crackled to life. "Alert, Alert, Alert. Explosion, front gate. Small arms contact east wall."

Jesse placed his cup of coffee down on the bar, and snatched his plate carrier and carbine off the ground at his feet. The gunfire turned from a muffled drumbeat to a sharp crackle as Jesse body checked the chow hall door open, his hands still buckling the armor around his body.

Incoming machine guns rounds ricocheted off concrete T-walls, zipping over his head with a banjo-like twanging sound. Jesse straddled the nearest four-wheel ATV, twisted the key hanging in the ignition slot, and revved the engine, speeding the quarter mile to the front gate.

By the time he got there, two guys from the Pro Det returned fire through the twisted remnants of the steel blast door that normally sealed the front gate. He screeched the ATV to a halt fifty yards from the hole and took off running, unslinging his Cobalt from across his back as he ran. As he got closer, he saw several black-clad insurgent bodies strewn across the opening, with close to a dozen more behind them.

An AK round snapped by his head as Jesse took a knee and raised his rifle, finger pulsing against the carbine's trigger as he squeezed off half a magazine of suppressing fire. The incoming gunshots paused, and he sprinted the last dozen yards to where the two Pro Det contractors huddled in a cement pillbox. One laid down measured machine gun bursts. The other pulled a multi-shot grenade launcher out of a lockbox on the ground. Three hollow *thumps* echoed in the pillbox as the grenadier emptied half of the launcher's drum magazine. The high-explosive rounds impacted outside the gate with a rapid succession of crunching explosions.

The machine gunner glanced over his shoulder, recognized King, and shouted, "Call for CAS, now!"

Jessie squeezed the talk button mounted to his shoulder strap.

**HILTON PIERCE
CALLSIGN "ALLEY CAT"
RECCE TROOP - WINDSOR KRAFT STRATEGIES
CLOCKTOWER BASE - TARKENT INTERNATIONAL AIRPORT
TARKENT, DARISTAN
0710 HOURS, LOCAL**

Hilton hadn't even pushed open the door to the ops center when he heard King's voice crackle over the radio speaker, popping gunfire coming through behind his voice.

"Clocktower, King. COP Nhahrullah under attack, multiple breach points. Requesting immediate close air support, over," King said.

"I fucking *knew* it!" Hilton snapped.

Mama grabbed her radio handset, her voice rock steady. "King, Clocktower, air support spinning up now. ETA one-two mikes. Over."

"Copy! Out!" King said.

Across the bullpen of desks, another support staffer alerted the pilots. Hilton threw the door open and sprinted toward the runway. Hugh Haughen saw him running and matched pace alongside him.

Not waiting for the question, Hilton told him,

"Nhahrullah just got hit. They're requesting CAS."

Hugh swore under his breath.

"This is it," Hilton said between huffs. "This is the play."

It took a few hundred yards to cross the Tarkent base

and reach their private ramp, which spilled out directly onto the main runway grid of Tarkent's larger international airport. Chests heaving and dripping sweat from their foreheads, the two men reached the ramp just in time to see a pair of slate-gray Super Tucanos pull out of their hangars. The planes taxied directly past Hilton and Hugh before turning out onto one of the main runways.

Hilton eyed them closely. A cylindrical rocket pod under each wing held nineteen AGR-20 guided rockets. Based on the 70mm Hydra rockets used by helicopter gunships in Vietnam, the AGR-20s were upgraded with laser-tracking guidance systems in their nose cones, allowing them to hit specific point targets up to five kilometers away. Below the fuselage was a single rack with four, two-hundred-fifty-pound Small Diameter Bombs. Like the ubiquitous JDAM but smaller, the high-precision, low-collateral-damage SDBs excelled at the kind of techno-augmented asymmetric warfare that was Windsor Kraft's specialty.

As the planes made their final run-up to take off, Hilton said, "How're your Owls looking?"

"One platoon stood down, one running battle drills in two-hour blocks, one sitting in the team room watching TV. Team room's less than thirty yards from the trucks. They rotate every eight hours," Hugh said.

Hilton nodded.

"Even if we start the trucks now, we'll never make it to Nhahrullah in time. That's a hundred clicks through contested terrain."

"Jimmy and Ben have the ground game covered up there. I'm worried about us."

"Al Badari just took the palace. You think he's going to start hitting bases and embassies inside Tarkent?"

"I don't know. But I think he's got help."

"Who?"

"Chechens, maybe? I was two blocks from the palace when they hit it. I saw a guy."

"What kind of guy?"

"Fair-skinned. Slavic looking. He sure as shit wasn't Daristani."

"You hear him speak?"

"No. Saw him through my scope."

"And he's still alive?"

"Not by choice," Hilton grumbled.

Hugh flashed a knowing smirk. "Incoming fire take the right-of-way?"

"RPG," Hilton answered.

"That'll do it."

"I keep thinking about how we would do this, if it was us."

"Al Badari isn't going to think like us. He's a tribal idealogue. His priorities are different."

"Yeah, but if there's a professional steering the ship…"

"But a stand-up fight against hardened targets? After he's lost the element of surprise?"

Hugh wasn't convinced.

Hilton countered. "It's happening in Nhahrullah right now. Maybe it's a blitzkrieg."

"Blitzkrieg needs a *lot* of bodies," Hugh said.

Hilton grunted, chewing on the argument.

"Besides," Hugh added. "They're not going after Nhahrullah. They're going after Maliki."

BILL WILLIAMS
CALLSIGN "SQUARE"
FORCE PROTECTION TROOP – WINDSOR KRAFT STRATEGIES
COP NHAHRULLAH
0712 HOURS, LOCAL

Still holding down the east wall, Bill took a knee next to the footlocker underneath his machine gun, sweeping aside a pile of brass and links to hoist up another square plastic ammo box. He squeezed it under one armpit, using the other hand to rip the empty box off the bottom of the Evolys. Hanging the fresh box on its mounting plate, he stood back up just as another mortar round whistled to the ground behind him, landing in an explosion that pelted him in the back with gravel. Dirt rained down into his hair as he fed the new ammo belt into the side of his machine gun and smacked the feed door closed. Behind the gun, he raised his neck to use the red dot sight—the insurgents were too close for the ACOG—and opened fire.

The four pickup trucks had arrayed themselves in depth, two trucks with machine guns only about one hundred yards from the wall. The other two stopped farther back, their mortar tubes arcing shells into the COP.

"One coming up!" a voice called.

Ben Gordon popped into the gunner's nest next to Bill, grenade launcher cradled in one arm. AK rounds chipped the edge of the stone wall in front of them. Ben held his calm, shouldering the grenade launcher and firing two rounds.

One grenade landed squarely on the hood of a mortar truck. The other flew wide and exploded harmlessly behind. Ben fired four more rounds, aiming his first round at the other mortar truck, and spreading the rest across the no-man's land between those trucks and the wall. Ben hunched over and opened the launcher's loading cylinder, turning it upside down to shake out the spent shells. The incoming fire stopped as he thumbed more grenades out of a bandolier to reload.

"Leave the launcher," Bill said. "I got this."

"Not a chance," Ben snapped.

"Where's Jameson?" Bill asked.

"Down at the front gate."

"Who's on Maliki?"

Ben looked up from the grenade launcher. Bill looked hard into his face and said, "Reload it and leave it here. Get on the HVT."

High Value Target.

"Fuck me," Ben muttered. He finished reloading, snapped the launcher closed, and dropped it on the ground, along with the bandolier of grenades. He looked at Bill one last time. "Are you *sure*?"

"Go."

"Shit."

Ben ran down the parapet while Bill turned back to his gun, sweeping for targets. The only insurgents he saw lay dead or dying in no man's land. None of the trucks fired. He let out a slow breath, palm sweating against the machine gun's pistol grip.

A flicker of motion off to the left drew Bill's attention. He pulled his head off the machine gun to look. The tips of an aluminum ladder poked up over the side of the wall.

An icy chill ran down Bill's neck as his fingers fumbled with the clasp of a grenade pouch on the front of his plate carrier. The pouch popped open, and he slipped the grenade into his palm – yanking the pin with his other hand. He let the safety spoon fly off and "cooked" the grenade for two seconds before he stood up to drop it over the wall.

Just as he let the grenade go, one of the pickup trucks fired a burst from its PKM. The force of the impact knocked Bill onto his back inside the gun nest. His armor absorbed several rounds, but one hit him just below the bottom of the carrier, tearing flesh and organs out one side of his body. The last round blew open the top of his left shoulder. His brain registered the grenade going off at the base of the wall, but a torso swaddled in black cloth already reached the top of the ladder.

Bill jerked his Staccato pistol free of its thigh holster and fired wildly, the pistol's butt braced against his chest. The insurgent swung his arm over the wall, clutching a Skorpion machine pistol. The Skorpion's muzzle flared, emptying its magazine in just over a second. The front of Bill's skull shattered. His body fell limp against the footlocker.

The insurgent froze atop the ladder, shocked by his success, before staggering over the wall and falling ten feet to the ground below.

**HILTON PIERCE
CALLSIGN "ALLEY CAT"
RECCE TROOP - WINDSOR KRAFT STRATEGIES
CLOCKTOWER BASE - TARKENT INTERNATIONAL AIRPORT
TARKENT, DARISTAN
1952 HOURS, LOCAL**

Hilton stood in the middle of the chow hall, arms folded, eyes glued to the flat-screen TV mounted on the wall. Formal dinner service ended at 1900 hours, but pockets of support staff and government agency liaisons—who manned Clocktower's tactical nerve center 24 hours a day—still picked at their plates or sipped coffee, waiting to start their overnight shifts in a couple of minutes.

Cossack and Crowbar, two of the contract shooters from Close Protection Troop, occupied one of those tables. They led the numerous armed escort and close protection missions that ran throughout the city. They already kitted up in their "tactical tuxedos," as the uniforms were jokingly called, chatting idly while their gazes remained fixed on the television screen.

It was just before a.m.noon in Washington, D.C., and the president prepared to give his first press conference since Al Badari seized the palace this morning—events that occurred overnight back in the United States. Americans went to bed grumbling about a military withdrawal already characterized as mismanaged and ill-thought-out. The situation they woke up to took a hard turn for the worse. Struggling to stare down a president he had little personal respect for, Hilton instead focused on the closed captions scrolling along the bottom of the screen.

[My fellow Americans, good morning. I wish I had better news to deliver. Last night, Ansar Al Badari and his forces entered Daristan's capital city of Tarkent. They took control of the Presidential Palace, the Daristani Hall of Government, and the National Courts. Our intelligence indicates that the prime minister, along with members of Daristan's parliament and their national justices, have been captured or killed by Al Badari's insurgent army.]

Off camera, a chorus of gasps and chatter rose so loudly that the president paused until the crowd's reaction subsided. After several moments, the commander-in-chief continued his address.

[Al Badari released a statement yesterday outlining a five-day timeline for all coalition forces and foreign diplomats in Daristan to depart the country. We are now entering the second day of this five-day edict. At the end of this period, once the ceasefire expires, Daristani airspace will be closed to all commercial and military traffic, and any foreign citizens remaining in the country will be subject to arrest or,in his words, 'summary judgement under the laws of the prophet.' In accordance with the fundamentalist code of Sharia, which Al Badari has advocated for many years, these judgements could include assault, torture, or even execution. We strongly urge all Western personnel inside Daristan to contact their embassies immediately to seek emergency evacuation. I instructed our military to assist in these efforts for all friendly troops and diplomatic staff to the greatest extent possible. After extensive discussion with the National Security Council, the secretaries of state and defense, and the Joint Chiefs–]

"Here it comes," someone said in the chow hall.

[We are issuing orders to all of our brave military men and women to focus their efforts entirely on evacuation and withdrawal. We will not, under any circumstances whatsoever, be conducting combat operations against Ansar Al Badari or his forces. Nor will we provide any direct support to the Daristani military to conduct the same.]

The chow hall erupted in loud groans and shouted obscenities. Several people slammed their fists on the table. Someone behind Hilton kicked a chair over.

[To be frank, the ball is in their court now. The burden of national defense rests squarely on the shoulders of the Daristani people themselves. Should any faction of the parliamentary government choose to mount a counter-offensive, it will be considered by the US government as a civil matter with which we will not intervene. Because a complete military and diplomatic withdrawal has been underway for several weeks, we see no need to redirect those efforts. Daristan must accept that there is a limit to the blood and money we can pour into their country and, if they are unwilling to fight for themselves, then it's time to bring our soldiers, sailors, airmen, and Marines home to their families. Home to America. So that they may enjoy once more the freedom and the liberty they have so valiantly attempted to bestow upon the Daristani people. My office will continue to update you as we're able. In the meantime, please pray for our brave servicemembers working tirelessly, even in this very moment, to bring each other back to the nation they serve. Thank you, and God Bless America.]

The president turned quickly away from his podium and exited the room, refusing to acknowledge the barrage of shouted questions and shutter flashes from the White House press corps stationed off camera.

Almost in unison, everyone in the chow hall burst out of their chairs and stormed off to their rooms or offices. Everyone except for Cossack and Crowbar, who hadn't moved an inch. They tapped their feet or drummed their fingers on the tabletop, but otherwise nursed their coffee cups in apathetic silence.

Hilton approached them and leaned against the back of an empty chair across from them. Sometime during the president's speech, Jimmy "Jameson" Tooms wandered into the chow hall and, following Hilton's lead, stood over his two counterparts from Close Protection.

The quartet shared a hard silence, soaking in the hum of industrial air conditioning and the smell of stale grease traps and dirty mops.

Hilton broke the silence. "Gonna be a busy week for you guys."

Crowbar nodded but said nothing.

Cossack looked up from his coffee. "NEO starts tonight. Phone's been ringing off the hook with extraction requests."

"Who's up first?" Jameson asked.

Cossack took another sip of coffee before replying, "Some NGO worker. College kid, parents with money. You know the drill."

"Either way," Hilton said. "Be careful."

Cossack and Crowbar pushed their chairs out and stood, filing out of the chow hall with a casual wave.

Hilton waited until they left, then turned to Jameson. "Any word on Flash?"

"He's down a leg, bunch of shrapnel wounds, but he'll survive. He's at the French hospital across the runway right now. They'll move him to Landstuhl tomorrow," Jimmy said.

After being transported from Nhahrullah to Tarkent, the company would put "Flash" Gordon on a military flight to Landstuhl, Germany, for treatment at the Army

Regional Medical Center there.

"Some good news in there, anyway."

"His callsign just got better," Jameson said with a smirk.

Hilton couldn't help himself, letting out a single, loud laugh—equal parts appreciation of the irony, and relief that their wounded man would survive.

Jameson's smirk faded, and he took a half-step closer to Hilton. "I need to show you something."

Jimmy dug into his pocket and pulled out the tattered shoulder patch he and Ben recovered off the fighter outside of Maliki's compound.

"Where'd you get this?" Hilton asked.

"We rolled up Mirwan Maliki last night."

"Yeah, I heard he got killed during the Nhahrullah attack this morning."

"He did. We also got ambushed on exfil the night before. After the fight, one of our Owls cut this off a guy in the ambush nest," Jimmy explained.

"Just the one?"

"Three of them, Hilton. And I think there were a couple at Hafiza, when we got overrun, but I don't have patches to prove that.

"Do you have anything from Hafiza?" Hilton asked.

"There was spent brass, in five-four-five. A lot of it. I've been working this country for five years, and I've never seen that ammo here. But the guys who ambushed us on the Maliki raid were also carrying tricked-out '105s."

Hilton knew that AK-105s—a shortened carbine version of the AK-74 rifle chambered in that same 5.45x39mm round Jimmy referred to—were a much newer iteration of the Kalashnikov product line. He also knew Russian Federation special operators favored the faster-handling, flatter-shooting -105 carbines.

"What'd the shooters look like?" Hilton asked.

"White guys. Square jaws, thick beards, tight haircuts."

"That's weird," Hilton said under his breath.

"The whole thing is weird," Jimmy replied.

"No, no. I saw a similar guy at the palace today. He was right on Al Badari's heels when they breached the palace. He looked scraggly, though. Shoulder-length hair, moustache. He had cammies on, and full kit. He moved like a pro, but also like he was bored."

Hilton took the patch out of Jimmy's hand, placed it on the table next to him, and snapped a photo of it with his phone. Then he held the phone up in front of his face, his thumbs tapping back and forth across the keyboard.

"Thanks for the heads-up on this. I need to go make a phone call," Hilton said.

Hilton and Jimmy bumped fists, and Jimmy walked out of the chow hall. Hilton glanced around, making sure the room was empty. Then he pulled out a chair, sat down, and dialed. Holly picked up on the second ring.

"Hilton?" Holly said.

"Check your email," Hilton said.

"Wait one," she said, manicured fingernails clacking on a keyboard in the background. "What am I looking at?"

"I'm not sure," Hilton said. "That's why I sent it to you. It's a patch we pulled off some bad guys last night. I need you to pass that off to an East Europe area analyst."

"You said East Europe?"

"Yeah. We think the guys wearing this patch may be Russian special forces. Just need to know if this unit patch is tied to someone outside of Al Badari's insurgency."

"Okay, yeah. I'll forward the email."

"Give them this number, if they want to call me back directly."

"Will do," Holly said. Hilton could hear more keys clacking in the background.

"Did you guy's see the White House press conference?" Holly asked.

"Oh yeah. Went over like a lead balloon here. How about there?" Hilton said.

"Depends on who you talk to. So far, the talking heads are going back-and-forth about whether it's an overdue end to an ineffective war, of if we're cowing to a terrorist for political expediency."

Hilton sighed.

"I suppose the two don't have to be mutually exclusive," he replied.

"Is five days really enough time?" she asked.

"For *us*, it's plenty. For the entire coalition force? Ask me again in four days."

Holly started to reply, but the phone beeped in his ear, drowning her out.

Hilton pulled the phone away from his face to see a second call incoming. "Holly, I got another call. See you in a few days." He tapped the button to switch lines and put the phone back to his ear. "Alley Cat, send it."

"Hey sir, this is Ronny, eastern Europe desk."

"That was fast."

"Yes, sir. Holly forwarded me your email. The one with the photo of a unit patch?"

"You called too fast to do any real digging. I'm assuming you recognize it."

"Uh, yes, we recognize it for sure. Can you tell me about how and where you guys found it?"

"We scooped it off some light-skinned guys who most definitely aren't from around here. They ran decked-out AK-105s. We're concerned it's Spetznaz," he said, using the term for Russian special operations forces.

"Well, I can confirm that patch is not from any Russian Federation military unit or intelligence agency. I'm not sure if that's good news or bad news."

"Why?"

"Because the artwork on that patch *is* connected to a Russian private military company called PMC Arkangel."

"Shit."

"One could argue they're the Russian version of us. On steroids."

"Define the *on steroids* part," Hilton said.

Ronny took an audible breath in. "There's this idea floating around in strategic think-tank circles called the Gerasimov Doctrine. It's kind of a misnomer because General Gerasimov never set out to design a cohesive warfighting doctrine, and many say he didn't coalesce any novel ideas about warfare at all. He tried to better understand the current strategies of Western militaries, and how the Federation could gain parity with or counter those strategies. The idea has also been referred to as New Generation or Hybrid Warfare."

Hilton sighed.

"Sorry. Anyway, it doesn't matter what you call it," Ronny said. "The general concept of Hybrid War incorporates a blended force of state and non-state actors. We obviously fall into the latter category."

In the Tarkent chow hall, Hilton nodded and said, "Okay, *now* I follow. So, this PMC Arkangel falls into the same non-state-actor category as Windsor Kraft. Essentially a privatized tool of homeland foreign policy."

"Yes, but there's more," Ronny said. "Gerasimov *specifically* proffered the concept of disguising military units as crisis-management or peacekeeping forces."

"Okay, wait. So is Arkangel an actual private contracting firm, or is it just a shell company to provide cover for bona fide Russian military units?" Hilton asked.

"That's the rub," Ronny said wryly. "Think-tanks are split on that question. Most of the intel community thinks Arkangel is simultaneously filling both roles. They are an actual corporate security force that pursues private contracts in areas of the world where Russia wishes to exert influence. It's believed they *also*, in certain circumstances, provide a cutout for small teams of Spetzsnaz and GRU operators conducting covered missions in politically denied areas. That brings us back to your original concerns of encountering Russian forces on the ground where you are."

Hilton's voice dropped low, and he spoke slowly. "Ronny, I need you hang up and get everything you have on these guys to Jack Young, right now. He'll know what to do with it."

Hilton knew Jack would take this information to Lisa Gregson at Langley. After that, it would be their call as to how to handle it.

"I put together a cursory info-brief and sent it over while I was talking. I will go up to his office and fill in the gaps for him, personally."

"Don't bother with his office," Hilton said. "He's in the GOC."

"Understood. Anything else I can do for you?"

"You're on top of it, Ronny. Thanks."

"Out here," the analyst said curtly.

The line went dead in Hilton's ear. He tucked the phone in his pocket, then stared at the wall as he anxiously cracked every knuckle on his hands.

**JACK YOUNG
WINDSOR KRAFT STRATEGIES
WILLIAMSBURG, VA
1400 HOURS LOCAL**

Two hours later, while Hilton showered for bed in Daristan, Jack Young and Lisa Gregson burned another pair of cigars in the sequestered alcove of their favorite meeting spot. Jack brushed the back of one hand against the rough-hewn surface of a 200-year-old limestone wall behind his chair. The benign tactile input represented a grounding exercise he'd learned from the performance psychology team at Army Special Forces Command—a period of his life that felt as old as the wall itself.

"You're telling me that your boys are trading bullets with Spetsnaz, who are directly supporting Ansar Al Badari, and the real-time collapse of our decade-long Daristan campaign? Do I have that right?" Lisa said.

Jack held up one hand in a cautioning motion, his smoldering cigar pinched between two of the fingers.

"I'm giving you, *verbatim*, the information I'm getting from the field, and the supporting analysis from my area team. Drawing conclusions is your job," Jack said.

Lisa pursed her lips, blowing a slow stream of smoke into the air between them as she collected her thoughts.

"Yeah, I know," she said with frustration. "I just needed to hear it out loud."

"Does this change anything?"

Her phone buzzed on the table between them. She picked it up, glanced at the screen, and silenced it. The phone clattered loudly as she tossed it back on the table.

"I doubt it," she said. "POTUS just publicly handcuffed everyone."

"That was for the masses. What's the inside track?"

"Exactly the same," she said. "Everyone's focus is solely on retrograde."

"Our enemy imposed a deadline and we've chosen to comply with it, then."

"By all orders and accounts, yes," she said.

"Even with proof of direct support from a foreign military?"

"So what, Jack? The Soviets backed Ho Chi Minh, Iran backed Al-Amiri in Iraq, Pakistan did it with Haqqani in Afghanistan. The list goes on. It's not any different from what we do. All the big players know asymmetric is a long con, and we've never gone toe-to-toe with the principles on the other side. Not out in the open, anyway. Just keep doing what you're doing, whether you like it or not."

Jack plucked the cigar out of his mouth and gave her a sharp nod. "Yes, ma'am."

Her tone softened. "Don't give me that shit, please. I'm not telling you anything you didn't already know."

"What do you want us to do if we run into them again?"

"Officially, this situation doesn't exist."

"Unofficially?"

"Handle business, exploit the leftovers as best you can.

Are your guys set up to collect biometrics?"

Jack shook his head.

"Okay," Lisa continued. "Then tell them to take photos and collect pocket litter. Unit patches, credentials, phones, flash drives, anything we can use to map out their people or org chart."

"I don't know how much we're going to get in three days," Jack said.

"I know. It's not a mission change. Stay focused on getting out of there. But, you know, targets of opportunity."

"I'll pass the word."

"Keep it close hold, Jack. Even among your own people. Remember, this is the long game. But I suspect once it's all said and done in Daristan, we're going to fight fire with fire somewhere else. We'll need a pretty specific tool for that job."

"A private army equipped to fight a private army," Jack said.

"If I've got a sense of this administration, the Russians won't be the only ones putting unofficial state-level support against the effort."

Jack took a long drag off his short, squat cigar. Leathery, slate-colored smoke spilled from his mouth as he said, "That is probably the best news I'm going to get all week."

GARY BOLCEWICZ AND FRANK RELYEA
CALLSIGNS "COSSACK" AND "CROWBAR"
CLOSE PROTECTION TROOP – WINDSOR KRAFT STRATEGIES
TARKENT, DARISTAN
2144 HOURS, LOCAL

The up-armored Land Cruiser rolled forward at a crawl behind a line of Suburbans, Excursions, Land Rovers, and Mercedes G-Wagons. The heavily-fortified, multi-stage checkpoints surrounding Tarkent's diplomatic district were colloquially known as The Hot Gates—a reference to the narrow pass leading to the Greek city of Thermopylae. Ironically, in Greek mythology, The Hot Gates also referred to an entrance to the underworld of Hades. Right now, it felt much more like the latter.

It had been like this for most of the last two days. Elite military and police teams from every Western country involved in Daristan streamed in and out of the diplomatic district, scooping up their intelligence and diplomatic officers and bringing them to the airport for outbound flights, as Al Badari's army marched closer to the city walls.

Co-located with the long stretch of foreign embassies and consulates were a series of NGOs—Non-Governmental Organizations—typically in the form of private-entity non-profits here to enact their best shot at solving some niche cultural problem. Education for women, orphanages, gender studies education, pediatric healthcare—name the issue, and a well-meaning group of volunteers living in Tarket tried to solve it.

The Land Cruiser crept one car length closer to the first inspection point. Frank saw the strobing of distant muzzle flashes over the rooftops.

"What's the over-under this kid cooperates?" he asked.

"Here's hoping," Gary said.

With the tension around Tarkent escalating quickly, and the odds of stopping Al Badari before he reached the city dwindling by the hour, Windsor Kraft's Close Protection Troop—normally tasked with close-protection and personal security missions—undertook the effort of evacuating American Citizens—AmCits—who did not fall under the responsibility of the US military or State Department. The military referred to this as NEO—Noncombatant Evacuation Operations, but they were too overloaded with last-ditch shipping and transportation operations, and managing the growing crowd of locals and expats gathering around the airport, to do the job themselves.

News broadcasts around the world pleaded with private citizens living as expats in Daristan to head to Tarkent International Airport as soon as possible and put their names on a roster for outbound evacuation flights. At this point, several major airlines from Europe and North America ceased all commercial service to Daristan. The options to get out thinned by the day, but many of the aid workers refused to run.

For some, it was a point of pride—the amount of their lives they'd given up to this country could not be for naught. Others felt genuinely invested in the close relationships they forged with Daristanis looking to better their quality of life. Others remained convinced that the news media exaggerated the likelihood of total collapse, or the punitive savagery that would come when Al Badari seized control of the country.

Gary and Frank eased up to the small, square guard shack channeled by concrete barriers and large welded roadblocks called Dragon's Teeth—four-foot lengths of steel I-beam welded into a three-dimensional X, strung together with braided wire cable. A local guard stepped out of the shack and gestured at them. Gary and Frank both held up the large, nylon badge holders around their necks. The holders had a clear, plastic window on the front containing both a NATO-issued ID card and their Windsor Kraft company IDs. These magic tickets allowed them to proceed into the diplomatic district.

The guard nodded and walked around the truck with his vehicle inspection mirror. He then waved the LC—Land Cruiser—through.

Gary eased the armored SUV through the first drop arm and approached the second guard house.

Frank plucked a radio handset off its dashboard mount. "Clocktower, Crowbar."

The handset crackled to life. "Send it, Crowbar."

"Crowbar plus Cossack, passing through Hot Gates time now."

"Copy Crowbar. Clocktower out."

Frank clicked the hand mic back into its mounting bracket.

At the second checkpoint, four British paratroopers stood on duty for the inner layer of security. They dressed in full combat gear, with helmets, body armor, and oddly shaped SA-80 service rifles. One wielded an eager Belgian Malinois on the end of a short, leather leash. The dog wore a lightweight mesh vest with his name and British Army corporal's stripes.

Gary popped open the driver's door, as the triple-thick ballistic windows didn't roll down. Frank peeled his badge holder off his head, and Gary handed both to the young paratrooper as the handler walked his dog around their vehicle.

"Evenin' mates," the soldier said with a nod.

"Tell me they have you boys on eights," Gary said.

"Twelves," the trooper replied. "Fuckin' brutal."

Frank leaned over in his seat and asked, "Do your dogs outrank you like ours do?"

The trooper chuckled. "Don't they always?"

He handed Gary back the badge holders. Frank took his and looped it back around his neck.

"Stay safe guys," Gary said. "See you at the next war."

"Cheers," the trooper replied.

Gary hauled the heavy door closed, and they rolled through the drop arm and out onto embassy row.

"Good thing we got the easy part over with first," Frank said sarcastically.

Gary said nothing, rolling slowly down the main drag as both men looked left and right for the small residence. Their target building was the staff headquarters for a small NGO focused on de-mining.

Prior to the international presence in Daristan, Al Badari loyalists made extensive use of landmines purchased from neighboring countries in the region, primarily to protect their various regional capitals, and sometimes to blockade entire villages that refused to pledge loyalty to their regime. The US military destroyed dozens of stockpiles of landmines and minefields laid years before the American invasion. Of course, when the supply of manufactured mines dwindled, the insurgents switched to IEDs.

However, the effort to fully demine the country, as well as establish a counter-mining education program for the local populace, eventually outsourced to a niche NGO with previous experience in Africa.

That's where people like Aaron Fisher entered the picture. Against his parents' wishes, Aaron, a nineteen-year-old college student from Colorado, took a year off from college to volunteer with the counter-mining NGO Tutum Terram—literally "Safe GroundEarth." When the writing on the wall became obvious to Mr. and Mrs. Fisher, they contacted Windsor Kraft to extract their son from the country. The company coordinated with a private equity firm funding evacuation flights and booked Aaron on a plane set to land at 3 a.m. the following morning. The pilots received instructions to remain on the ground for sixty minutes to refuel and load passengers. After that, they were free to take off with or without the full manifest.

After some back and forth in the Clocktower station, Gary and Frank teamed up to get Aaron from the diplomatic district to their private terminal at the edge of the airport. From there, they would drive him across the runway to meet the charter plane.

Frank pointed to a small building that looked like Tarkent's answer to a fraternity house. A dozen such houses sandwiched between the larger diplomatic compounds that dotted this stretch of road.

Frank recognized the plaque with Tutum Terram's logo on it. "Hey, that's it."

Gary parked the LC with two wheels up on the curb, and both men got out. Gary rang the doorbell. Frank, out of habit, turned his back to the door to watch the street. Several moments later, the door opened a foot, and a woman's face filled the gap.

"Can I help you?" the woman said.

"Yes, ma'am," Gary said. "We're with Windsor Kraft Strategies."

"Mercenaries," the woman said with clear contempt. "What do you want?"

"We're looking for Aaron Fisher."

"What for?"

"He's booked on an evacuation flight later tonight. We're his ride to the airport."

"He didn't tell us anything about that."

"Maybe not, but it's the truth."

"Am I supposed to take your word on that?"

"I have a satellite phone, if you'd like to speak with his parents."

"He's a legal adult and can make his own decisions about whether he leaves or not."

"All the more reason we should speak with him directly."

"Well, you'll have to come back. He's not here."

"Ma'am, time is of the essence on this."

"*Your* time is of the essence. We're here doing…"

A voice from behind the door cut in. "Give it a rest, Kathy." The door opened further, and a younger woman appeared in the doorway. "Are you taking all of us?"

"Unfortunately, it's just us, and we're only here for Mister Fisher," Gary said.

"What are we supposed to do?" the younger woman said.

"Ma'am, there are evacuation flights leaving every hour. All you need to do is get to the airport."

"Have you seen it out there?" the younger woman asked. "It's not that easy."

Gary reached underneath his gear and pulled out a business card, which he held out to the younger woman. "This is my direct line, local cell phone. If anyone here needs help getting to the airport, we'll do everything possible to come back for you."

Kathy looked hard at the younger woman. The younger woman looked at the card in Gary's hand.

"You don't have to use it, but at least you'd have it. Just in case," Gary said.

The younger woman tucked the card into the back pocket of her jeans. "Aaron's not even here."

"Where is he?"

"The German embassy. He heard there's a party over there tonight. Some *girl* invited him."

Gary sensed a lover's quarrel, but it wasn't his problem. He did his best to soften his face. "Thank you. If any of you need a ride, I'll do what I can. My name is Gary, and I'm with Windsor Kraft."

She held out her hand, and they shook.

"Thanks, Gary. I'm Alyssa. It's like three embassies down, on the left."

"Stay safe, ladies."

"I hope you find another war after this one," Kathy said tersely.

"Likewise," Gary replied.

Kathy closed the door on him.

Frank looked over his shoulder. "That could have gone worse."

"Let's go crash an embassy party," Gary said.

"Don't act like it's your first," Frank said.

They got back in the LC and rolled several blocks farther down the road until they saw the walled-in compound with a spotlight shining on a German flag flapping in the night breeze. They parked across the street and walked up to the pedestrian gate. Frank could already hear heavy bass pounding and see colored light flickering from inside the walls. A German Bundeswehr soldier with a G36 rifle slung over his back met them at the entrance. Both men held up their badge caddies.

"You are a guest of whom?" the German guard asked.

"There's an American here. Aaron Fisher," Gary said.

"He is American military?"

"No. He's an aid worker."

"No rifle," the guard said.

Gary and Frank looked at each other.

Frank looped his arm under the carbine's sling and peeled it off his head, holding it out for the German soldier. Gary followed suit. The guard took both rifles.

"Wait here," the guard said. He disappeared inside his armored booth and came back out a minute later with two white, plastic cards with numbers printed on them.

"Don't lose these," the guard said.

The two contractors took their check cards.

The guard pushed hard on a rolling steel blast door. He stood aside once it opened. "This is German land. Cause trouble and you will be subject to German law."

Gary and Frank filed through the gate, which rumbled closed behind them. The courtyard in front of them looked like a discount version of a European house rave. KMFDM blared over speakers. A couple tabletop strobes wheeled back and forth on small motors, sweeping beams of colored light across the open area. There sat fifteen or so round, metal patio tables with matching chairs, all piled with paper plates of food and plastic drink cups. Fifty or sixty people milled about, some bobbing their head to the music, others huddled in small cliques talking or laughing loudly.

"Jesus H…," Gary muttered.

Frank grinned and said, "Don't tell them there's a war going on."

"They wouldn't believe me if I did," Gary said with a shake of his head.

They pushed their way through the crowd, who largely took no notice of them, trying to find a face that matched the photos they'd been given of Aaron. It took almost ten minutes of interrupting conversations and tapping strangers on the shoulder, but they found him.

"Aaron?" Frank asked.

"Yeah! You guys need a drink?" Aaron said.

"Nah, man. We're here to take you to the airport."

"What? Did my fucking parents send you?"

"They did."

"I *told* them I wasn't leaving yet. The city is still fine. We can still do work here!"

"They already booked you on a flight."

"When?"

"Tomorrow morning."

"Fine. I'll go to the airport in the morning."

"You don't understand. The flight takes off at four AM."

Aaron checked his watch. "There's still plenty of time."

"The airport is getting pretty crowded. We waited as long as we could."

"Yeah, well, you can remind them I'm a big boy. I'll get to the airport when I'm ready."

Frank put a hand on Aaron's shoulder. "Get ready now. We're going."

Aaron slapped Frank's hand away. "Don't fuckin' touch me, dude. I'm not going."

Gary grabbed him by both shoulders and leaned in close. "You can come with us, or we can take you with us. Your call."

A small knot of people started to form around them.

"Let him go, Gary," Frank said. The last thing they

needed was to get arrested on sovereign German soil.

Gary released him and stood there staring. Two long bursts of machine gun fire could be heard over the music. Everyone looked up, and a flurry of green and red tracers crisscrossed in the night sky over the courtyard.

Frank put one shoulder between them and said to Aaron, "This is real, amigo. If you don't go now, you won't get another chance."

"Even if you make me go home, I'll come right back tomorrow," Aaron said.

"That's a fight for tomorrow," Frank said.

Aaron looked down at his feet.

Frank felt a palpable sense of relief as he watched the younger man cave inside.

Just then, Aaron stood up straight and looked Frank in the eye. "Fuck this. Tell my parents…"

Aaron suddenly doubled over hard with a grunt.

Frank caught him before he hit the ground and got under one of his arms. Gary quickly took the other and, out of the corner of his eye, Frank saw Gary drop the small stun gun back into the cargo pocket of his utility pants. The crowd around them murmured.

"It's fine," Frank said to the bystanders. "He can't hold his liquor. We'll get him back to the house."

The two dragged Aaron toward the front gate. The guard gave them a curious look when they showed back up, ready to leave.

"Is he alright?" the guard asked.

"Kid partied a little too hard. We're gonna get him back to his bed. It's just down the street," Gary said.

After looking them all up and down for a few seconds, the guard said, "Okay"

"We'll be right back for our rifles," Gary said.

They hobbled Aaron across the street and folded him gently into the backseat of the LC, buckling him into the center seat.

"Fire it up," Frank said. "I'll grab the guns."

He took off across the street and came jogging back moments later with a Cobalt carbine in each hand. The truck idled when Frank got in and tucked both their rifles in the footwell next to his leg.

Gary waited for a pause in the two-way stream of armored SUVs and U-turned into the street, heading back toward the checkpoint they'd entered through.

"I need my shit," Aaron mumbled from the back seat.

"You got your wallet?" Gary said.

"Yeah."

"That's all you need."

Frank grabbed the hand mic off the dash. "Clocktower, Crowbar."

"Go for Clocktower."

"Crowbar plus Cossack RTB with package in…"

The front of the LC heaved into the air, throwing the vehicle up on its back wheels like a bicycle trick. Frank saw nothing but night sky and flames billowing up over the front bumper from the blast. Temporal distortion made it feel like they were hanging in the air for minutes before the front of the vehicle crashed back down under its own weight.

Frank felt an icy, searing bolt of pain go directly up his

spine when the front of the truck landed. The nose went below ground level into the blast crater, leaving Frank and Gary hanging forward against their seatbelts. The hand mic dangled by its thick, squiggly cord somewhere under the dash.

Frank grabbed the cord and pulled it hand-over-hand until he got the mic back. "Break-break-break, contact, IED, inside Hot Gates. I say again, contact IED."

The radio operator at Clocktower came back. "Status?"

Frank looked over at Gary and asked, "You good?"

Gary blinked both eyes and dabbed at the blood on his upper lip, sniffing the rest of it back up into his nose. "I'm good."

Frank looked into the backseat at Aaron. "You awake back there?"

"What the fuck was that?" Aaron asked in a panic.

"Are you hurt?" Frank asked.

"Huh? I don't think so."

Frank keyed the mic again. "Clocktower, Crowbar. Minor injuries, vehicle down hard. Moving to hardpoint. Standby."

"Clocktower copies."

"Alright," Frank said. "Pack out and burn it."

Gary pulled down the GPS tracker Velcroed to the ceiling above the center console.

Frank braced both legs against the footwell to put slack in his seatbelt and unbuckled. Once free, he heaved open his door and climbed out. He heard the popping of semiautomatic gunfire from somewhere on the street. He grabbed both carbines and slung them across his back, crisscrossed. By then Gary was unbuckled and climbing over the console toward Frank's open door.

Frank helped him out. "I got the kid. Pop the tracker and grab the SAW." He pulled open the rear passenger's door.

Gary dropped the GPS tracker on the ground, drew his Staccato from its drop-leg holster and fired two rounds into the center of it before kicking it into the blast crater. Frank and Aaron were halfway out of the car when he shuffled around them. As they came out of the back of the LC, Gary crawled in and reached over the back seat.

Frank shoved Aaron onto his knees. "Get down right here, behind the wheel. Don't move!"

He plucked a soda-can-sized thermite grenade off his kit. Pulling the pin, Frank tossed the canister into the front of the vehicle. It landed on the dashboard and ignited with a hissing *pop*.

The front of the vehicle lit up with a white-hot glow as the aluminum/magnesium incendiary burned at over 4,000°F. Molten slag would trickle down through the dash, melting all the communications and electronics equipment it met. The fiery sludge would drip down through the floorboards, melting the drive shaft, axles, and any other part of the vehicle's mechanics it touched. If it burned all the way through the bottom of the vehicle, it would even melt the asphalt below.

Gary took one knee next to Aaron. He had pulled the vehicle's bailout bag—a small sling pack full of ammo, grenades, radio batteries, parachute flares, and a backup satellite phone. With it, he had pulled out the FN Mk 46

Squad Automatic Weapon stowed behind the back seat. He tugged on the telescoping stock, snapping it into fully extended position.

Gary slung the bailout bag across his chest and clamped the SAW's stock under his armpit, holding the weapon on-handed with muzzle straight up.

The individual pops escalated to bursts of full-auto AK fire. The other armored SUVs had sped away toward the Hot Gates, pulled off into side streets, or rested up on the sidewalks to hold in place.

JIMMY TOOMS
CALLSIGN "JAMESON"
COMBAT ADVISORY TROOP
"CLOCKTOWER" – WINDSOR KRAFT CONTROL CENTER
TARKENT INTERNATIONAL AIRPORT, DARISTAN
2208 HOURS LOCAL

"All callsigns report to the team room. I say again, *all* callsigns to team room, troops in contact."

Jimmy let his finger off the PA's talk button. The operations center buzzed with activity. Several of the company's support staff talked on their respective phones, holding simultaneous conversations with local US military units, the American embassy, and the company's GOC back in Virginia.

Jimmy turned to one of the support staff, who had a phone pressed to her ear. "I'm heading to the team room. Channel two if you need me."

She pinned the phone with her shoulder and gave him a thumbs up. Then she grabbed the phone with her hand again and leaned into it. "No, no, this is *on* embassy row, David. I know it's not possible, but it fuckin' happened. Can you see anything from…"

Her conversation faded as Jimmy shoved open the door to the control room and ran across the parking lot. He counted eight other contractors already huddled outside, in front of the team room. He could see more guys inside through the open door, pulling padlocks off the gray, metal arms lockers containing all their heavy weapons—more of the SAWs, plus heavier Evolys machine guns in 6.5 Creedmoor, multi-shot grenade launchers, shotguns, and sniper rifles.

One of the guys saw Jimmy coming and whistled loudly. The guys inside filed out into the parking lot. They made a horseshoe formation around Jimmy as he jogged to a stop. He took one breath to settle himself and briefed the group.

"Cossack and Crowbar are in contact in the diplo district. They've got a private extract with them, some NGO kid. They hit an IED on the way out," Jimmy said.

Hilton Pierce cut him off. "They hit an IED *inside* the diplomatic district?"

"Right on embassy row," Jimmy said.

"Fuck me," Hilton said.

"Yeah. The Brits are running the Hot Gates, and they've sealed off the entire quarter."

One of the other guys asked, "How do we get QRF in there if they've sealed the gates?"

The Quick Reaction Force—QRF—of contractors and Owl commandos stood ready to drive into the city within five minutes of an emergency call to rescue their own. Because of the more stringent rules of engagement inside the diplomatic district, they waited on pause unless approval came from the joint coalition command.

Jimmy replied, "Clocktower is fighting that fight right now. It's joint territory, and NATO is saying that 2 Para is the only authorized QRF inside the gates. All the individual embassies are buttoned up, with their own guard forces. A bunch of other coalition SOF were in there performing extracts when Cossack and Crowbar got hit, and they're all stuck inside now. It's too many guns on the ground as it is. They know it's us who caught the IED, but the Paras are in a TIC with squad-sized elements of active shooters right now."

The vernacular for TIC—Troops In Contact, meaning an active firefight—was understood.

"Hilton, you're Recce Troop, right?" Jimmy said.

Hilton nodded.

"Get on the horn with your local assets. Find out what the fuck is going on with that ceasefire."

"Rog," Hilton said tersely. He turned away from the group and dug his local burner phone out of his pocket.

Jimmy looked at Hugh Haughen, callsign Rook, the commander of Tarkent's Owl detachment. "Hugh, where are the last of the Owls?"

"Two, fifteen-man chalks camped out in a hangar with their trucks and gear," Hugh said.

"Give their commanders a WARNO."

"But don't stand them up yet. Everyone else, prep heavy weps and trucks. Park just inside the front gate and leave the engines running. As soon as we can get clearance, you're out of here."

The group dissolved into a flurry of moving bodies as some men ducked back into the team room to stage guns, while others ran to the line of armored Hiluxes and Land Cruisers parked in a row for just this occasion.

Jimmy turned around and started walking back to

the Clocktower control center, but Scott Booth took up a quick stride next to him.

"Hey Jimbo," Scott asked. "What about air?"

"I don't think they'll clear it," Jimmy said.

"Yeah, but what if we just *do it*?"

Jimmy stopped and looked at him.

Scott added, "It's not like they have air defense set up over there. Nobody can shoot us down."

"Even if we did, those buildings are so close together you'd never get an MI-17 down in there," Jimmy said.

Scott shook his head. "I'm not talking about an MI. I'm talking about a Little Bird."

"How? We put four guys on the benches, plus three on the ground? Not enough room to bring anyone out."

"So we insert light," Scott said. "Just you and me. We touch down, throw the kid inside the bird, put Gary and Frank on the benches with us. Then there's just enough seats for everyone."

"That's some *Black Hawk Down* shit, Scott."

"Go raise Frank and Gary on comms. They just need to find a rooftop and pop an IR strobe. We'll never even touch the street."

Jimmy stroked his beard in contemplation. Finally, he said, "Go get a pilot. I'll get back on the radio and see if Clocktower can clear airspace."

"Tell them not to call until we're already in the air."

GARY BOLCEWICZ AND FRANK RELYEA
CALLSIGNS "COSSACK" AND "CROWBAR"
CLOSE PROTECTION TROOP – WINDSOR KRAFT STRATEGIES
DIPLOMATIC DISTRICT
TARKENT, DARISTAN
2215 HOURS LOCAL

Gary and Frank heard AK rounds clanking into the thick armor on the other side of the LC. The armor stopped the 7.62x39mm slugs dead in their tracks, but the longer they stayed crouched behind the vehicle, the more likely they'd be pinned down behind the vehicle until they could be surrounded.

Gary leaned around the rear bumper and fired short bursts whenever he saw muzzle flashes from behind them.

Frank glanced over his shoulder, trying to find some place for them to go. He spotted several NGO residences on the near side of the street with small, mud alleyways between each one.

"Aaron, you're coming with me. See that dark alley between those two houses? Go just far enough in that you can't see down the street and crouch down. Ready?" Frank said.

"Yeah." Aaron didn't sound ready, but they couldn't wait any longer.

"Okay," Frank said. He turned to Gary. "Moving."

Not taking his face off the machine gun's stock, Gary

replied, "Move."

Frank hauled the kid to his feet and pushed him in the direction they needed to go. Both took off running. Aaron slipped between the two houses. He ran halfway down the alley before he stopped and turned around.

Frank held right at the corner of the house and fired his suppressed carbine.

"Moving!" Gary called.

"Move!" Frank said.

Gary hoisted himself up—laden with both machine gun and bailout bag—and jogged toward Frank, who fired a steady stream of controlled shots toward the bright, orange muzzle flares of multiple AKs.

"Down the street or down the alley?" Gary asked between machine gun bursts.

"Let's skirt the street, try to work our way to the gate," Frank said.

"Reloading," Gary said. He took a knee and snapped up the SAW's feed tray cover. Frank stood over him, one knee in Gary's back, and continued firing shots with his carbine whenever he saw a muzzle flash.

Gary pulled a plastic box of belted ammo out of the bailout bag, clipped it to the bottom of the gun, and pulled a foot of linked rounds out of the box. He laid the first three rounds onto the feed tray and slapped the cover closed on top of them.

"I'm up," Gary said.

Frank took his knee off Gary's back, and Gary stood back up.

"Reloading," Frank said. The empty magazine

dropped out of his carbine. Before it hit the ground, he pulled a fresh mag off his plate carrier, inserted it into the magwell, and tapped the bolt release with his thumb.

When the bolt snapped forward, Frank said, "I'm up."

"On you," Gary said.

"Ready Aaron?"

Aaron nodded hurriedly.

"Moving," Frank said.

"Move."

The two took off at full speed, passing three more houses before they ducked into another alley, out of earshot of each other.

Frank keyed the Push-To-Talk on his plate carrier and quietly said, "Set."

His earpiece crackled softly right before Gary's voice came through it. "Moving."

"Swing wide so I can cover you. Move."

Gary bolted out of the alley into the middle of the street before he turned and sprinted toward Frank and Aaron. This allowed Frank to lay covering fire. Gary zigzagged through the armored SUVs sitting idly in the street. Some still had people inside, and Gary could hear the metallic *swack* of AK rounds hitting the vehicles as he ran. He ran just past where Frank and Aaron crouched down. He button-hooked in behind them.

"Next building down is the Italian embassy," Gary said, huffing from his dash.

"I saw," Frank said. "Gonna be a long bound."

"I'm good on ammo. Just get there."

Frank clapped Aaron on the shoulder as he said,

"Moving."

Gary started shooting. Over the suppressed machine gun's muffled chugging, he replied, "Move."

Frank and Aaron took off once more. The ten-foot concrete wall of the Italian embassy loomed over their right side as they ran. The heavy, steel blast doors rested shut, creating nearly seventy feet of solid wall with no side street or alley for them to duck into. They needed to run past the embassy, exposed the whole time, and hope that there were more smaller residences with access paths to hide in.

Frank made it about twenty feet from the end of the embassy wall, with Aaron several yards behind him, when the world in front of him exploded into white flashes.

A sound like branches snapping filled his left ear. He dropped to one knee and raised his carbine before the streak of red tracers cut the white-out in his vision. Just as he realized what was happening, Aaron ran into him at full gallop, sprinting in a blind panic. Aaron toppled over top Frank, landing face-first on the sidewalk and blacking out.

Frank felt Aaron hit him and then saw him go down, as more twigs snapped in his ears. The young man splayed flat on his stomach, and when Frank rolled him over, blood covered his face. Frank held his hand on the PTT button to call Gary when Aaron fluttered his eyes and tried to sit up.

"Am I dead?" Aaron said.

Frank chuckled. "Not if you have to ask. C'mon, back the other way."

They ran back the way they came, the embassy wall now towering on their left. The miniature, laser-like beams of red machine gun tracers sailed past them, bouncing off the asphalt and zinging erratically up into the night sky.

Frank squeezed his PTT as they ran. "We're coming back."

"Roger," Gary said.

Seconds later, Aaron collapsed into the alley at Gary's feet. Frank put one hand against the side of the house they hid behind and dry heaved several times.

"Who's back there?" Gary asked.

Between heaving breaths, Frank said, "Paras."

Realizing they were now in the middle of a firefight between Al Badari insurgents and British paratroopers, Gary knew they needed to be anywhere else.

"Alley," Gary said.

"Moving," Frank said.

Without waiting for Gary's reply, Frank took off at a much slower jog down the alley between two houses. Aaron scurried behind him.

Just as Frank reached the end of the alley, someone crashed into him coming the other way. The two men bounced off each other, and Frank immediately thrust his carbine forward, smashing the other person in the face with the end of his suppressor as if it were a bayonet. He snapped the stock into his shoulder and tapped the pressure switch on his Surefire weapon light.

The person staggering in front of him wore light-colored, local clothing. An AK hung limply across his chest as he covered his face. Frank fired two rounds through the backs of the man's hands. The man toppled over backward, dead before he landed.

Frank clicked off the weapon light. He heard multiple voices shouting in Arabic.

"Contact," Frank said. "One down, multiple inbound."

Gary stood next to them, having come running when he heard the scuffle.

"They're cutting through the backyards," Gary said. "Trying to flank the Brits."

Frank nodded in agreement.

Gary gestured toward the two houses they were in between. "Who lives here?"

Aaron pointed to one of the houses. "This one is ours."

"Inside," Frank said.

Aaron turned to go back down the alley, to the front of the house. The Brits laid in hard with their machine gun teams, and the sidewalk would be a human blender with one misstep.

Frank grabbed the back of Aaron's shirt and turned him around. "*Back* door."

Aaron swung his leg over a thigh-high decorative fence. Frank and Gary followed behind him, up to the back door. They weren't sure if it was unlocked, or if Aaron was just fast with the key, but he ducked inside.

Gary said, "Lock the door, get everyone behind furniture. If you hear us banging, be ready to let us in."

"Got it," Aaron said.

The door slammed on them, and the two contractors ducked back into the alley.

Gary unslung the bailout bag and dropped it between them, unzipping every compartment. He pulled the last box of ammunition for his SAW and swapped it into his gun. Then he unfolded the machine gun's bipod and laid down in the dirt, leaning his weight into the stock and "loading" the bipod.

Frank pulled two fragmentation grenades out of the bag, hooked one to his plate carrier, and pulled the pin on the other, holding the safety spoon down with his palm.

Then they waited.

The insurgents proved not to be stealthy, chattering to each other in hurried Arabic as they moved like a gaggle of geese down the row of backyards. They peered down each alley, trying to find the British fire teams.

Frank waited until they were within fifteen feet and lobbed the first grenade high so that it landed behind the insurgents. Gary fired before the grenade hit the ground. AK rounds chewed away the corner of the house they hid behind when the frag detonated. The gunfire paused, replaced by screaming, and Frank tossed the second grenade in a soft underhand. It landed right in front of the insurgent team, close enough that both Frank and Gary pulled back into the alley to avoid blast fragments when it went off a two seconds later.

Dirt showered down on them as Gary rolled back behind the machine gun and fired an extended burst—at least twenty rounds—into the heap of insurgent bodies, raking his muzzle back and forth until he could see his barrel smoking in the dark.

Frank and Gary held their sights on the pile of bodies,

waiting for movement, when their earpieces crackled.

"Cossack, Crowbar, this is Jameson, over."

"Cover me," Frank said, lowering his carbine to click his microphone on. "Crowbar, send it."

"SitRep?" Jimmy asked.

"Cossack is with me. British QRF in heavy contact, one block west of our position. Our package is intact. Looking for egress routes, over."

"Hold fast," Jameson said. "We're coming to get you."

Frank's brow furrowed. "Jameson, Crowbar, uhh… the Hot Gates are sealed, and embassy row is a two-way range right now, over."

"Crowbar, roger. We're coming by air. How copy?" Jimmy said.

"They cleared airspace, over?" Frank asked.

Jimmy paused before coming back. "We're not sure. But we're coming."

"Good copy," Frank said. He let off the mic and said to Gary, "Someone is gonna get an ass chewing tomorrow."

Gary smirked behind his machine gun. "There might not be anyone left to yell at us by sunrise."

Frank squeezed his PTT again. "Jameson, Crowbar. It's gonna be a tight fit down here."

"We're sending a little bird plus two pax."

Gary took his face off the stock and looked up at Frank, brow raised.

Frank shrugged, and said into his radio, "Copy, little bird plus two. What do you need from us?"

"Find a flat roof and put an IR strobe on it. You have ten mikes."

"Solid copy," Frank said.

"Crowbar, we can make one pass. If you miss the window, you're stuck in there until they open the gates. Understood?"

"Crowbar copies all. We'll be ready."

"Jameson out."

Frank popped out of the alley, stepped over the short fence into Tutum Terram's backyard, and hammered on the door with his fist. He heard the deadbolt unlatch. Aaron swung the door open.

"Let's go," Frank called.

Gary got up to his knees, zipped the bailout bag, threw it over his shoulder, and jogged to meet them at the back door. They piled in and locked the door behind them.

Inside, the remaining aid workers huddled behind tables or couches. Gunfire still crackled in the street out front. Gary saw Kathy, laying in the fetal position, curled around an old recliner chair. Alyssa sat cross-legged on the kitchen floor, up against the refrigerator.

Gary turned to Aaron. "Can we get up on the roof?"

"Yeah, just take the stairs all the way up," Aaron said.

"Alright," Gary said. "You have exactly five minutes. You can fill a single backpack with belongings. No electronics larger than a laptop. Meet us on the roof."

Aaron nodded and left the room at a quick walk.

"What's going on?" Alyssa asked.

"We're leaving," Frank said.

"In the middle of that battle?"

"Nope. Over top of it."

"I don't understand."

"There's a helicopter coming."

"Are we all going?"

"No, ma'am."

Alyssa got to her feet and took off after Aaron.

Frank and Gary traded glances before crossing into the living room and ascending the narrow staircase, clearly not built for weight-lifting Americans in full combat gear. At the top sat an angled door that opened upwards onto the roof. They looked like storm cellar doors on the side of a farmhouse in Kansas. The roof itself was set up as a patio, with a wrought-iron table, a matching set of four chairs, additional plastic chairs, and a folding card table weathered by the sun.

"We gotta clear this shit off," Gary said.

They laid their weapons down and grabbed the wrought iron table. Lifting it in unison, they walked it to the edge of the roof and threw it over. It landed in the backyard with a crash. The two men crossed back and forth around each other, hurling the individual chairs and card table over as well. In front of the house, a British tracer ricocheted off something and zipped straight over the roof into the night sky.

"Gonna be a dicey approach for the pilot," Frank said.

"All we can do is give them an LZ," Gary said.

With all the furniture clear, Gary opened the go bag. He pulled out an MS-2000 strobe light about the size and shape of a small TV remote, and a bundle of infrared glow sticks. He handed Frank the glow sticks.

"Mark the corners," Gary said.

Frank cracked all four sticks in one, hulk-like bending

motion. He rolled one to each corner of the roof.

After watching where they landed, Gary positioned himself as close as he could to dead center. He snapped the IR shield over the top of the strobe before turning it on and placing it down.

"Go get the kid," Frank said. Gary disappeared down through the storm door and Frank keyed his radio. "Jameson, Crowbar. LZ marked. What channel is the bird on?"

Frank heard wind rushing in his earpiece as Jimmy yelled over the whipping air, "Crowbar, I'm on the bird. We're two mikes out."

Frank heard Gary and Aaron before he saw them. They emerged from the roof access door in a hurried racket, with Gary pulling the younger man along with him. Two steps behind them, Alyssa clamored up the narrow staircase onto the roof. Aaron turned to her and brushed her hair out of her face.

"This isn't how it was supposed to be. You said you were staying. You were going to stay with me, no matter what," Alyssa said.

"If it makes you feel any better," Frank said to her, "it wasn't his call."

The young woman ignored him. She and Aaron clutched each other, kissing with desperate passion.

Frank and Gary traded glances. Frank shook his head but let them have their long goodbye until the distinct, lawnmower buzzing of the little bird grew louder. The two men looked up. Through their night vision goggles, they saw the teardrop-shaped fuselage of the small helo skimming over the city in a beeline toward them.

Gary turned to the star-crossed lovers. "I'm sorry. It's time to go."

Aaron broke the kiss to face Gary. His back stiffened. "I'm not leaving without her."

"What?" Alyssa yelled. "I'm not going anywhere!"

"We only have room for you," Gary replied firmly.

"I already told you I didn't want to go," Aaron said.

The helicopter slowed down a block away, preparing for the hot landing.

"You can come with us, or we can take you with us. Your call," Gary said.

"You can't do this to him," Alyssa said. Rotor wash blew her long hair wildly around her face. Behind them, the little bird's nose bucked upward as the skids touched down onto the roof. Jimmy and Scott hopped off their benches and ran up to the four people on the opposite edge of the rooftop.

Jimmy had to yell over the buzzing of the rotors. "You guys ready?"

"Yeah!" Frank yelled.

"No!" Aaron shouted. "I said I'm staying!"

Jimmy looked at Aaron, then at Alyssa, then the other two contractors.

"You have five seconds to unfuck this!" Jimmy said to Frank, who immediately gave Aaron a light back-handed punch to the abdomen.

Aaron hunched over, and Gary wrenched one of his arms behind his back. Frank took the other arm, and they started toward the helicopter. Aaron went dead-weight, but they dragged his ankles across the rooftop as he screamed in protest.

Jimmy and Scott walked behind them, Alyssa scurrying alongside, slapping at the two SEAL veterans. They reached the helo, Aaron sobbing in defeat as Frank and Gary stuffed him inside behind the pilot's seat.

Scott spun around and gave Alyssa a stiff-armed shove, knocking her back two steps. As Scott turned away from her, she surged forward and punched him in the back. It felt little more than a nudge to Scott. Alyssa recoiled in pain when her knuckles smashed into the hard armor plate, her angry yelp lost to the buzzing rotorwash.

Gary could still hear Aaron crying out for her as the four men hooked themselves onto the Little Bird's assault benches. The helicopter popped off the roof, bolting into the darkness at full speed.

DAY THREE

**HILTON PIERCE AND JIMMY TOOMS
CALLSIGNS "ALLEY CAT" AND "JAMESON"
WINDSOR KRAFT STRATEGIES
TARKENT, DARISTAN
0540 LOCAL TIME**

Hilton and Jimmy stood silent on the flightline, watching the first rays of watermelon sunlight pierce the perpetual veil of dust that hung over Tarkent. In the distance, muezzins sang their morning prayers over loudspeakers. A calm haunted the dawn. No beating blades of helicopters, or distant gunfire, or formations of troops running around the perimeter singing cadence. The quiet made Hilton nauseous.

"Hilton?" Jimmy said.

"Huh?" Hilton said.

"Did you hear me?"

Hilton blinked slowly, then shook his head.

Jimmy repeated himself. "This may be the last time we ever get this."

"Get what?"

"This quiet. In Tarkent, anyway. The mil airlift is supposed to be insane."

"Oh. Yeah." Hilton finally caught up. "An aircraft every sixty minutes for sixty-six hours, right? I remember it being something catchy like that on the news."

"That's not even counting all the private charters,"

Jimmy added.

As if on cue, the growing rumble of a C-17 descending through the dust undercut the prayer.

"When do they start letting locals manifest on flights?" Hilton asked.

"Noon today. It'll be all US citizens until then."

They continued watching as the C-17 grew larger and louder before its wheels screeched against the runway on touchdown. Behind them, a phalanx formation of would-be passengers took shape. They formed a mix of military personnel, diplomatic staff from allied embassies, and non-profit NGO workers. Some wore business casual attire, others dirty camouflage fatigues. All looked defeated. Each waited laden with luggage: green canvas duffel bags or assault packs covered in MOLLE webbing.

At the back of the group sat a stretcher with an IV bag dangling from its support pole. At the front rested a single coffin. Hilton glanced over at Jimmy, who stared over the crowd, his eyes glued to the coffin.

"You sure you want to stay?" Hilton asked.

Jimmy nodded, gaze still fixed on the coffin.

Hilton's eyes narrowed behind his Oakley shades. "Why?"

Jimmy focused on his own reflection in Hilton's sunglasses. "I can't help him now, but I can help you."

Hilton turned away from him to watch the C-17 lumber across the tarmac to the Clocktower ramp, which butted right up to the edge of the runway. The plane pivoted on its landing gear, its tail pointing directly at them. Hydraulic pistons whined as the ramp lowered and a US

Air Force crew chief walked up to meet them.

"This everyone?" the chief asked, motioning toward the crowd behind them.

"Far as we know," Hilton said.

"That K-I-A one of yours?"

"Yes, chief," Jimmy said.

"Okay. We'll take him first."

Hilton and Jimmy looked at each other, nodding in unison. They turned around and walked up to the casket on its own rolling stretcher. A Windsor Kraft flag draped across the box. Drab tan, with black stitching—the company logo of a double-edged dagger, point down, through the outline of a globe. The company name arced about the top of the emblem. The motto mirrored across the bottom: Pax Requirit Vires—Meaning, "Peace Requires Strength."

Hilton and Jimmy took up post at the front corners. Four soldiers in tattered camouflage filled in behind them. Hilton stepped off first, everyone else following. Without a word between them, they rolled Bill Williams past the crew chief, up the ramp, and all the way to the front of the plane.

Inside, the air crew snapped thick, canvas cargo straps into loops on the plane's floor. They pumped the ratchet handles until the casket and its wagon were secure just behind the cockpit. The soldiers turned and jogged back down onto the ramp, both contractors planted in place with the flag-draped coffin between them.

"Can't help him now," Hilton said softly.

"But we can help them," Jimmy replied, looking out

the back of the aircraft.

They walked slowly out of the plane.

Hilton patted the crew chief on the back. "Load 'em up, chief."

The chief pointed to the crowd and motioned them forward with both arms. Hilton expected them to file off one column at a time. Instead, they trudged forward all together. Some carried everything they owned. Others lugged a change of clothes and the weight of a collapsing campaign they'd sworn allegiance to, missing birthdays and anniversaries and piano recitals for something they decided served a greater good. Rumpled clothes and dirty faces held questions to be answered much later, if ever at all.

Hilton clenched his teeth, and wondered what Corrine was having for dinner back in Boston.

At the back of the crowd, Hugh and Scott walked up to the ramp. Jimmy assumed control of the Tarkent Owl team in their absence, until those Owls could be evacuated on the last day. Hugh and Scott would escort Ben to Germany before doing the same for Bill on his final trip back to the States.

"You guys gonna stay with Ben?" Jimmy asked.

"Until we can't," Scott said.

Two French military nurses pushed the stretcher forward. Jimmy reached out for Ben, but placed his hand on the metal railing instead when he realized Ben had been sedated for the flight. Underneath his green, wool blankets, the stump over Ben's left knee was wrapped in a spool of fresh gauze.

One of the nurses pulled aside the crew chief and rattled off instructions or a status update—Jimmy wasn't sure which. One of them wore a rucksack on her back. She went up the ramp with Hugh and Scott. The crewmen strapped down Ben's stretcher as they had Bill's casket. The nurse waited to take her seat on the floor next to him until they were finished. Hugh and Scott dropped their bags beside her.

The crew chief shook hands with Jimmy and Hilton in turn before heading up the ramp and pulling a headset down over his ears. He said something into his mic lost to the sound of turbines before the ramp folded up behind him.

The plane accelerated halfway down the runway before Hilton said, "That a storm moving in?"

Jimmy looked across the horizon. Thick, high-topped clouds gathered on the other end of the city.

"Worried it's gonna spoil your plans?" Jimmy said.

"I've gotta head to the embassy," Hilton replied.

"A storm is appropriate, then."

"You good?"

"I'm good," Jimmy confirmed.

"See you at lunch."

Hilton squeezed Jimmy on the shoulder and walked away.

Jimmy stood at the edge of the runway until he couldn't see the plane anymore. Even then, he stayed a little longer.

HILTON PIERCE
CALLSIGN "ALLEY CAT"
RECCE TROOP – WINDSOR KRAFT STRATEGIES
US EMBASSY
TARKENT, DARISTAN
0728 LOCAL TIME

A steady, pattering rain drummed off the roof of Hilton's Hilux pickup. The heavy armored truck threw water to both sides as it rolled through the blast gate at the American embassy. As the contract guard hauled the steel door closed behind him, Hilton's stomach clenched at what he saw. Computer towers, laptops, portable hard drives, and phones littered the parking lot in front of the embassy. The clover-green splinters of fractured circuit boards scattered across the wet pavement.

At the far end of the lot, two US State Department staffers used an up-armored LC to run over electronics. When they crushed one piece, they simply kicked the pieces across the lot and dropped another item down in front of the truck. Three, fifty-five-gallon barrels lined up on the sidewalk in front of the main entrance, fires burning in each one. The flames sputtered and flickered against the steady rain. The front doors of the embassy swung open and closed like those in a wild west saloon as a stream of diplomatic staff came in and out with reams of documents that they dumped into the barrels. The shovel-loads of burning, wet paper left a thin veil of sooty smoke hanging over the parking lot.

Hilton parked his truck and stepped out. The smell of wet cement and burning paper touched something deep in the core of his brain he couldn't place. Maybe a distant memory of a high school bonfire. Or maybe *this* would be the distant memory, forming in real time and forever tied to the smell of burning paper.

Hilton entered the lobby and wiped the rain off his arms. Stepping up to the front desk, he saw it was bare. The same two American contractors posted behind the desk. One of them had bloodshot eyes. The other bounced his leg almost uncontrollably in his chair.

"Hey guys," Hilton said calmly. "No sign-in book?"

Bloodshot Eyes looked up at him, as if he hadn't seen Hilton walk in. "Logbook? We burned the logbook this morning."

"Should I just go ahead?"

"It's all gone, man. I dunno where you're going to."

Hilton started to walk down the hall but turned back. "How long have you guys been here?"

The two just looked at each other. The one bouncing his leg said, "A while, I guess. Some of the other guys won't come out of their rooms. We're here until they can find two guys to take our spots. What's Windsor Kraft gonna do when this is all over? You guys got other contracts?"

"I don't know," Hilton lied. "I'm just the help."

"If you see any of our guys, we could really use a shift change."

"I'll see what I can do," Hilton said and left the desk, heading for Kelly's office.

The door next to Kelly's office rested partially open. Music blared from inside. Hilton stopped in front of the door, looking up and down the hallway. People passed each other gruffly in the corridor on their way to or from the parking lot. They carried boxes of paperwork or awkward armfuls of electronics to be destroyed outside. A dumbbell from the gym propped open the front door of the embassy, which was normally sealed with an electromagnetic lock. Hilton put two fingers on the office door and slowly pushed it open the rest of the way.

A heavyset man sat slumped in his office chair, back to Hilton. He stared out the floor-to-ceiling sheet glass window. Gray raindrops, loaded with dust and ash, splattered against the window and ran down the pane in steady channels. Beyond the stripes of dirty water, the fire barrels in the parking lot looked blurry, the orange flames climbing out of them whipping back and forth like flags in the wind.

A mostly empty bottle of Johnny Walker Blue Label sat front-and-center on the desk, its cap removed and discarded. Hilton recognized the song, "Black Hole Sun," by Soundgarden, blasting through a Bluetooth speaker too loud to have a conversation. The man's arm came up to his face, then back down. He spun around slowly and placed a cut. crystal tumbler down on the desk. Then he picked up the bottle and refilled his glass halfway to the top. No ice cubes. Placing the bottle back on his desk, the man looked up at Hilton as he grabbed his glass.

"Help you?" the man asked. He spoke loudly, fighting the music, and concentrated hard on each word.

Hilton shook his head.

Unprompted, the man yelled his sour retort anyway. "Can't help anyone here. Too late for that now."

Hilton held up both hands, as if to say, "sorry, wrong office," and backed himself out. He opened Kelly's office door halfway and leaned in. She sat at her desk with two stacks of papers almost as high as her head. She robotically pulled papers off one pile, smashed a red-rubber stamp onto them, and then placing them on the opposite pile.

Hilton rapped on the doorframe. Kelly looked up, irritated, as if she'd already told twenty other people to keep her door closed. Her expression softened when she realized who it was.

"Hilton! What are you doing here? Close the door, please," Kelly said.

He did. Kelly shook her head and said, "Mike has been blasting that fucking racket for like thirty minutes. I don't know how far down that bottle he's gotten, but it was sealed this time yesterday."

Hilton pulled up a chair across the desk from her. "Kel, *what* is going on here?"

"People are freaking out over this Al Badari thing."

He raised an eyebrow. "*This Al Badari thing*? He's occupying every major city in the country, and just blasted through Parliament last night. The country's government collapsed."

"Correction, Hilton. *A* government collapsed. Not *the* government. It's just a transition," Kelly said.

Hilton rubbed his forehead with one hand as she continued to stamp papers. He couldn't decide if he thought she was the bravest or stupidest American woman in Daristan. "I assume you're stamping visa applications?"

She nodded, still stamping.

"Why?" he asked.

"Because the governmental transition taking place right now doesn't change the fact that these people followed the procedure in place when they started it. We have one week to finish our work here before the new government ends its diplomatic relationship with the US. I would like to uphold our commitment to as many Daristanis as I can. Every one of these sheets of paper is a person who trusted the American immigration process. I owe them that much, even if the ambassador is hiding in his room."

Despite their differences in worldview, Hilton regretted his previous thought about Kelly being stupid. She dedicated herself to her mission as much as he did to his, regardless of how he felt about it.

"You never did tell me what you were doing here," she said.

His eyes narrowed.

"I need one of those," he said, nodded his head toward her finished stack.

"Your guy? Daoud?"

"You see his name yet?"

"Honestly, Hilton, I'm not even looking at names right now. Feel free to start digging through the finished pile."

Hilton got up and dragged his chair to the corner of

her desk. He slid the stack toward him and peeled them off, scanning the name and placing them back into a new pile. He and Kelly fell into a rhythm. Neither spoke for ten minutes. The only sounds came from Kelly's stamping, Hilton's shuffling of paper, and Mike's music—Nirvana's "Heart-Shaped Box" now—blaring through the adjacent wall as he continued to drown his feelings in a couple hundred dollars' worth of cliché.

Two-thirds of the way through Kelly's finished pile, Hilton still hadn't found Daoud's SIV. He began to think he'd rather be in a gunfight than stuck behind a desk while the country collapsed around this bubble of American ideocracy. A thought occurred to him, and he looked up from the paper in his hand. "What are you going to do with all these approved visas?"

Kelly let out a big breath. "The new government asked all civilians leaving the country to head to Tarkent airport. I need to get these to whoever will be screening passengers."

"How you gonna get there?"

"They were supposed to send a helicopter over to pick a few of us up, but I'm pretty sure the weather grounded that flight."

Hilton looked past her, out the window, into the parking lot. At his truck.

"Oh! Here he is!" She enthusiastically stamped the visa packet in front of her and held it out to Hilton. He scanned it, trying to make sure all the signatures were there, and double-checking that Kelly stamped in all the required spots. He quickly folded the packet, unbuttoned the top half of his flannel overshirt, and tucked the papers between his plate carrier and undershirt.

"How much longer to finish that stack?" Hilton asked.

"That's not the last of it. I have two more file drawers full of these," Kelly said.

"I understand. But, that stack."

Kelly paused to size up the unfinished pile next to her right arm. "Twenty, thirty minutes, maybe? Why?"

"The 82nd Airborne is standing up a pax processing team at the airport right now. Finish those up, I'll run you over there to get all these where they need to go."

"How do I get back?"

"If flights are moving by then, catch one. Otherwise, I can bring you back."

"I'll have to let my department head know."

"I'll let him know. Where is he?"

Kelly shrugged. "Around here somewhere. Haven't seen him all day."

"If he doesn't turn up by the time you're done, grab your cell and we'll call him en route."

Kelly opened her mouth to answer, but an explosion in the parking lot cut her off.

Hilton watched a geyser of dirt and concrete chunks blossom out of the ground. She yelped and ducked her head. He shot out of his chair, knowing the large window behind her was three-inch-thick, blast-resistant laminate. By the time he stood at full height, a second blast erupted, this one flipping a US State Department Land Cruiser and knocking over two burn barrels. Glowing, red embers and sheets of scorched paperwork spilled out onto the ground. Klaxons sounded throughout the entire building.

"Get under your desk," Hilton said.

Kelly pushed her chair back and crawled under the heavy, wooden desk. Hilton pulled her office door open and poked his head into the hallway. No movement whatsoever.

He turned back to Kelly's desk. "*Do not* leave this room. No matter what. I'll be back for you."

Her head popped up from under the desk. "What if they…"

"I said *don't*."

She nodded. Then she grabbed her rubber stamp and the stack of unfinished visa applications, and pulled them under the desk with her.

Hilton closed the door behind him and jogged back down the hallway to the front desk. Only one of the guards, the one with bloodshot eyes, remained.

"Indirect?" Hilton asked.

"I think so," the desk guard replied.

"Where's your partner?"

"Left for help."

Hilton pointed at a metal mesh locker behind the desk. "Lay out your belt fed and get me a radio."

"I'm pretty sure it's just rockets, man."

Hilton shook his head and crossed behind the guy, throwing the locker open. He grabbed a radio, turned it on, and clipped it to his pants pocket, opposite his own Windsor Kraft radio. Then he hauled out the M240 machine gun and dropped it on the desk in front of the junior contractor. He flung the feed tray cover open, laid a belt of 7.62 ammo into the feed chute, and slapped the cover closed. He charged the weapon and clicked the safety on.

"Is the ambo off site?" Hilton asked.

Something clicked inside the kid's brain. "No, sir."

"Good." Hilton pointed to the double front doors and said, "If you see that blast door open, waste anyone who makes it this far."

The guy nodded.

"Now let me out," Hilton said.

"What?"

"Buzz me out."

The locks buzzed, and Hilton ripped one of the front doors open. He took one deep breath and burst into a sprint across the parking lot. He made it halfway to the small, square shack that housed the gate guard when a third blast knocked him off his feet. Ahead of him, the sliding blast gate blew off its track.

Hilton scrambled to get his legs back under him as four black-robed men squeezed through the fresh gap at the edge of the blast gate. Hilton snatched the front of his flannel shirt, pulling it halfway up his ribs as his other hand jerked the Staccato free of its appendix holster.

The gate guard loosed a burst of machine gun fire through the port in his bulletproof window. Three of the four insurgents fell to the ground by the time Hilton got his first shot off. A 9mm hollow point snapped the last man's head back, crumpling him to the pavement.

Hilton ran to his truck, ripped the passenger door

open with his left hand—keeping his pistol in his right—and fished his carbine out of the footwell. In one fluid motion, Hilton holstered his pistol and looped the carbine's sling over his head, pushing the truck door closed before shouldering the rifle and sprinting to the guard shack. He pounded on the door. It popped open just enough for Hilton to slide into the armored cube.

The guard inside, another American contractor, breathed a little heavy but otherwise seemed sharp-eyed and collected.

"You good, brother?" the contractor asked. "I saw you go down."

Hilton nodded, also panting. "Yeah man." He looked down at the M240, a whisp of smoke still rising from the muzzle. "Thanks for the quick trigger finger."

The guard nodded toward the pistol still in Hilton's hand and smirked. "Likewise."

Hilton slung the carbine across his back and leaned down toward the desk. He eyed the monitor showing camera feeds from outside the blast gate. Without looking up, he asked, "Was that indirect, or did they throw charges over the wall?"

The guard, who was back behind the stock of his machine gun, shook his head. "Rockets. I heard them come in."

Hilton nodded. He grabbed the computer mouse and clicked a couple different windows on the computer screen, panning the cameras around.

Outside the gate, an old man with a long, gray beard pointed at the blast gate. He repeatedly smacked one of his subordinates in the side of the head, speaking rapidly and gesturing angrily.

Hilton pointed to the screen, and put on his best "Cool Hand Luke" impression. "What we have here is a failure to communicate."

The guard looked at the monitor and smirked. Hilton looked at the guard and said, "See that big, long gray beard?"

The guard nodded.

Hilton ran a hand through his own close-cropped facial hair. "See how short mine is?"

The guard nodded again.

"Look for the beard first. If it's longer than mine, open fire."

"What?"

Hilton opened the door to the armored shack and disappeared. Shifting his rifle back into the low-ready position, he stormed to the blast door and pushed himself through the gap, out into the street.

The old man stopped berating his lieutenant and looked at Hilton, eyes wide. He put both hands up in front of him.

Hilton took his left hand off his carbine, holding it out to his side and shaking the watch around his wrist. Then he threw his arm up in the air as if to say, "What the fuck, man? Badari said five days!"

Hilton didn't speak a lick of Daristani, but he hoped his gestures broke the language barrier. The old man waved both hands out in front of himself and shook his head violently. Hilton started to turn around, but he stopped short.

A rust-speckled AK materialized from under the old man's robe. The old man fired a point-blank burst into the younger insurgent next to him. The black-clad insurgent collapsed. A bright-red pool of blood spread from under the body. The old man let his AK hang from the sling and gave Hilton a thumbs-up, hoping that his gesture, too, would break the language barrier.

It did. Loud and clear.

Hilton returned the thumbs-up, and the old man shuffled around the corner. Hilton slipped back through the blast door, where the guard came out of his shack to meet him.

"What the fuck was *that*?" the guard said, eyes wide.

"Fog of war, I guess," Hilton said dryly. "Can you get this gate open? I need to get out of here."

The guard eyeballed the gate. "I think so."

Hilton nodded. "Someone needs a ride to the airport. I'll be back in five."

"Roger that," the guard said, still stunned.

Hilton walked back to the embassy entrance and stood there. The doors buzzed, and he walked back inside. Hilton handed the embassy radio back to the desk guard, whose partner had returned now that the shooting stopped.

Hilton pointed at him. "Where the fuck were you?"

"Looking for my guys!" the younger man said defensively.

"You guys know Kelly?"

They both nodded.

"She needs to get visas to the pax team at the airport, and your pilots called the game for rain. I'm taking her over. Questions?"

"Nope," one said. The other just shook his head.

Hilton walked past them without another word and opened Kelly's office. "It's me."

Kelly popped up from under the desk.

"We're good. The attack is over," Hilton said.

"Are you sure?" she asked.

"Positive. Grab your finished pile and your body armor. Leave everything else. We're moving."

Kelly stood up, swept the pile of approved visas into an empty cardboard box, shrugged awkwardly into her wraparound armor vest, and followed him out of the office.

They passed the desk guards in silence, who unlocked the doors. They got into the armored Hilux, and Hilton rolled his truck slowly to the blast gate. He put it in park, hopping out to help the gate guard haul open the blast door. Hilton thanked him and jumped back behind the wheel of his truck.

The twelve-minute drive to the airport fell silent, save for the squeaking of windshield wipers and pattering rain. Neither spoke, even as they passed burning vehicles, toppled street carts, and black-robed Al Badari loyalists shaking down shop owners on the sidewalk.

They pulled up to the outermost gate of the airport compound. Hilton lowered his visor, which had a large American flag sticker taped to it. He pulled his Windsor Kraft ID badge from under his flannel and held it up to the window. A young paratrooper in Multicam utilities walked around his truck, dragging a wheeled bomb-search mirror underneath the pickup. When he finished his search, he raised a drop-arm and waved them through.

Hilton flipped the visor back up and slowly circled the airport compound on its outermost service road. They rolled up to a gate with a large crowd of locals milling around dual barricades of sandbags and concertina wire. A fire team of 82nd soldiers kept the locals at bay on the edge of the road.

Hilton threw the truck into park. "Wait here and lock the doors."

Hilton hopped out and pushed his way through the restless crowd. He felt hands grabbing on his shirtsleeves and belt as he forged his way through hundreds of Daristani civilians waiting to get manifested on a refugee flight. He held his badge up to the first soldier he saw when he reached the checkpot.

"This gate is for locals only, sir," the trooper said firmly.

"I'm with Windsor Kraft. I've got a US State Department official with a stack of approved visas to help screen these people. I'm guessing someone on your side is gonna need those papers."

"You'll need to speak with the S3, Major Kraut."

"Cool." Hilton pointed past the wire. "Is he in there?"

"Somewhere, sir."

"Then I need to get in."

"Is he expecting you?"

"Is he expecting anyone?"

"I'm not his secretary, sir."

"When did you guys get in-country?"

The paratrooper became annoyed. "Forty-two hours ago."

"I've been here two hundred days a year, for the last four years. Let me help you guys."

"Where's your Statie?"

"See my truck over there?"

The paratrooper looked past him and eyed the Hilux. "Roger."

"Can you get us through this crowd? I'll handle the rest."

"I'll radio for him."

Hilton rolled his eyes. "I'll wait."

The trooper looked him up and down. Then he said, "Get your truck, we'll clear the crowd."

"Thank you."

Hilton heard the soldier talking on his radio as he pushed his way back through the throng of panicked people to the Hilux. By the time he was back behind the wheel, a team of soldiers forcefully corralled people off to one side of the entrance.

"Are we in the right place?" Kelly asked.

"To start," he answered. "Major Kraut is their lead ops officer. We'll need to get with him once we're inside."

Kelly shifted in her seat. They eased the truck gently past the crowd and through the sandbagged entrance to the airport proper. The soldier from moments before came up to the driver's side door. Hilton cracked it open.

"Quarter mile straight down, there's a cluster of tents. He's somewhere in there. Stay off the tarmac," the soldier said.

"Copy all," Hilton said. "Thanks for your help."

The soldier turned away, and Hilton pulled the door closed. They took off down the road. They parked in front of a row of olive-green, US Army-issue GP Medium tents. The area crawled with clean-cut paratroopers ten to fifteen years younger than Hilton. The troopers unpacked large, plastic crates full of radios, weapons, and collapsible furniture.

This time, Kelly got out with Hilton, the box of visas cradled in her arms.

"Hilton, this box isn't waterproof," Kelly said.

Hilton nodded. Then he called out, "Major Kraut!"

An exhausted female sergeant approached. "Who are you with, sir?"

"US State Department. I'm looking for your three shop," Hilton said.

"No offense, sir, but you don't look like diplomatic staff."

"I'm not. But she is," he raised his chin toward Kelly. "We've got a stack of visas for locals approved to fly. I was told at the pax gate that Major Kraut was who we needed to see."

She hooked a thumb toward one of the tents.

"Much appreciated," Hilton told her. He walked with the easy confidence of entirely too much time in-country. Kelly shuffled quickly behind him, trying to keep her paperwork dry.

Hilton parted the flaps of one of the tents and waved Kelly in ahead of him. The inside of the tent was even more chaotic than the outside. Lower enlisteds scrambled to set up tables, plug in computers, and scribble priorities of work on easel-mounted white boards.

A tall officer with ramrod posture crossed the tent to intercept them. Hilton scanned his chest and saw the gold oakleaf of a major's insignia and "Kraut" on the name tape.

"This is the operations tent. No civilians," Major Kraut said curtly.

"Sir, this young woman has paperwork for you," Hilton said.

"Who are y'all?"

"Hilton Pierce, Windsor Kraft, this is…"

"A merc. There's no gunfight here, son."

Hilton ignored the jab. "*This* is Kelly Rowland. She's with State."

Major Kraut turned to face her squarely. "What do you want, ma'am? We're still trying to get established."

Kelly's sense of diplomatic entitlement kicked in instantly. "Yes, sir. I'm here to help with that. These are State Department-approved visas. You'll need them to help screen those folks out there looking to complete their government-endorsed immigration to the United States."

The major let out a short sigh. "Put them under my table. That one over there." He pointed.

"Thank you, sir," she said.

"Then what?" Hilton asked.

"Then let us do our jobs, and go back to doing yours," the major said.

Hilton ignored him and looked at Kelly.

"I got it," she said, and crossed the tent to place her box down. She came back to Hilton and Kraut. She pulled a business card out of her pocket. "Major, this is my direct, local cell."

He took the card and dropped it into the Velcro pocket on his upper arm.

Kelly continued, "I'll leave if you insist, but State Department protocol is to have a liaison on-site to verify proper processing of our issued documentation."

"Well, ma'am, all due respect, we're still trying to find our asses with both hands here. It'll be another couple hours before we can start pushing bodies through the gate. So either head back to the embassy or pull up a chair."

A soldier interrupted them. "Major Kraut, I've got the XO on SIPR phone for you."

"Miss Rowland," the major said before walking away.

"What do you want to do?" Hilton asked Kelly.

"What I came here to do," she told him.

"You gonna be okay?"

Kelly hugged him, their armor plates clicking against each other.

"Thanks, Hilton. I'd get Daoud here sooner than later. Things are going to get bad, quickly."

She let him out of the hug and looked up at him. He looked around the tent, pulsating with activity, and ran a hand through his wet hair.

"You're one of the good ones," Hilton said.

"You, too," she replied with a smile. "Go on. I'm good here."

Hilton hesitated.

"They're just soldiers," she quipped.

"Yeah." After a beat, he added, "You've got my cell?"

"I do."

"If you need it, don't hesitate."

"Roger that," she said, with a mock salute.

Hilton pulled himself away from her and left the tent. The rain pounded down sideways now, and lightning forked through distant clouds. Kelly was in for a long day.

Hilton dropped himself into the Hilux and slammed the door hard behind him. He sat behind the wheel for almost a full minute, listening to the rain and watching paratroopers scuttling about in the storm. Then he wiped the rain off his face and started the truck.

GARY BOLCEWICZ
CALLSIGN "COSSACK"
CLOSE PROTECTION TROOP – WINDSOR KRAFT STRATEGIES
CLOCKTOWER BASE
TARKENT, DARISTAN
1333 LOCAL TIME

Gary sat half-asleep in the team room's worn-out recliner. A TV across the room played the inescapable news coverage about Daristan, but Gary only heard unintelligible chatter.

Until his cell phone rang.

Gary snapped up out of the chair and dug the phone out of the cargo pocket of his fatigue pants. He didn't recognize the number.

"Send it," he said into the phone.

"Gary?"

"Elise? Are you still here?"

Elise Marceau worked as a freelance war correspondent who sold stories to news outlets all around the world. She specialized in conflict zone reporting, working in many of the same places Gary had, from Iraq and Afghanistan to Haiti and the Balkans.

"I'm not sure," Elise said.

"What do you mean *you're not sure*?" Gary asked.

"I planned to stay. I have connections inside Al Badari's camp. I'm not so sure now."

Elise was Corsican by birth, and her French Mediterranean looks combined with her taste for danger proved intoxicating for Gary. They worked in Daristan for the last three years, forming the kind of romantic partnership that thrived in war: habitual if not committed, full of hormones, and void of structure. They cared for one another, but not enough to stick it out beyond a common conflict zone. Certainly not enough for either one to walk away and be the bedrock.

"There's not much time left to decide," Gary said.

"I heard your company is conducting extractions," Elise said.

"You need to tell me you want to get out. For sure."

"I don't know if I can leave these people," she told him.

"You can, Elise. I think you should."

"What will happen to them?"

"I don't know, and you can't stop it."

As a journalist, Elise shed light on the humanity of war. Gary's entire job depended on blocking humanity out to accomplish a fixed objective. The dynamic fueled their passion when bombs fell, but it wouldn't survive too many average nights in suburbia.

Elise went quiet on the phone.

"Ellie?"

"Okay."

"Okay, what?"

"I want to go. I am sure. Can you help?"

"Where are you?"

She gave him an address for a hotel just outside the Hot Gates called The Denton—a favorite for aid workers and journalists.

"I will be there in less than an hour," Gary said.

He hung up without giving her a chance to change her mind. Gary plucked the radio off his hip. "Crowbar, Cossack."

"Go for Crowbar," Frank said through the radio.

"Team room."

"En route."

"Tango Mike," Gary said.

In other words, "Thanks Much."

Gary stood up, stretched, and cracked all his knuckles. The team room door creaked open, and Frank filled the frame.

"We got a customer, amigo," Gary told him.

Frank furrowed his brow. "I didn't hear anything come over the radio."

"She called me direct."

Frank raised an eyebrow. "*She*? What are you guys?"

Gary shrugged. "We're whatever you call the thing that happens in a place like this."

"Is she NGO or journo?"

"She's a reporter."

"What outlet?"

"Freelance."

"Where is she?"

"The Denton."

Frank knew it well. "Should be a walk in the park, then."

"Here's hoping," Gary said.

"Does she have flight?"

"I doubt it. This sounded like a snap decision."

"You got a plan?"

"Ask Mama if she has a seat on our flight."

"What if that doesn't work?"

"Take her over to the Army terminal and let her figure it out."

"Best you can hope for. She American?"

"French."

"Like, French national? You know the Legion is here for that."

"She didn't call the Legion. She called me," Gary said.

Frank glanced at his watch. "Our flight is in less than four hours. It's at least an hour round trip with traffic. If we get into a dust-up, we might miss it."

"If we get into a dust-up, missing that flight won't be my first concern."

"Let's go talk to Mama."

Gary squeezed Frank's arm on his way out the door and said, "Thank you."

Frank smiled and threw his arms out wide. "Bullets and broken hearts turn the Ferris Wheel, baby. I'm just along for the ride."

"A hopeless romantic," Gary said, straight-faced. "That's why I like you."

Frank grabbed his partner by the shoulders and shook him playfully. "*Love*, brother. It's why you *love* me."

"I'll talk to Mama," Gary said. "Go sign out a truck and put us on the movement board."

Twenty minutes later, they rolled out the airport gate. Their Land Cruiser crawled through a jostling mob of

Daristanis who gathered around every entrance and gate leading into the airport. The military recently opened space available—"Space-A"—seating to Daristani citizens who wished to leave the country before Al Badari's deadline. The crowds were already a hundred deep, and growing, at every gate.

"This is insanity," Gary said under his breath.

"You think they realize there's no way we have enough seats for everyone?" Frank said.

"Honestly? I hope not."

"You think false hope is better than no hope?" Frank asked.

"For me? No. For these people? False hope is the only hope they've got right now."

"That's kind of a downer."

The LC nudged its way onto the first main thoroughfare headed toward The Denton.

"You think there's any *real* hope for these people?" Frank said.

"What if someone pops old Ansar before the end of the week?"

"Who's gonna do that?"

Frank blew out a loud breath.

Gary continued. "It would have to be locals. POTUS already declared the military isn't gonna do anything. If we're not doing anything, no one is."

"I guess we're off the board, too," Frank said, the defeat creeping in.

"Yes, for two reasons. One, we lose all our USG contracts if we go unilateral. Two, we don't have the manpower."

"To kill one dude?"

"To kill one dude holed up in a fortified palace compound that we built, surrounded by would-be martyrs and a bunch of ex-Daristani military that we trained. Even with every one of our guys, and all the Owls, fifty-fifty odds is being generous."

"When you put it like that…"

"It needs to be locals. Really, it would only take one Daristani military officer who's close enough to him and willing to make the sacrifice. I don't have any indication the world will get that lucky."

"What good is victory if you can't live long enough to enjoy it?" Frank said.

Gary shrugged behind the wheel. "Not my flavor of bravery but, yeah, I guess."

VIKTOR
PRESIDENTIAL PALACE
TARKENT, DARISTAN
1402 HOURS LOCAL

Viktor leaned back in his plush roller chair, his Asolo mountain boots kicked up on the massive conference table. The sole of one boot touched a messy stack of papers several inches high.

Two of his subordinates entered the other end of the room. Each cradled a heap of banded bricks of US dollars that reached from their chests their chins. As soon as they reached the edge of the table, the men dumped their loads of cash onto the conference table, pushing them into an existing pile already two feet high.

Blowing out a long stream of heavy smoke, Viktor tucked a stray lock of hair behind his ear. He swapped his Apollo-Soyuz cigarettes for the pleasure of a Cuban cigar from the dead president's desk. While Al Badari held a series of mostly ceremonial war councils, Viktor and his men undertook a thorough search of the palace. It turned out to be both a literal and figurative treasure trove.

Based solely on the height of the money pile, Viktor estimated there were several million dollars in cash accrued from various coalition governments and humanitarian aid organizations—and the men weren't even done searching yet. Even more valuable were the decades of signed contracts, diplomatic cables, and official memos documenting the president's private communications with everyone from the United Nations to European corporations seeking oil and mineral rights, to multiple American intelligence agencies.

While he felt happy to pack out a couple duffle bags of dollars that Al Badari would have no use for, Viktor knew the information provided his employers strategic leverage for years—if not decades—beyond the failure of the world's campaign in Daristan. The thought made the corners of his thin lips bowed upward into a grin that looked like bent rebar.

Viktor's two lieutenants stacked the bricks of banded bills into neat cubes, a separate cube for every million dollars. Four cubes rested on the table, with two more being built.

"Have you ever been to Cuba?" Viktor asked.

One looked up at him dumbly. The other, a Marlboro cigarette dangling precariously from one side of his mouth, shook his head without looking up from his half-built cash cube.

"What's it like?" the non-smoker asked.

"Warm, but not hot like here. The air is softer, and there's always a breeze. Old American cars. Desperate brown women," Viktor said.

The smoker's mouth twisted into a wry smile with missing teeth on either side. He, too, worked in tropical territories and experienced the companionship of peasant girls.

"Paradise," he said with Marlboro smoke spilling

from the gaps in his smile.

"I miss it," Viktor said. Maybe he would take some of this money and go back to the southern hemisphere. He spent too much time in the desert. Daristan, Libya, Syria—too much sand with no water.

Al Badari entered the room with long, confident strides. His robe flowed around his legs, giving him the appearance of gliding from place to place with an air of regality that betrayed his sense of entitlement to the very ground he walked on.

"This is my palace," Al Badari snapped. "You will take your feet off the table."

Unbothered by the tone, Viktor dragged his bootheels along the tabletop as he lowered his feet, maintaining eye contact with Al Badari the entire time.

Al Badari gave no reaction, disrespecting Viktor's protest by refusing to acknowledge it. "I need some of your men."

Viktor raised an eyebrow, switching seamlessly from Russian to English. "For what? The country is yours."

"We will attack the airport," Al Badari said curtly.

Viktor made a face like he bit into a lemon. "Why?"

"To show the world that the West will not dare retaliate against me, even when we kill them."

The two lieutenants looked up from their counting, each trying to catch Viktor's eye. He saw them and dipped his chin toward the remaining pile of uncounted money. Both men resumed working.

Looking back up at Al Badari, Viktor said flippantly, "We gave you your land. Our work out there is finished."

Al Badari's tanned face turned brick red at the cheekbones. "You did not *give* me anything! This nation has always been mine, and *I* took it *back*!"

Viktor's smile spread high and wide across his face. He took a long drag off his cigar, then spoke slowly and with naked contempt.

"You were hiding like a mouse in a Lebanese slum. This land is yours because of my aircraft, my money, my weapons. You *took it* by climbing over the corpses of martyrs. Syrians, Yemenis, Pakistanis, Jordanians. Young men that we trained, we housed, and we moved for you. You would do well to not mistake my assistance for obligation," Viktor said.

"You *communists*," Al Badari spat the word, "know nothing of my kingdom, or my god."

More Cuban smoke spilled from Viktor's mouth when he replied, "Your god didn't help you, Ansar. We did."

Al Badari pointed at the table full of money. "Your god is made of paper. You decry America to your factory workers and your old women on the tundra, but you count their money with hungry eyes when no one is looking."

Viktor leaned forward in his chair. "How many of the widows and orphans you created will you let sleep in your new palace?"

"We attack tonight," Al Badari said. He spun around to leave the room when Viktor called after him.

"At night? Like a coward?" Viktor said.

Al Badari turned back and glared at Viktor but said nothing.

"Do it tomorrow. In the day. Less than twenty-four hours before they leave for good. There will be no consequence, and it makes a stronger statement."

"I do not need your men," Al Badari said.

"On that, we agree."

Al Badari stormed out.

Viktor looked at his lieutenants, placing his feet back up on the table. The man with the cigarette blew smoke out his nose and flashed another gap-toothed smile.

GARY BOLCEWICZ AND FRANK RELEYA
CALLSIGNS "COSSACK" AND "CROWBAR"
CLOSE PROTECTION TROOP – WINDSOR KRAFT STRATEGIES
THE DENTON HOTEL
TARKENT, DARISTAN
1437 LOCAL TIME

Gary eased the Land Cruiser to a halt at the front gate. Like several of the hotels and restaurants that served as hub locations for Westerners, The Denton used its own private security force. Some places employed locals for protection, but others relied on Gurkhas, South Africans, or Colombians ultimately employed by European or Israeli security firms.

The gate opened, and they rolled into the vehicle search area—an artificial alley lined on both sides by concrete walls and closed off from the hotel courtyard by a solid, steel blast door.

Two guards approached the truck, one dragging the ubiquitous wheeled mirror-on-a-stick behind him. Short-barreled Galil rifles slung over their shoulders. They wore green, canvas chest rigs over their khaki uniforms.

Gary and Frank pressed ID cards against their windows. The guards glanced at them before flashing a thumbs-up. They dragged the mirror slowly around the vehicle, crouching down to eyeball the wheel wells. Satisfied, they heaved the blast door open and gave another thumbs-up.

The LC rolled past a modest fountain in the lush courtyard. The road—a narrow, dirt track—ran up to marble front steps flanked by a pair of stone columns. Gary nosed into a parking spot made with white lines painted into the dirt. Both men left their carbines in the truck but kept their plate carriers on. Frank let out a low whistle as they mounted the steps together.

"Nice place," Frank said, eyeing the architecture.

"Doric columns and everything," Gary replied.

Frank grinned. "Good effort, but these are actually Tuscan, not Doric."

"What's the difference?"

"These are smooth. Doric columns have longitudinal grooves, like a fluted rifle barrel."

Gary's eyebrows went up. "I learned something today."

"My work here is done."

"Why do you know that?"

"I'm an architecture nerd."

Gary rolled his eyes. "You and my dad both with that shit."

"Sounds like your dad is also a man of culture. What happened to you?"

Just as they reached the front desk, Gary told him, "I rebelled," before turning to the desk clerk. "Elise Marceau, please."

The clerk picked up a landline phone and dialed. A moment later she said, "Miss Elise, you have guests in the lobby. Of course, ma'am. Thank you."

The clerk hung up her phone and told them the room number before directing them to an elevator.

Inside the elevator, Frank asked, "Should I wait outside?"

"Why?"

"I dunno. Maybe she'll give you one more for the road."

"If that's the case, you won't be waiting long."

"Still don't wanna be standing in the corner for it."

"I doubt that's the mood today."

"Don't be a pessimist."

The elevator door opened before Gary could respond. When the door to Elise's room opened, Gary felt thankful he didn't have any romantic expectations. Luggage, laptops, and camera equipment strewed across the floor. Duffel bags spilled out on three of the four beds in the large room. Frank felt a pang in his stomach that felt uncomfortably like jealousy when he saw Elise.

"You ready to go?" Gary said to Elise .

She looked at Gary, straightened her posture, and rolled her shoulders back. "Get me out of this goddamned place."

"With pleasure," Gary said.

They left the room in a hurry, slamming the door behind them, and stayed quiet until they buckled into the Land Cruiser.

Gary navigated the cross-town trip back to Clocktower. Half a mile from their destination, traffic ground to a halt. Three cars ahead, four black-clad men with AKs haphazardly directed traffic and inspected each vehicle before letting it pass.

Gary squeezed his hands on the steering wheel. "That checkpoint wasn't here on the way over."

Frank pulled his carbine up from between his legs, resting the buttstock against his armor.

They inched forward, one car length at a time, until they stopped at the threshold of the intersection. One of the black-clad men rapped hard on the triple-thickness driver's side window. Gary held up his ID. The man took one step back and motioned for them to get out of the truck. Two more men planted themselves in the middle of the intersection, blocking the path. Gary shook his head, tapping his ID against the inside of the window.

"All you have to do is hit the gas," Frank said.

The man at the window shook his own head in response, waving them out of the vehicle again.

"Let me talk to them," Elise said from the back.

"Absolutely not," Gary said.

"He's right," Frank added.

Gary tapped the gas pedal, and the armored truck jumped forward a foot. The two men in front raised their rifles.

"Is this car bulletproof?" Elise asked.

"Yes."

One of the men in front yanked the charging handle on his AK, sending one round flying out the side of the gun. The guy at the driver's door hammered the glass with his fist. Gary put his left foot down on the brake and held eye contact with his man as he revved the engine up. The heavy truck pushed against its brake pads.

Frank raised his carbine, pressing the muzzle against the inside of the windshield as a show of force. He wouldn't fire, as the bullets would only ricochet back on him after hitting ballistic glass, but the choreographed performance of gestures served as a universal language in conflict zones.

The man at the driver's door raised his own AK, muzzle to the sky, shaking it in Gary's face. In response, Gary pressed the gas pedal down further, and the Land Cruiser jumped forward an inch, tires screeching in protest. The two men in front jumped in opposite directions to avoid being hit. Frank knew in that instant they wanted a shakedown, not a gunfight.

"Go!" Frank snapped.

Gary let off the brake, and their truck catapulted through the intersection in a whelping squeal of burned rubber. Honking his way through red lights, Gary didn't slow down until they returned to the crowd outside the airport, which had grown even larger.

"Oh my God," Elise whispered. "All these people."

"It's only going to get worse," Frank told her.

They drove through the same mirror and ID checks at the front gate of the airport complex. Only when the airport blast door clanked shut behind them did Frank finally let go of his carbine again.

Minutes later, they rolled through another security gate—this one manned by Windsor Kraft contractors.

"This isn't the check-in terminal," Elise said.

"No, this is our terminal," Gary told her.

"How do I catch a flight from here?"

"I already took care of that. Frank and I are leaving tonight. You're coming with us."

"Where are you going?"

"I can't say, but you'll be able to find your way home from there."

Depending on what plane the company sent, they would most likely wind up in Amman or Abu Dhabi—possibly even Kuwait City. Regardless, all offered massive international airports with a buffet of flights for Elise to get back to Europe or wherever she planned to go next.

"When do we leave?" she asked.

Frank glanced down at his G-Shock watch. Almost 1530.

"Ninety minutes," Frank said. Looking at Gary, he added, "We need to rally for out-processing in like thirty-five mikes."

Gary let out a breath. "Just made it."

"Just."

250 TOM MARSHALL

**JACK YOUNG
WATCH CAPTAIN
GLOBAL OPERATIONS CENTER - WINDSOR KRAFT STRATEGIES
CHESAPEAKE, VA
0650 HOURS, LOCAL**

Jack woke up to the soft sound of a keyboard clacking. He cracked his eyes open, staring at one of the GOC's sterile white walls. His breath felt cold and smelled of ozone. He rolled over, pushed the top of the sleeping bag off himself, and pressed his bare feet down on the scratchy, brown carpet. He blinked a few times, glanced at watch, and then looked toward the clacking sound.

Holly sat cross-legged in her chair wearing baggy sweatpants and an oversized fleece pullover. She cradled a wide, bowl-shaped coffee mug painted in pastel colors in both her hands. One corner of Jack's mouth turned up. If you took her out of the office chair and dropped her on a big, plush couch, she would look like a poster for some kind of cozy cabin rental in New England. Despite being late spring in southern Virginia, the GOC felt downright chilly. The air conditioning ran cold to keep the banks of electronics properly cooled. It also helped keep everyone awake throughout the day.

"How long have you been here?" Jack's voice still sounded hoarse from a night of breathing in chilled static.

"Little less than an hour. I couldn't sleep," Holly said

with a shrug.

Jack yawned and rubbed his eyes.

"I have work clothes with me," Holly added. "I'll change before people start coming in."

Jack grunted, dismissing the concern with a casual wave. He crossed one ankle over the opposite knee and picked up a sock from the floor. The military-issue cot he slept on was little more than a framework of aluminum legs with a sheet of olive drab nylon pulled taut between the beams. It groaned and creaked as he put his dress shoes back on. He stood, stretched his arms, and tried to smooth the wrinkles out of his slacks with his hands. It was a futile endeavor. He rolled up the fluffy, gray sleeping bag and stuffed it back into its storage sack, cinching the drawstring closed before he collapsed the frame of the cot with rehearsed ease.

Next to Holly's keyboard rested a large, brushed aluminum thermos. Jack walked up to her desk, unscrewed the lid to the thermos and breathed in the steam from the fresh brewed coffee inside.

"Washed your cup out. It's in the back," Holly said.

He carried the thermos to the back of the room. He returned with it in one hand and his full mug in the other.

"Thank you," he said, draining half the mug in one long gulp. He perked up after the coffee's heat hit his stomach.

"FYI, we have a flight landing at Clocktower in about forty-five minutes."

"Mil flight, or one of ours?"

"One of the Gulfstreams."

Jack nodded. "You check the news yet?"

"Not yet. Didn't want to wake you up."

Jack picked up a TV remote off one of the desks, aimed it at a flat screen, and pressed the power button. After a few seconds of warm up, the sound kicked on and dropped them right into the middle of yet another news report.

"With just over twenty-four hours left for coalition forces to completely evacuate the country, Russian officials have released an official statement recognizing the validity of Al Badari's insurgent forces as the legitimate governing body of Daristan. They also confirmed that their embassy would remain open past the five-day deadline to evacuate without persecution. While there has been no public response from Al Badari or his lieutenants, Russia is the first and—to date—*only* world power to recognize this coup as an actual transfer of state power…"

Jack thought back to his last conversation with Lisa. Asymmetric warfare was a long con. Never go toe-to-toe with your actual opponents out in the open. The Russians acknowledging Al Badari's insurgency as a legitimate government made a bold statement to the NATO-driven world hurrying to wash their hands of the entire situation.

It was, in that way, an international strategic victory for Russia, gained without firing a shot—plus or minus some ex-Spetsnaz contractors.

Jack didn't have much room to talk about that from

the safety of Windsor Kraft's million-dollar GOC.

"It's a smart move. Tells the world they're not afraid to tackle the issues we're running away from, even if everyone else is running, too." Holly said.

"Exactly."

Jack clicked his molars together and remembered Lisa's last directive: "Just keep doing what you're doing. Whether you like it or not."

GARY BOLCEWICZ AND FRANK RELEYA
CALLSIGNS "COSSACK" AND "CROWBAR"
CLOSE PROTECTION TROOP – WINDSOR KRAFT STRATEGIES
CLOCKTOWER BASE
TARKENT, DARISTAN
1652 LOCAL TIME

As a private charter flight, the customs and immigrations procedure could be abbreviated but not foregone completely. The process to get nearly twenty people squared away and ready to board took the better part of an hour, moving at the speed of bureaucracy. Fortunately, the plane landed less than ten minutes earlier. The huddle of anxious passengers shepherded across the base to the private ramp where their plane awaited.

Frank squinted through his shades. The shallow horizon angle and perma-haze of dust and air pollution turned the daylight a flamingo pink that radiated over the city in thick, angular bands. The wheels of his roller-bag clacked on the cement as they approached a small, armored pedestrian gate. It measured a fraction the size of the large vehicle blast doors that guarded every private compound around the city.

Frank and Gary had already turned in their weapons and kit, but Hilton and Jimmy still dressed in full gear with carbines limp across their chests, acting as escorts for the dozen-plus unarmed passengers.

At the head of the group, Hilton unlocked one bolt on the pedestrian gate, his hand already on the second, when his radio burst to life.

"Airport breach, east wall. I say again, airport breach, east wall," the voice on the radio said.

Hilton plucked the radio off his belt. "Clocktower, Alley Cat. Is there gunfire?"

"Negative, Alley Cat. Civilians overran an entry point and appear to be moving toward the runway."

"How many?"

"Three-zero to seven-zero pax."

"That's a big range," he said with frustration.

"It's a big crowd," the radio replied, matching his tone.

Jimmy ran to Hilton's position at the door when he heard the radio call.

Another voice came over the radio. "Clocktower, Spartan Two-Two. We need pax in sixty seconds or we hold until it's over."

Hilton and Jimmy traded quick glances before Hilton worked the second lock and pushed the door open. He stepped through the threshold and brought his carbine to the low-ready.

Jimmy stood in front of the passengers and called out loudly, "Do *not* try to run with all your luggage, but you better walk with a quickness." Then he keyed the mic attached to his plate carrier. "Spartan, Jameson. Pax are here. Drop your ramp, we'll make it quick."

"Spartan copies."

"Okay!" Jimmy yelled to the group. "Move now!"

The passengers hustled between Hilton and Jimmy

out onto the ramp. Jimmy walked alongside them while Hilton pulled the gate closed behind him and locked it up from the outside. When he finished, he jogged to catch up to the line of passengers. He glanced off to the east and could already see the front edge of the crowd of civilians.

"Jimmy…"

"We're here!"

The jet's staircase lowered, and the co-pilot waited on the ramp. Checked luggage loaded while the passengers processed. Everyone was down to backpacks and rollerboards. By the time Hilton reached the co-pilot, half the passengers already boarded.

"This everyone?" Hilton asked.

"Roger, sir. Full flight," the co-pilot said.

"Quick work, thank you."

Hilton gave the co-pilot a casual salute as he climbed the staircase. Moments later, the door closed, and the plane turned toward the runway.

Dropping her backpack on a chair, Elise looked around wide-eyed. "This isn't a plane. This is a yacht with wings. You travel like this?"

Gary chuckled. "Not usually, no."

The Gulfstream 650ER could travel close to 9,000 miles at just under the speed of sound. The ER model specifically set world records for the farthest, fastest business aviation flight. Windsor Kraft favored them for this combination of range and speed, which made them an ideal tool to get into or out of remote areas, or for moving small teams of contractors around the world on time-sensitive operations.

The cabin speakers crackled to life as the plane rolled slowly forward. "Ladies and gentlemen, this is your captain speaking. We're going to skip the formalities and tell you to buckle up. We are taxiing for take-off immediately. Thank you."

Already strapped in, Gary looked out his porthole window to see Hilton and Jimmy sprinting back toward the steel pedestrian gate, carbines raised to high port. He pressed gently back into his plush, leather seat as the posh Gulfstream reached full ground speed.

Through the porthole, he saw one terminal of the airport fully on fire. Civilians overran adjacent runways to get to an aircraft. They sprinted for their lives, directly toward his window it seemed. A stream of khaki-painted Humvees and MRAPs raced to meet them from down the runway, some of them already firing warning busts from their top-mounted machine guns.

Even if someone from the crowd did manage to catch a plane, they would inevitably die in transit—whether from falling or asphyxiating at altitude—but, for many, even that would be preferrable to the tidal wave of public executions, punitive gang rapes, and radical Sharia law that would descend on Tarkent in just over forty-eight hours.

However, the flock of terrified farmers and merchants running for their lives in robes and sandals never caught the sleek Gulfstream.

In the seat ahead of him, Elise held a camera with telephoto lens to her window, its shutter clicking like a prize wheel at the county fair. Gary dropped his seat back and closed his eyes as the nose of the aircraft tilted toward the sky.

On the ground, Hilton and Jimmy each worked one throw-bolt of the steel ped gate. With both locks secured, Hilton slumped back against the sealed door. "They said thirty people."

"That was over a hundred, easy," Jimmy said.

"What do you want to do about it?"

Jimmy thought for a moment. "Park a truckload of Owls out here on overwatch, rotate them every hour. Two people in ops control watching radios and cameras. You and I on roving patrol. Everyone else shelters in place until the military gets this shit under control."

Hilton pondered the plan for only a moment. "I don't have anything better."

"When we get back, you head to the ops room. Get everyone locked down. I'll find Jazz and have him push at least a squad out here."

"Heavy weapons," Hilton added. "Just in case."

"For sure."

Even through the steel door, and over top of the high concrete walls, they heard a chorus of shouting like the massed charge of troops in a medieval war movie. Without another word between them, the pair took off in a jog toward the inner sanctum of their compound.

DAY
FOUR

**HILTON PIERCE
CALLSIGN "ALLEY CAT"
RECCE TROOP - WINDSOR KRAFT STRATEGIES
TARKENT, DARISTAN
1440 LOCAL TIME**

Hilton parked his truck in a mostly empty lot behind a wedding hall. He spent most of the morning calling Daoud's cell phone on repeat and getting no answer. A day passed since he'd been able to reach his source. Every call that went straight to voicemail brought Hilton closer and closer to the thought that Daoud could already be dead.

When he couldn't reach the man by phone, Hilton left Clocktower to drive loops around the city checking all of their agreed-upon meeting spots. The only place he hadn't looked was their primary rendezvous spot: the café inside the Hot Gates. After the massive running gunfight Gary and Frank had been involved in two nights prior, 2 Para put a rifle squad at every intersection. No one could get in without prior authorization directly from their own chain of command.

But they weren't stopping people from leaving. With just over thirty-six hours left before Al Badari and his forces declared the West's presence wholly illegal, most coalition embassies closed shop, their personnel either out of the country already or sitting at the airport waiting for one of the dwindling number of flights left.

The national government compound in the center of the diplomatic district—which housed the Presidential Palace, National Court, and Parliamentary House—all remained occupied by Al Badari and his forces. The Paras left a two-block radius around the compound unoccupied as a show of good faith, but the rest of the district was essentially a British Army garrison.

Hilton pulled his local cell phone out of the cup holder in his truck and pressed a key to light up the screen. No missed calls or new messages. He dropped the small, rectangular Nokia back into the console and thumped his head against the headrest.

After ten more minutes of sitting in the idling truck, he pressed the clutch and shifted into first gear. The phone began buzzing and chirping in its cup holder before he made it out of the parking lot.

Hilton popped the Hilux out of gear and yanked the e-brake, snatching up the phone. "Alley Cat!"

"Hilton, it's me!" Daoud sounded out of breath.

"Where are you?"

"I think they're following me."

Hilton told Daoud where he was parked. "I want you to pass by here. Don't stop! Just drive past and keep driving. Exactly five minutes later, I want you to double back past me again. Understood?"

"Yes."

"See you soon."

Hilton ended the call and scrolled through his contacts for another number. It rang twice before Jimmy picked up.

"Yo, where are you?" Hilton asked.

"Where are *you*?" Jimmy said.

"Out in town."

"I know. Where?"

Jimmy rattled off the nearest intersection and said, "I've got a section of Owls with me on presence patrol."

"How many is that?"

"Eight guys, three gun trucks."

"I've got a source headed to me, thinks he might have a tail. Can you move to intercept?"

"Is he on foot or in a vehicle?"

"Vehicle."

Hilton gave him the description and plate number of Daoud's sedan.

"We'll make a pass by him and see what we can see," Jimmy said.

"Switch to radio when you get here."

"Roger."

Hilton hung up. An earpiece for his radio plugged one ear, Micro Chest Rig partially hidden beneath his unbuttoned flannel. His carbine tucked up against the driver's door panel. He reached down and wrapped his hand around the pistol grip, checking for ease-of-access. Satisfied he could grab it in a hurry, he slid his seat back to make space between his rig and the steering wheel. Then he waited.

Agonizing minutes passed before he saw Daoud's car roll past the parking lot, turning at the intersection and disappearing in front of the wedding hall.

"He just passed me," Hilton said into his radio.

"Eyes on," Jimmy said. "We're travelling the opposite direction."

"Anything?"

"Two cars behind him, but it could be street traffic."

"Copy."

The Owl convoy turned into the parking lot, stopped yards in front of Hilton and pulled a hard U-turn in unison. They poured back out onto the street and followed Daoud's path.

"How's he look?" Hilton asked.

"He looks clean from here."

"Okay, I'm going to bring him to me. Follow him in and set a tight perimeter."

"Understood."

Hilton re-dialed Daoud on his cell phone.

"There are more of them now," Daoud said.

"Three tan pickups?"

"Yes! Yes!"

"That's my people. They're following to make sure you're okay."

"The car following me went a different way."

"Probably just a coincidence they were behind you. Come back to me and pull into the parking lot behind the wedding hall. Drive straight up to my truck and park right next to it."

"I will."

Hilton hung up the phone again. Seconds later, Jimmy's voice came through his earpiece. "En route to you. He still looks okay."

"Bring him in and close us off tight," Hilton said.

"Standby."

By the time Daoud pulled into the parking lot, Jimmy's lead truck was feet from the sedan's rear bumper. Daoud sped across the parking lot and braked hard next to Hilton's passenger side door, facing the opposite direction. The gun trucks circled around them, only feet away. Owls leapt from every truck bed, each one taking a knee facing outward, customized AKs at the low-ready.

Hilton snatched his Cobalt and bailed from the Hilux. Daoud flung open his driver's door, brushing it against Hilton's leg, and popped up out of the car without turning off the engine.

"Let's go," Hilton said.

Hilton kept a hand on Daoud's back as the younger man piled into the passenger's side of Hilton's truck.

Jimmy pushed open his own door and leaned out.

"Airport?"

"Yeah," Hilton said.

"You're three truck."

"Got it!"

Hilton slammed his driver's door and watched the Owls re-mount their respective vehicles before opening up the circle to form the pickups into a loose column. Hilton nosed his truck into the third spot. They pulled out onto the street and drove back to the airport, doing highway speeds on surface streets, Owl commandos leaning hard into the stocks of their truck-mounted PKM machine guns. They finally stopped at the back entrance to the airport, their column locked securely between two sets of blast gates. Local guards dragged bubble-shaped mirrors on wheels around them to check for IEDs or magnetic mines under the trucks.

Hilton keyed his radio. "Once we're through, you guys are good. I gotta take my package to the foot gate and get him on a flight."

"Copy all," Jimmy replied.

Hilton turned to Daoud. "We made it, buddy. You're fine."

Daoud wiped sweat from his forehead.

The guards waved and hauled open the second set of steel blast doors. All four trucks rolled slowly through. Hilton turned left as the rest turned right. Jimmy and his men headed back to Clocktower, on the opposite end of the airport.

Hilton continued a steady drive along the service road until they reached another gate. This one was designated for coalition personnel lining up for flights out of the country. It took another fifteen minutes of waiting in line until they were at the drop arm, manned by a squad of airborne soldiers. Hilton pushed open the truck's heavy armored driver's door and held up his ID badge. The soldier looked at it, and raised an arm to wave him through, but dropped it when he saw Daoud.

"Are you guys flying together?" the soldier asked.

"Negative. I'm just dropping him off," Hilton said.

"Coalition pax only at the gate. He needs to go to the local civ gate."

Hilton reached underneath his chest rig to pull out Daoud's Special Interest Visa with Kelly's stamp on it.

"He's got an SIV."

"He can show that to the guards at the local gate and they'll front load him. But he's gotta go through there."

Hilton rolled his eyes behind his shades. "It's a zoo over there."

"They'll let him in with the visa."

"If we can get to the front."

"Adapt and overcome, sir."

"Call Kelly Rowland from State. She's in your hangar."

"I don't know who that is, sir."

"Major Kraut. Call Major Kraut at ops."

The soldier let out a sigh. "Wait one, sir."

Hilton eased his door closed as the guard returned to his shack for a radio.

"What the problem is?" Daoud asked, his English faltering with anxiety.

"They want you to go to the other gate. The one for locals looking for a flight," Hilton said.

"But I have a visa. I heard there are hundreds there waiting."

"Me too. I'm working on it."

The soldier walked back up to their truck, and Hilton opened the door again.

"I can't reach him," the soldier told them.

"Try again!" Hilton snapped.

"Sir, he has to use the local gate."

"I'm cleared to get through here."

"Not with a local."

"He's *got* a visa! I have it."

The soldier spoke slowly and calmly. "I'm sorry, sir.

He needs to go around."

Hilton blew a hard breath through pursed lips.

"That's our orders."

"Fuck your orders," Hilton said as he slammed his door in the grunt's face.

Daoud stuttered something.

"We'll get you in. Don't worry about it."

Hilton jerked the shifter into reverse and backed out of the search lane, returning to the service road. It was a quarter-mile to the walk-up gate designated for all Daristani locals looking to flee. Hilton stopped the truck halfway there. Civilians blocked the road, gutter to gutter. Hilton felt his stomach twist.

There weren't hundreds of people.

There were over a thousand, if there were any at all.

"Let's go," Hilton said tersely.

"What do you mean?" Daoud said.

"There's no way I'm getting through this in a truck. We're walking."

Hilton unhooked his chest rig, laying it across the console between them. Daoud didn't move.

Hilton pushed the door open and stepped out. The smell hit him before the heat did: a seething mass of terrified people, waiting over a day in desert heat with no access to hygiene. Intermittent screams or sobbing without resolution punctuated the dull roar of idle chattering. A day's worth of human waste turned the khaki-colored dust beneath their feet to a charcoal slurry that filled the shallow drainage gutters on either edge of the dirt road. The shimmer of innumerable black flies crawled back and forth across the excrement.

Hilton grabbed Daoud by the wrist and stepped up to the edge of the crowd. He did his best to move gingerly through them, twisting his hips and shoulders to avoid bumping people. A small girl shrieked next to him. When Hilton stepped back, the child pulled her foot out from under his boot. He tried to step toe-heel to avoid repeating the mistake.

An elderly woman doubled over and vomited on one of his shoes as he brushed past her. Hilton pulled his work shirt up over his nose to stifle his gagging as he pushed forward. Daoud coughed loudly behind him.

Halfway to the entrance, Hilton felt Daoud's arm rip free from his grasp. He spun around to see another Daristani man shouting at Daoud from inches away. The man gestured angrily at Hilton, then back at Daoud, clearly berating him for either cutting in line or being too good to suffer with his own countrymen.

Hilton inched closer, but the language barrier forced him to stand idle while Daoud put both hands up in pacification as he seemingly tried to explain his situation. Then the man in the crowd slapped Daoud across the face with an explosive stroke of the arm that shocked Hilton, as there was no room to wind up in such tight quarters.

Hilton sprang into action, grabbing the man's shoulder and spinning him. In the instant they came face-to-face, Hilton crashed an elbow across the man's jaw, sending the man crumpling to the ground.

The crowd roared in anger. Hilton felt the weight of a dozen bodies press his armor plates against his ribs. Before he could contemplate the potential of his mistake—picking a fight in a hostile crowd—a flurry of warning shots sailed over their heads. A man next to Hilton yelped in pain when a small can hit him in the head and tumbled to the ground.

Hilton shoved himself away from it and pressed his palms over Daoud's ears. The rapid blasts of a multi-charge "nine-banger" flash grenade drowned his whole world in a sea of concussion.

An instant later, three more stun grenades detonated across the crowd in a daisy chain of flickering explosions. Civilians screamed in fear or pain from flash burns. Several collapsed into the black paste of dust and shit. The tight knot of people pressing against Hilton and Daoud pushed and punched each other aside.

Hilton took a deep breath as soon as the crowd opened up around him, but choked as he inhaled a mouthful of black flies rousted from their gutter buffet by the blasts. He retched into the blind blackness that surrounded him. Before the crowd could close in any tighter, he coiled his arms against his chest and shoved his way toward the muffled sound of warning shots being fired at the gate.

**JACK YOUNG
WATCH CAPTAIN
GLOBAL OPERATIONS CENTER - WINDSOR KRAFT STRATEGIES
CHESAPEAKE, VA
0737 HOURS, LOCAL**

Jack curled his toes into fists, released them, and repeated. His bare feet scraped the GOC's harsh rug with a dull, crunching sound. He focused solely on the tactile feedback of the carpet, his diaphragm moving rhythmically inside his abdomen. He couldn't get more than two breaths in a row with proper focus, as his mind kept pulling him to the female voiceover on the television.

"We understand that a brigade of paratroopers from the 82nd Airborne Division are managing the ground component of what many are calling the largest military airlift operation since the Second World War. The footage you're seeing is live from Tarkent International Airport as soldiers struggle to control the unprecedented crowds of Daristani citizens who are eagerly awaiting what they perceive as their last chance to flee their country before the imminent takeover by Ansar Al Badari and his fundamentalist government. While priority is clearly being given to coalition personnel needing to return to their home countries,

Pentagon officials have stated that they are committed to providing as much opportunity as possible for Daristanis who wish to emigrate."

A male co-anchor chimed in.

"This live footage from local correspondents shows the military making extensive use of non-lethal stun grenades and warning shots in attempts to subdue a desperate and unruly crowd. It appears some kind of disturbance broke out among the locals there. The soldiers working there must ensure that people are processed thoroughly to minimize security risks, and a mass breach of the gate could halt evacuation flights until order is restored. It's already late afternoon in Daristan, which means the coalition has just over twenty-four hours to complete its withdrawal. Al Badari has stated firmly that any foreigners left behind after that time will be subject to the laws of the new government. The United Nations has publicly denounced this edict, saying that Al Badari is risking a severe humanitarian crisis in the aftermath."

Jack breathed in deep and compressed his toes one last time. When his feet relaxed, he bent over and put his socks and shoes back on before standing up off his cot and crossing the room. Two analysts sat quietly at their desks monitoring less eventful company missions elsewhere in the world. Jack crossed his arms against the cold and rocked on his heels in front of the monitor showing drone feed from Tarkent. The bird skirted the edge of the airport, giving Jack a clear view of the human swarm outside the local access gate. Through the Predator's thermal camera, the crowd appeared as a white blob, like an electron microscope zoomed in on a single human cell.

Jack squinted, trying to make out individual heads or bodies, when the silent screen flashed white. A tiny, dark cloud billowed up toward the camera lens.

JIMMY TOOMS
CALLSIGN "JAMESON"
COMBAT ADVISORY TROOP – WINDSOR KRAFT STRATEGIES
"CLOCKTOWER" OPERATIONS CENTER
TARKENT, DARISTAN
1537 HOURS, LOCAL

Jimmy leaned over Mama's shoulder, one hand on the desktop next to hers, as she clicked her mouse back and forth across open tabs on her computer.

"Wait, so organic air is off limits now?" Jimmy said.

"Not yet. Midnight tonight," Mama said.

Jimmy rubbed his forehead in frustration. "Explain it to me again."

"The military controls all air traffic now, and they are shutting down access for commercial flights twenty-four hours before the withdrawal deadline to prioritize what's left of the military airlift."

"We're not commercial."

"We're private. They don't want to make a distinction."

He grunted in frustration. "Is DOD still saying they will land a bird every sixty minutes? Even tomorrow?"

Mama shrugged. "That's what they're saying. With the chaos outside the airport, I don't know if they can maintain that tempo without security halts. Everything after our Gulfstream was grounded for two hours yesterday."

"How many seats can we get on those mil birds

tomorrow?"

"I'm trying to get a straight answer out of Major Kraut over at the 82nd. He's trying to tell me government employees have first rights, and we don't qualify for priority seating. None of our clients are making that distinction on their end. They're listing us all as supporting employees."

Jimmy nodded. "So let's reach out to those clients and get them to slot us on their end. Take the Army out of the decision loop altogether on this."

"Some are easier than others," Mama replied. "You and Hilton will be fine since the Combat Advisory and Recce Troops fall under OGA or JSOC contracts already. But some of the support staff are assigned to State Department or USAID charters, and those guys aren't going so far out on the limb for us."

Jimmy stood upright to his full, 6-foot-3-inch stature. His back cramped from hunching over while wearing a fully-loaded plate carrier. He stroked his thick beard.

"If the black side guys are the easiest to get on board, we might slot them first, but I don't want to front-load all our combat power and leave the support staff without guns around them," Jimmy said.

"Not to be selfish, James, but if you guys are guaranteed seats, then maybe we should focus on fighting for the people who don't have seats first."

"What about other coalition planes? Or other PMCs?"

"I'm not opposed to using either of them, for sure, but that coordination must come from headquarters. Especially for foreign military planes."

"I guess it's time to call Jack and see…"

A rumbling blast interrupted Jimmy. It shook every computer in the Clocktower. Seconds later, someone burst through the door.

"Where was it?" Jimmy asked.

Between heaving breaths, the man at the door said, "S-Vest clacked off at the west gate."

"Get a head count," Jimmy told him. "Do we have anyone on that side of the airport?"

"Hilton's over there, trying to get one of his sources on a flight."

HILTON PIERCE
CALLSIGN "ALLEY CAT"
RECCE TROOP - WINDSOR KRAFT STRATEGIES
TARKENT INTERNATIONAL AIRPORT
TARKENT, DARISTAN
1542 HOURS, LOCAL

Hilton leaned back, placed a knee on the man's chest, and pried his knife free. He sheathed the blade on his belt and climbed off the corpse, scrabbling around on all fours to find his handgun as more bullets snapped overhead.

Smearing the blood out of his eyes, Hilton crawled frantically and scooped his Staccato HD up off the ground. The stippled grip slipped in his bloody hands, so he placed it down, wiped his hands on the front of his shirt, and picked the gun up again, climbing to his feet. Glancing around to gain his bearings, he heard a burst from the M240 machine gun on the wall behind him. After that, the gunfire stopped.

Hilton raised his Staccato and aimed across the street. The insurgent gunmen laid on the ground in heaps, their weapons scattered across the pavement. Realizing the fight was over, he holstered his pistol and pulled his shirt tails down over it.

"Hilton!" someone called.

He snapped his head and saw Daoud crouched down on his heels, arms over his head as the mass of panicked civilians swirled around him. Hilton shoved his way through the surging crowd and hauled Daoud to his feet, pushing him forward.

"Are you okay?" he yelled over his own ringing ears.

"I think so!"

"Keep moving!"

Hilton put his shoulder into Daoud's back, forcing the man forward through a swarm of pushing, panicked people. To their left, a group of women collected at the base of the cement wall, sobbing and holding their children up toward the paratroopers manning their guns. The soldiers created a human chain. A female soldier, stripped of her battle gear, hung over the edge, one arm flailing desperately into the crowd to grab one of the toddlers.

"Stop!" Daoud yelled over his shoulder.

Hilton looked up and nearly ran into one of the clear, plexiglass riot shields protecting the entrance to the runway. Hilton groped his chest until he found his military contractor credentials hanging from a lanyard around his neck.

"Americans!" he yelled.

At first, the riot force wouldn't yield, even after Hilton identified himself two more times. Finally, he stepped around Daoud and pressed his creds up against the full-body shield. Finally, the grunt behind it dropped one elbow, allowing his shield to shift just enough for them to push through. Hilton heard a click of shields hitting each other as the line closed up behind them.

He and Daoud took off in a dead sprint until they skidded to a stop at the end of the runway. Twenty yards in front of them, the massive gray C-17 started its lumbering taxi down the tarmac. Daoud slumped in defeat.

Still huffing from the run, Hilton clapped him on the back. "It's okay, buddy. You'll make the next one. Let's go talk to the manifest coordinator."

"Who is this?"

"An Army guy, he'll get you a seat for tonight."

Hilton walked toward the 82nd Airborne ops hangar, where he dropped Kelly off yesterday. Once they showed his visa, they'd get him slotted on another plane. It wasn't ideal, but it would work.

He'd taken several long strides when he realized Daoud was not with him. Hilton turned around and saw the younger man still planted in place, eyes fixed on the plane, which was slowly gaining speed.

"Hey!" Hilton called out. "Let's go! Now!"

Daoud didn't look at Hilton. He just watched the plane, jaw clenched as he wiped his eyes with the back of one sleeve.

Hilton walked back over to him, his tone softer. "The hard part is over. You just need wait 'til tonight."

"I can't."

"That one is already leaving."

"It's not gone yet," Daoud said to himself. "It's not gone."

"What?"

"I have to leave. They will kill me."

"Daoud, look at me."

Instead of looking, Daoud took off in a full-out run, his sneakers slapping the pavement with each bounding step. He headed directly for the plane.

Hilton shouted his name and took off after him, but Daoud was ten years younger than him, muscles pumping on sheer terror and unencumbered by body armor or weapons. The ringing in Hilton's ears grew louder, his vision blacking out around the edges until he could only see Daoud's back through a toilet paper tube of clear sight.

Hilton's foot caught a seam in the pavement and his whole body gave out. He toppled to the cement runway. Searing pain shot through his palms and knees as he hit the ground, rolling over to one side as he gasped for air, mouth wide open and wheezing like a fish out of water.

Hilton craned his neck to watch Daoud, but a wall of Army-issued desert boots blocked his view as a team of soldiers crowded around him. He felt warm water pouring over him as a young airborne corporal emptied his canteen over Hilton's head. Hilton pushed a cloud of arms out of his way, rolling back onto his hands and knees, trying to find Daoud through the tangle of camo-clad legs around him.

Daoud had made it to the plane. He ran directly under one of the wings, his wavy hair tousled by jet exhaust. What happened next seemed to unfold in slow motion. Hilton felt himself floating higher—in reality, a pair of soldiers dragged him to his feet—and his view of the flightline opened up just in time for him to watch Daoud being pulled under the C-17's landing gear.

Daoud's body slammed to the ground, crushed like an empty beer can by the massive wheels. The plane didn't even hiccup as its nose coned aimed skyward.

Hilton surged forward on both legs, knocking the soldiers back on their heels. They recovered quickly, pinning his body to a dead stop. He screamed so loud that the soldiers closest to him turned their heads away. A pair of hands clenched around the back of his belt, and Hilton felt himself being dragged backward, away from the flightline. Another hand darted into the front pocket of his jeans, digging out his local cell phone.

Hilton quit fighting and watched one of the soldiers talk on a phone. *His* phone. The soldier said something that Hilton couldn't hear, and then held the phone out to him.

"It's for you," the soldier said.

Hilton pressed the phone to his ear.

Jimmy's voice sounded muffled and distant. "Hilton! Are you okay?!"

Thirty minutes later, Hilton perched bare-chested on the back bumper of a Humvee, staring off into the dusty horizon while an Army medic used forceps to push her hook-shaped needle through the flesh around his stab wound. He winced as she tugged on the black thread. It would be a few more rounds of pierce-pull until she could lace the wound closed. She didn't ask him what happened, and he didn't make small talk. They stayed silent until Jimmy came up from behind.

"What happened?" Jimmy asked. The medic flicked her eyes up at him, brow crinkled in confusion. He caught her gaze and quickly added, "Besides the obvious."

Satisfied Jimmy wasn't a complete idiot, the medic returned to stitching.

"I returned fire when someone in the crowd jumped me," Hilton said.

"What'd he stab you with?"

"A goddamn sharpened-down screwdriver."

"Wow. Straight-up prison shank."

"Yeah."

Without looking up from her work, the medic asked, "You up to date on your tetanus booster?"

"Roger, sergeant," Hilton responded.

She grunted acknowledgement while pulling the thread taut again.

"You get him?" Jimmy asked.

Hilton tapped the handle of his knife, a Colonel Blades Contingency, sticking out of the waist of his jeans. "Paid him back in spades."

"Well done. Sorry to hear about your man."

"Yeah...," was all Hilton could muster in reply.

Jimmy looked down at the medic. "Yours as well."

She glanced up just long enough to thank him before tugging one last turn on the stitching thread. She put down her forceps and picked up a set of shears to cut the thread off at Hilton's skin. "The stitches will dissolve on their own. Don't play with them."

"Understood. Thank you again."

Hilton picked up his button-down work shirt and fished a thin, metal card out of the breast pocket with his contact info on it. He held it out for the medic, who dropped it into the sleeve pocket of her combat uniform blouse. "Call us if there's anything we can do for you."

"Will do," the medic said.

Hilton pulled his bloody undershirt down over his head and strapped on the low-pro armor carrier. Both of his shirts sported a palm-sized blood stain just inside the left shoulder. Hilton touched the dark red patch, which felt cool and wet against his skin. "What's the deal with flights?"

"For us?" Jimmy asked.

"Yeah."

"We've got another Gulfstream landing in about an hour for a dozen more support staff and the last of the shooters. Besides us, I mean."

"Good for them," Hilton snapped. "I can't wait to get out of this fuckin' country."

The sentiment made Jimmy think about Ben. A small pang flared in his stomach as he wondered whether he should have gone with him. Ben was *his* partner, after all.

Hilton must have caught the look on Jimmy's face. He quickly added, "You, too, I know."

"Yeah."

"For what it's worth," Hilton told him, "I respect the guilt, but I'm glad you stayed, selfish as it is."

Jimmy waved it off. "I'm glad I stayed, too."

"It's what Ben would have told you to do."

Changing the subject, Jimmy said, "Let's get you some clean clothes. Looks like you came from a bum fight. Smells like it, too."

Hilton shrugged.

"I mean, kind of."

JACK YOUNG
WATCH CAPTAIN
GLOBAL OPERATIONS CENTER - WINDSOR KRAFT STRATEGIES
CHESAPEAKE, VA
1852 HOURS, LOCAL

Holly held one hand on the door, about to walk out of the GOC for the evening, when she turned back around. Her hand slid off the doorknob.

Clothes wrinkled, hair ruffled, chin stubbled, Jack stood cross-armed in front of the bank of flat-screens high on the wall. His eyes darted back and forth between screens, working each one bottom to top and back down again as if appraising a piece of fine art. In a way, Holly thought, this was his art. And like all great artists, Jack let the craft consume him.

"Hey, boss?" Holly said.

He twisted to meet her gaze.

"You need to leave here for a few hours," she said.

"I'll be fine."

Her eyes narrowed. "That's not what I asked."

"You didn't actually ask anything," he replied.

"That's my point."

Jack never needed to be pushed toward chaos, but he did need to be pulled back from it.

Jack threw his arms up. "And go where? My whole world is here right now."

"It sure feels like that," Holly said.

"I'll take a few hours when you come in tomorrow. I promise."

She dipped her chin. "We both know your promises are bullshit when it comes to self-care."

Jack rubbed his temples with both hands.

"Your cell phone works fine, and you're less than an hour away. You don't have to go home," she said.

He smirked. "But I can't stay here?"

"You got it."

"Okay," he conceded. "I'll be right behind you."

"You better be in fresh clothes the next time I see you."

Eventually, A couple hours later, Jack did go home, and he did put on fresh clothes. Then he got in his truck and drove across the Virginia state line, all the way to in Knotts Island, North Carolina,. Jack felt his stomach flutter as he turned vehicle'soff his headlights off and stepped out onto the gravel driveway. He tried to tell himself it was just exhaustion. That was half true, but not more than half. He placed a hand on the railing outside a screened-in front porch, pushing himself up three wooden steps that creaked under the soles of his Belleville jump boots. He found the storm door unlocked, which led him to a porch complete with two-person swing, potted plants, and driftwood art. Dim, amber light shined through the half-moon window in another door, this one leading inside a housefrosted glass front door.

Jack rapped lightly on the door with scarred knuckles. The door opened, but only a foot. A thick terrycloth robe swaddled the woman inside. Her hair was wet and down, dark ringlets splayed across the robe's thick lapels.

"You shouldn't be here," she said curtly.

"Is this where you remind me that you're half my age, and I make an observation about how you maybe have a kink for that?" Jack said.

Straight-faced, she said, "Technically, it's a little less than half."

He smirked. "I know you like it rough, but go easy on an old man's ego."

Not swayed, the woman told him:

"This is where I remind you that we *agreed* once was enough."

"I distinctly remember agreeing under protest."

She gave him a slow look up and down, clucking her tongue and shaking her head. "Jesus Christ. Look at you."

"What?"

"Is that a pearl-snap shirt? And Wranglers? You know we don't have cowboys this close to the coast."

"You can take the boy out of west Texas...," Jack said with a shrug.

"The quintessential cowboy operator. Somebody warned me about your type."

"Pretty sure that was me," Jack quipped.

The woman's smile vanished as she met his eyes. "I gotta warn you, Jack. The way this week is going, I'm liable to cry when we're done."

"The way this week is going," he replied, "we might cry together. I ain't afraid of it."

The front door swung all the way open, and Holly stepped aside to let him through.

She did cry when it was over, sobbing softly into the crook of his neck. He didn't. Instead, he held her tightly and silently, chin buried in her wet hair while he stared at the ceiling.

DAY FIVE

HILTON PIERCE
CALLSIGN "ALLEY CAT"
RECCE TROOP – WINDSOR KRAFT STRATEGIES
TARKENT, DARISTAN
2302 HOURS, LOCAL

The last day proved eerily quiet. No more attacks. No more breaches around the airport, despite the lingering mob of civilians. Windsor Kraft spent a lot of packing, destroying documents and equipment they couldn't take with them, and collecting a final set of cell phone photos for the memories that would accompany them into whatever was next for the company.

Hilton stood alone in the empty bullpen of cubicles. For years, this room served as the heart of Windsor Kraft's operations in Daristan. Now, the room colloquially known as Clocktower, looked like a burnt husk of its former self. Computer monitors smashed with hammers. Desktop terminals melted into globules on tabletops by thermite grenades or oxy-acetylene torches left behind by fleeing construction workers.

Hilton held the company's last thermite grenade in his right hand, index finger fiddling idly with the pull ring. With the toe of his left boot, he tapped anxiously against the side of a square, tan, plastic fuel can filled with diesel he siphoned out of an abandoned Humvee left behind by the 82nd Airborne guys.

The door squeaked ever so slightly as it opened behind him. Hilton knew it was Jimmy Tooms. They represented the last two Windsor Kraft operators left in Daristan. Only half-a-dozen support specialists remained, gathered in the chow hall to stare anxiously at the clock.

Jimmy stayed partly to help Hilton as final security element, but also because this flight carried out the last twelve Owl commandos—Jazeeri and his platoon—fleeing to the US on emergency visas. Jimmy helped recruit and train them nearly a decade ago.

Without turning his head, Hilton asked, "You confirm the final flight specs?"

"It's an Air National Guard C-17 out of South Carolina, with a DAGRE team from Hurlburt. Wheels down at 2345, ten minutes to load, ramp closes at fifty-five, wheels up midnight-plus-one-minute tomorrow morning," Jimmy said.

Hilton glanced at his watch. Forty-three minutes to wheels down. "Did we fail, Jimmy?"

"We're contractors, Hilton. We don't win wars, we pull jobs. We did this job to the bitter end. There are Americans in the air headed home, right this second, because of us. The assholes who failed all work in big white buildings in Washington, brother."

Hilton shook his head again, this time without any amusement. "And they'll never face the full scope of this failure."

"No. They won't," Jimmy said. He stepped up right behind Hilton, putting his hands on Hilton's shoulders and giving him a reassuring squeeze. "Leave the grenade here.

We'll knock that can over and pull the pin right before we walk up the ramp."

Hilton gently placed the brick-red canister on a desk next to him, and they walked out of the room.

JACK YOUNG
WATCH CAPTAIN
GLOBAL OPERATIONS CENTER - WINDSOR KRAFT STRATEGIES
CHESAPEAKE, VA
1506 HOURS, LOCAL

Jack leaned over, placing a plastic go-tray of salad next to Holly's keyboard. She caught a whiff of heavy, earthen smoke. She knew he'd spent most of his lunch break puffing down one of the stubby, brown cigarillos from his office humidor.

"Thanks Jack, I'll eat it later," Holly said.

"Now, Holly. Please. You've been running on coffee and apples for two whole days," Jack said.

"The last flight is in less than an hour," she countered.

"And you're going to be sitting right here at your desk that whole time. Might as well get something in your stomach."

She looked down at the tray. The sight of food made her stomach and throat tighten.

Jack grabbed an empty roller chair and pulled it up next to the desk. "How are you?"

"No offense. boss, but that's kind of a dumbass question."

Jack chuckled, shrugging his shoulders. "I know."

"I appreciate it, though."

"It's almost over."

"I'm not sure if that makes me feel better or worse," she said.

He sighed. "Yeah."

"How about you?" she asked.

"It's a dumbass question both ways."

She cracked a weak grin.

"I know."

"Flash is in the air now. He's going straight to Walter Reed when the ramp drops. He's down a leg, but he'll be okay."

"He's got Square's body with him, too?"

"Yeah. Casualty notification team already spoke to his parents. They're getting escorted to Dulles to receive him."

"What else needs doing?"

"Air Force is running the last flight. All we can do is wait for confirmation when they go wheels down. Did Hilton call in yet?" Jack asked.

"Not yet. I suspect we won't hear until they're about to board."

HILTON PIERCE
CALLSIGN "ALLEY CAT"
RECCE TROOP – WINDSOR KRAFT STRATEGIES
TARKENT, DARISTAN
2310 HOURS, LOCAL

Only thirty minutes left.

The remaining support staff packed only what they could fit into a single backpack—nothing larger than a college book bag, messenger tote, or three-day assault pack. The C-17 would be loaded to the brim with a combination of military personnel, locals, and contractors. Spare clothing, hygiene supplies, souvenirs, and company equipment were all superfluous at this point.

To Hilton's relief, everyone followed his instructions. They sat huddled around one cafeteria table, munching nervously on candy or granola bars, since the kitchen had long gone cold. The table smelled faintly of alcohol, something never allowed in any other situation. Some tried to read books or absently scrolled social media on their phones. Half of them just stared off into space.

Per Hilton's instructions, each one carried a loaded Staccato holstered to their hip. The two senior staffers also kept their short-barreled carbines on the floor next to their chairs.

Hilton walked out of the chow hall to find whatever busy work remained, when he saw Jazeeri and his men across the courtyard. They leaned against their armored Hilux pickups. Even in the dark, Hilton could see the barrels of PKM machine guns pointing skyward from the bed of every truck, belts of ammo hanging out the side of each gun. The men wore their full kit. PVS-7 night-vision goggles jutted from the brim of every helmet like unicorn horns.

Hilton turned around and poked his head back into the chow hall. "Jameson!"

Jimmy strode quickly across the hall, leaning in close to Hilton.

"Jim, did you tell the Owls to jock up?" Hilton asked.

"What? No. I gave them the same direction as support staff. Guns and carry-ons only."

"You might want to see this."

Jimmy stepped out onto the porch with Hilton, who pointed to the trucks. "What the…?"

Hilton took off in a brisk walk. Jimmy's longer legs carried him past Hilton as they approached the Owl platoon. He arrived three full steps in front of Hilton, calling out, "Jazz! What the fuck, man?"

Jazeeri stepped in front of his men, almost toe-to-toe with the taller SEAL veteran.

"We're staying," Jazz said.

Jimmy looked at Hilton in disbelief, then back to the Owl commander. "I'm sorry, *what*?!"

Jazeeri's face stayed flat and emotionless. "We're staying, Mister Jim. This is our country. We must fight for it."

"Jazz, there's twelve of you. No offense, but what are you going to do?"

"There are others," Jazz said. "I know it. Other Owls, army soldiers, policemen. People who do not support Badari. We will find them."

"They control the entire government, Jazz. There are already insurgent fighters patrolling the land borders. In thirty minutes, they're going to close the airspace and lift the cease-fire. They'll hunt you like dogs."

"It was this way before America came. So it will be when you leave."

"You won't make it out of the city."

"We will."

"To go where?"

Jazz pointed to a distant, craggy ridgeline. "We'll head north, to the mountains."

Jimmy spun around and walked away from Jazeeri. Hilton caught him a few steps away and grabbed him by the arm.

"This is fucked, Hilton," Jimmy said.

"I know," Hilton said.

"They're gonna wind up with their heads on the palace sidewalk, right next to the parliament guys!"

"Probably."

"He's being foolish! It's suicide!"

Hilton put his hands up. "I'm not arguing with you, but we can't make them get on the plane."

"The fuck we can't. I say we zip 'em and bag 'em," Jimmy said, referring to the flex cuffs and black cloth hoods they put on captured insurgents.

Hilton side-stepped so he was fully in front of Jimmy, who looked frantically back at the Owls, then again to

Hilton.

"They're not going," Hilton said. "It's done."

Jimmy jaw clenched and unclenched in frustration. Finally, he let out a long breath and asked, "What do we do?"

"I'll go to the 82nd hangar, tell them a dozen seats just opened up and see if they have locals who want to go. You take the Owls and start scouring the other hangars for abandoned supplies. Jazz is gonna need every bullet and bottle of water you can find."

"We've got less than thirty minutes," Jimmy said.

Hilton held up a fist and replied, "See you on the ramp."

They bumped fists, and Hilton took off running.

Moments later, four Owl pickup trucks sped across the empty runway at highway speed. Jimmy pointed, and Jazz swerved the lead truck hard left, beelining for the large, corrugated metal hangar that occupied by 2 Para until yesterday afternoon. The trucks screeched to a halt in unison, just in front of the large bay doors. Men spilled out of all four trucks, with a pair of Owls running to the bay doors and pushing them apart.

Jimmy and Jazz walked between them as the doors slid open. Jimmy plucked a flashlight off his belt and clicked it on, panning it back and forth across the bay. Jazz let out a short, bird-like whistle.

The Brits left everything.

A literal pile of black guns rested in the center of the cement pad. GPMG machine guns, SA-80 and M4 rifles, SIG pistols, and MP5 submachine guns all piled waist-high like discarded trash. Next to it was a smaller pile of PVS-14 night-vision goggles, rifle scopes, handheld thermal optics, and binoculars. At the back of the bay, olive-green web gear and Bergen packs sat in heaps. Unopened wooden crates of hand grenades and shrink-wrapped cases of bottled water stacked four high and three deep in one corner. Against the opposite wall perched a neat row of Javelin antitank missiles and mortar tubes.

Jazz looked at his American counterpart. "What do we take?"

Without hesitation, Jimmy said, "All of it. As much as you can carry."

Jazeeri barked a rapid string of commands in Daristani, and the men went to work. They paired off to lift crates and boxes, and heaved Javelins onto their shoulders. Jimmy walked to each pile, looking for the small things he knew the men would forget: batteries for the electro-optics, spare plates of body armor, and knives and machetes still clipped to abandoned web gear. He knew they couldn't take all of it, but he also knew whatever they didn't take would be seized by Al Badari's insurgent forces when they re-took the airport after midnight. He wondered how many other hangars across the airport were left just like this one.

Outside the hangar, Jimmy heard the clatter of heavy weapons dropping unceremoniously into truck beds. It took them nearly twenty minutes to fill the trucks, inside and out. With nowhere to sit in the cabs, the men perched themselves on the roofs or walls of the truck beds, legs hanging precariously above back tires that sat low and heavy on the shocks.

Jimmy glanced nervously at his G-Shock watch. He said to Jazz, "Time's up. I've got a plane to catch."

Jazz whistled and circled his hand in the air above his head, the universal grunt hand signal for "rally up, we're leaving." Jimmy jumped back into the passenger seat of Jazeeri's truck, his legs tight to his chest since two crates of grenades occupied the footwell. The engine of their Hilux whined under the weight of excess load as they crept back across the runway. Jimmy looked up through the windshield just in time to see the silhouette of a blacked-out C-17 cross in front of the crescent moon.

On the opposite side of the runway, the brightly lit 82nd Airborne's hangar bustled with activity, the bay doors wide open. Non-commissioned officers barked profanity-laden orders to line up to the mass of men and women clad in Multicam uniforms or local garb.

Hilton stepped in front of the first person he saw wearing sergeant's stripes. "Is Major Kraut still here?"

The man pointed to the back corner of the hangar. Hilton power-walked to the back of the building and found the man leaning over a desk reading lists of names.

"Major," Hilton said.

The man looked up.

"The merc," Major Kraut said curtly. "You're not on my lists."

"I've got my seat," Hilton said. "A dozen more just opened up."

"I didn't hear about this."

"I know. The locals slated on our manifest aren't leaving."

"Talk about a last-minute mix-up."

"Not a mix-up, sir. They had a change of heart."

"Change of heart?" the major said incredulously. Hilton shrugged. "Their funeral."

"Moot point," Hilton snapped. "If you've got people on a waiting list, fill those seats."

"We've got way more than a dozen," Kraut said.

"I don't care how you pick 'em. Fill those seats."

"Last I check, we don't answer to corporations."

Hilton smirked. "Sir, if that's how you feel, then you don't know how the military-industrial complex really works."

The major's cheeks turned red.

Hilton kept talking before the officer could blow his lid. "That's twelve more lives you can save, major. You won't get a medal for it, but it might be the most meaningful thing you can do for these people."

"*These people* had their chance to change the course of…"

"Major!" came a voice.

Both men snapped their heads. Neither one saw Kelly approach, her eyes narrowed and cheeks flushed.

"You may be running the airlift, but the US State Department is in charge of the humanitarian operation. Are you refusing to comply with standing directives to…"

The major put his hand up. "Spare me, *miss*. You've got twelve seats, and just about twelve minutes to fill them."

Without a word, Hilton turned on his heels and left

the hangar. His hand wrapped around the driver's side door handle when Kelly caught up to him, panting lightly.

"Hilton, what happened?" Kelly said.

"Our local commandos dropped out."

"What? Why?"

"It's their country," Hilton said.

Kelly looked down at her shoes for a moment, then back up at Hilton. "What about Daoud?"

Hilton shook his head.

Kelly's face went slack. She threw her arms around him and whispered, "I'm sorry."

Hilton accepted her embrace without returning it. "Don't forget to book yourself a seat."

She pulled back from the hug, pressed up on her toes, and kissed his cheek. Then she grabbed two fistfuls of his shirt. "I'll save you the seat next to mine. Don't be late. That's an order, soldier."

They both looked up, attention pulled by the growing whine of massive turbine engines. Hilton gently pried her grip off him. "See you soon."

Kelly nodded, wiping her eyes with the backs of her hands. He turned from her and sat down behind the wheel, slamming the door closed behind him and gunning the engine into a hard U-turn back toward Clocktower.

Meanwhile, Jimmy shielded his eyes against bright, red lights as the C-17 lowered its rear ramp. He saw Hilton's truck, flashing its high beams as it sped toward the plane. The aircraft lumbered down the runway, stopping halfway between Clocktower and the Army's hangar.

The truck leaned forward as it slid to a stop behind the

plane. Hilton jumped out, engine still running. Glancing over his shoulder, Hilton saw columns of people from the military side walking hurriedly toward them.

Jimmy jogged up to Hilton. "Didn't your command ever teach you to be on time, shit bird?"

"How'd the scavenger hunt go?" Hilton asked.

"Fuckin' paydirt," Jimmy said excitedly. "2 Para left *everything*. Jazz can outfit a battalion."

Hilton sighed with relief.

The first two columns from the military hangar walked up the ramp. Hilton watched a pack of locals sprinting out of the hangar toward the back end of the last column—the ones granted a last-minute miracle. Kelly touched his arm as she passed him to board the plane.

Hilton and Jimmy watched as the last Windsor Kraft staffers merged their way into the line of passengers, both men counting heads as they passed. When the last one set foot on the ramp, the two contractors turned toward Jazz and his men, who watched stoically as the massive jet filled with people. Jimmy stuck his hand out, and Jazz gripped it hard, giving Jimmy an exaggerated handshake.

"Inshallah," Jimmy said, meaning "As God Wills It."

"Inshallah," Jazeeri replied. Then he turned to Hilton, who shook his hand but didn't say anything.

One of the Owls let out a loud sob and fell to the ground. The man next to him crouched down and hugged him hard, both men crying loudly. Jazz pushed past his team and stood over them. The two men on the ground looked up at their commander, babbling in panicked

Daristani. Jazz hauled them to their feet and slapped one hard enough to snap his head sideways. Hilton and Jimmy shouldered themselves into the trio as Jazz wound up to strike the second one.

"What is it?" Jimmy asked.

Jazz waved him off as the three men shouted Daristani back and forth at each other.

Finally, Jazz turned to Jimmy and said, "It is fine. These men are cowards."

Hilton cocked his head. "Talk to us, Jazz."

Jazz grunted loudly before explaining. "These men are brothers. This one," Jazz pointed, "his children left three days ago. He doesn't know if his wife made it with them. He wants to get on the plane."

Jimmy wiped his face with one hand. "What the fuck, Jazz? I thought you guys settled this."

"We did," Jazz said coldly. "Your jet is here. This is our business now."

Jimmy shoved the Owl commander hard enough to stumble him back two steps.

"Fuck you!" Jimmy shouted. "His kids are probably orphans in America right now!"

Jazz leaned in, stepping up to Jimmy.

Hilton pushed the two apart and shouted, "Calm down! Just wait, will you? Wait!"

Hilton turned around and jumped up onto the ramp. He grabbed the C-17 crew chief by the sleeve of his flight suit, yelling over the engines.

"We've got two extra!" Hilton yelled.

The crew chief swiped his hand back and forth across

his throat. "No go, sir! Everyone is accounted for!"

"We can't leave them!" Hilton said.

"Sir, this is it! War's over! I have orders to repel intruders with deadly force!"

Hilton kicked the inside wall of the C-17. "*Fuck!*"

The crew chief collected his nerve. "Whoever you are, you did your best. Now, with all due respect, get on my fucking plane and let's get out of here."

Hilton put both hands up in a stopping motion. The chief shook his head and held up two gloved fingers.

Two minutes.

Hilton jumped back off the ramp. He pulled Jimmy away from the Owls and said, "They won't take them."

"That's what it looked like."

Hilton looked into the plane, then to the group of Owls. The two brothers still sobbed. Still looking at the Owls, he said quietly, "Jim, it's two seats."

"I know. Goddamn Air Force."

Hilton looked hard into Jimmy's face. He poked the man in the chest with one finger, poked himself in the same spot, then held up two fingers just like the crew chief had.

Jimmy stared at Hilton's hand. "That's suicide, Hilton."

"We have a contingency."

"What are you talking about?"

"Jack had me set it up a few days ago. The old Olympic village, across the city. The LZ is marked, with a full TRP deck for cover fires," Hilton said.

"Cover fires are *gone*, Hilton!"

"The landing strip is still there."

"This is the last flight!"

"There's a company jet in Dubai. Right now, Jimmy. It's two hours, wheels up to wheels down. All we need to do is call the GOC on sat phone."

Jimmy glanced back at the Daristani commandos behind them. "We still have ten good Owls."

"Ten *great* ones. And four trucks. And all that firepower. It's the middle of the night, only six percent illum."

The hangnail crescent of moon above them only shined at six percent of its full brightness, and Al Badari's forces were not known to have large quantities of night vision. Hilton looked over at the crew chief. The man held up one finger.

"Shit," Jimmy muttered.

Hilton ran past him, past Jazz, and hauled the two sobbing men to their feet. The brothers looked at each other in wide-eyed confusion as Hilton ripped the helmets off their heads and unbuckled their plate carriers. The Owls shrugged out of their armor and dropped it on the tarmac. Hilton grabbed them by the collars of their fatigues and dragged them hurriedly to the edge of the ramp.

"Last two!" Hilton yelled.

The crew chief stepped back as Hilton pushed them up the ramp. "What the fuck is this?" Halfway down the plane, Kelly shot to her feet. She scrambled to step over the rows of soldiers and local civilians seated between them.

Hilton avoided her terrified face and forced the Owls into the hold. He spun around, running down the ramp at full sprint and jumping onto the tarmac. He turned back and gave the crew chief two thumbs up. The crew chief hit a large, red button on the inside of the plane. The ramp hummed loudly as its massive hydraulic arms retracted.

Hilton watched Kelly cup both hands around her mouth and shout something he couldn't hear as the ramp folded slowly up between them. The beams of red light from inside shrank to slivers before cutting out completely.

Hilton clicked a button on his watch, and the Suunto's face lit up bright turquoise: 23:58. He heard whooping and celebratory gunfire from the far side of the airport. He turned around to see Jimmy and Jazz, shoulder to shoulder, speechless.

Hilton said to Jazz, "Tell your men to shuffle some gear around so we have a place to sit."

"Where are we going?" Jazz said.

"Olympic village."

"That's all the way across the city."

"Then you better work fast."

Hilton turned to Jimmy. "Burn down Clocktower and grab your shit. I've gotta call the office."

Jimmy and Jazz took off in separate directions. Hilton watched the C-17 lift into the night. He slipped the satellite phone off his belt and pressed it to his ear.

**JACK YOUNG
WATCH CAPTAIN
GLOBAL OPERATIONS CENTER - WINDSOR KRAFT STRATEGIES
CHESAPEAKE, VA
1602 HOURS, LOCAL**

Jack saw the sat phone on his desk vibrate. He snatched it up immediately and said, "Go for GOC."

"Jack, it's Hilton."

"What's the hold-up? You should have been taxiing seven minutes ago."

"No hold-up. Plane took off without a hitch. All support staff on board."

"Without a hitch? If the plane took off and you're on it, why do I hear gunfire in the background."

"We're not on it."

"Who the fuck is *we*?"

"Me and Jameson."

"Don't say it, Hilton."

"We're still in-country, Jack."

Jack felt a wave of nausea rise from his hips to his throat. He swallowed hard and said slowly, "*What* is going on?"

"Contingency time, Jack. We need the jet."

"What happened?"

"It's after midnight and you have two behind the lines. Get that jet in the air. The emergency LZ is still in play.

We're moving to secure it in five mikes."

The line fell silent.

"Jack?"

Jack swallowed again. "GOC copies."

"Alley Cat out."

The line went dead. Jack lowered the phone and looked back at Holly.

"What happened?" Holly asked. "You look like you just talked to a ghost."

"Not if I can help it," he said. "Call Dubai."

"The jet? Wha...*why*?"

His voice cracked when he replied, "Call them now."

DUBAI INTERNATIONAL AIRPORT (DBX)
DUBAI, UNITED ARAB EMIRATES
2307 LOCAL TIME

The cell phone on Rick Stahl's nightstand chirped four times before he stuck an arm out from under the covers and grabbed it.

"Stahl," he said drowsily.

"Rick, it's Holly."

Rick looked at the bright, red LED lights of his bedside clock. Tarkent ran an hour ahead of him. He sat up in bed, irritated that headquarters felt the need to call him just to tell him to stand down. Then again, it wasn't even midnight in Dubai, which meant most of the nightclubs would be open for another five or six hours. Maybe he'd throw some clothes and roust his co-pilot for a couple celebratory drinks.

"Holly, how'd it go?"

"Spin up, Rick."

Rick swung his legs out of bed and bolted upright on the edge of his bed. "It's already past midnight in..."

"Shut the fuck up and go hot, Rick. LZ Pantheon is in play. Right now."

Pantheon was the code name for the old Olympic village on the edge of Tarkent. Rick studied imagery of it for days, prepping pre-loaded flight plans with false routes and dummy stops under redundant charters held by

Windsor Kraft shell corporations.

"Al Badari has the country. Airspace is closed," Rick said.

"Do you think we don't know that?" Holly said.

"They could have air defense setup by the time we get there."

"There's a commando unit moving to secure the field. I'll update you in the air."

Rick jumped into his pants, phone pinned to his ear with one shoulder. "Yeah, I'm moving. I'll give you a call when we're ready for taxi."

The line went dead in his ear.

Zipping his pants up, Rick grabbed his shoes and dialed his co-pilot, staying two hotel rooms over. He put the phone on speaker while he laced his shoes.

"Why are you call…," the co-pilot started to say.

"Get dressed. We're going," Rick said.

"It's already after midnight there."

"Exactly. We're going."

The co-pilot's voice changed. "Meet you in the lobby."

HILTON PIERCE
CALLSIGN "ALLEY CAT"
RECCE TROOP – WINDSOR KRAFT STRATEGIES
TARKENT, DARISTAN
0012 HOURS, LOCAL

Hilton buckled the D3 chest rig over his button-down flannel, securing a row of rifle magazines and medical gear in addition to the hard armor plates under his shirt. The sling bag across his back held smoke and flashbang grenades, as well as his PVS-14 night-vision goggles and a mesh-nylon "Night Cap" which allowed him to wear the night vision without needing an actual helmet.

In contrast to Hilton's plainclothes look, Jimmy wore a heavily laden plate carrier over his 5.11 combat shirt. His full combat load included three frag grenades and half a dozen mags lashed down via MOLLE webbing. A matching battle belt with additional ammo and ordnance also held his Staccato HD in a drop leg holster. A second belt stacked over his battle belt held a dozen high-explosive 40mm shells, their dull, gold noses glistening in the faint moonlight.

"Where'd you get that?" Hilton asked.

Jimmy held an M4 carbine with M203 grenade launcher attached under the barrel. It was not a Windsor Kraft issued weapon.

"Courtesy of our British allies," Jimmy said.

"Nothing like international cooperation."

"I'll take second truck," Hilton said. "You ride trail?"

Jimmy nodded. The four Owl trucks lined up, pointed toward a side gate to avoid the growing mob of Al Badari loyalists pouring in through the airport's main entrance. The commandos manned their machine guns, waiting to go.

"Hilton, every Al Badari fighter knows these trucks. We're instantly recognizable," Jimmy said.

"This airport is littered with abandoned equipment from every army and contracting company that's ever had a presence here in the last ten years. I think we'll be hiding in plain sight," Hilton said.

"Speaking of hiding, take this." Jimmy held out a black balaclava. All the Owls wore them.

Hilton grabbed the one being offered to him, and Jimmy pulled another out of the leg pocket of his fatigues. That's when a thought hit Hilton so hard he almost felt it. Not even a thought. A memory. A cursory glance of something he'd seen at the 82nd Airborne's hangar across the tarmac.

Hilton ran to the last truck in the convoy and hurriedly gestured for the Owls to get out of the vehicle.

"Come with me," he said to Jimmy, almost panicked.

Jimmy hesitated. "We gotta roll brother. Time fuckin' now."

Ignoring him, Hilton climbed into the driver's seat of the now-empty Owl truck. "Let's go!"

Jimmy stuffed himself into the passenger's seat, his assault gear digging into every joint and fleshy pocket of his body as he struggled to wedge the door closed. Hilton stomped the gas pedal, and they shot down the empty tarmac. Seconds later, Hilton slammed the brakes so hard his chest rig bumped the steering wheel.

Both men rolled out of the parked truck. Hilton waved him around the side of the hangar. Parked by itself was an extra Hilux truck, with a heavy canvas tarp draped over some kind of superstructure sticking up out of the bed.

Hilton ran up to the truck and ripped the tarp away. "If we're going to secure an airfield…"

Jimmy cut him off. "Yeah, that would work."

The Vehicle-Agnostic Modular Palletized ISR Equipment—affectionately dubbed VAMPIRE by its designers at L3 Systems—was a man-portable modification kit made for commercial vehicles like pickups or flatbeds. The kit came with a multi-spectrum camera, target-designating laser, rectangular four-tube launcher, and remote-control system. All of which could be installed on almost any small truck with common hand tools. Each of the four tubes came loaded with an AGR-20 Advanced Precision Kill Weapon—the same laser-guided rockets used on Windsor Kraft's Super Tucano attack aircraft.

"You drive it back, then ride the bed," Hilton said.

Jimmy pulled the unlocked driver's door open and leaned in. The keys sat right on the driver's seat. He crawled into the truck and slammed the driver's door. The diesel engine chugged to life.

Hilton went back to his own truck and jumped in. The two Toyotas took off simultaneously, racing each other back up the tarmac where the Owls waited.

They briefed the convoy change to Jazz, who put two Owls in the cab and two more on the back with Jimmy. They now acted as the trail vehicle at the rear of their convoy.

Hilton and Jimmy rolled the masks down over their faces, bumped fists, and climbed into their trucks. Hilton unrolled the Night Cap, strapping it over top of his balaclava before clicking his single-tube PVS-14 night vision onto the cap. He lowered the tube over his eye. The PVS painted his surroundings in white phosphor luminescence.

With his one naked eye, Hilton saw muzzle flashes in the rearview mirror as they started moving. He took a deep, deliberate breath as their convoy rolled through the abandoned service entrance into the streets of Tarkent.

Next to Hilton, one of the Owls whispered in English, "Fucking animals."

The city blocks around the airport looked like a scene from one of those "Purge" movies. Parked cars had been set on fire at almost every intersection. Chips of glass fanned out into the street from shattered storefront windows. Bodies were strewn across the sidewalk at odd intervals, some of them stripped naked.

The radio earpiece in Hilton's ear crackled softly.

"You seeing this?" Jimmy said.

"Affirmative." Hilton's voice sounded distant, his mind lost in the pandemonium.

A convoy of three US military MRAP vehicles passed them going the other way. Insurgent fighters hung off both sides of each truck, clad in baggy black pajama sets with white shemaghs around their faces. Some hung off the vehicles by one hand, using the other to fire AKs or captured M16s into the air while the trucks moved. Others shot randomly into buildings and cars.

Hilton watched one insurgent fire his M16 into a corpse on the sidewalk until the weapon ran empty, which he threw it into the street while the vehicles kept rolling.

As they rounded the next turn, Hilton's driver took one hand off the wheel and pointed. "Mister Hilton."

Hilton followed the man's finger.

"Sir, they're…"

Hilton cut him off. "If we stop now, we all die,"

"But sir…"

"I know."

"Sir, they are raping that woman."

"I *know*."

"What do we do?"

"You know what."

From the backseat, Hilton saw the driver stiffen. The man fixed his gaze directly forward, gripping the steering wheel tightly with both hands."Yes, sir."

Hilton clenched both hands around his carbine, looking out his window. He did his best to scan the surroundings for potential threats. He tried not to look too closely at any of it.

**HOLLY TOMASSI
OPERATIONS ASSISTANT
GLOBAL OPERATIONS CENTER - WINDSOR KRAFT STRATEGIES
CHESAPEAKE, VA
1618 HOURS, LOCAL**

Holly's phone buzzed again. She looked at the name on the screen, the same one as last time, and her stomach twisted again. Shaking her head, Holly accepted the call and pressed the phone to her ear.

"Holly?" a voice said from the phone.

Holly stayed quiet.

"Can you hear me? Hello?"

Finally, barely above a whisper, Holly said, "Hey, I can't really talk right now."

"I know," Corrine said. "I'm sorry. Did he make it on the flight?"

Holly blinked the tears out of her eyes. "He's okay, Corrine. We just heard from him."

"Oh, thank God. Do you know what time they'll land here?"

"Uh, no, not yet. The flight is going to land in Germany first."

"Okay, yeah, I guess that makes sense. But he's on it?"

"He's fine."

Corrine's voice changed on the other end. "Holly, I didn't ask if he was okay. I asked if he made it on the flight."

"He…um…he got delayed."

"What? It's all over the news. The last flight took off. Everyone is saying it's the last one. That all US forces are out of the country. Hilton's *on* that plane, right?"

With her free hand, Holly grabbed the crucifix hanging around her neck and rubbed it with her thumb.

"Corrine, listen to me…"

"No! What's going on? Where's Hilton *right now*?"

"He's still on the ground."

"I'm not a soldier, Holly. What do you mean *on the ground*?"

"He's still there. He's in Daristan."

Holly heard a single sob before the line went dead in her ear.

"Shit," Holly whispered, pulling the phone away from her ear and frantically re-dialing the number. She put the phone back to her face just in time to hear the call go straight to voicemail.

Holly's thumbs tapped out a text message explaining that they were sending a plane for him, and it would only be another couple of hours. She deleted the text and started over twice, desperately unsure of how much information to put in a written message that could be intercepted, screen-shotted, transcribed, or subpoenaed later. When she finally hit the send button, all she had was:

We're going to get him. His ride is already on the way. He's not alone, and he's going to make it. Talk when I can.

Holly stared at the sent message for almost a full minute, waiting for a reply from Corrine that never came.

JIMMY TOOMS
CALLSIGN "JAMESON"
COMBAT ADVISORY TROOP – WINDSOR KRAFT STRATEGIES
TARKENT, DARISTAN
0024 HOURS, LOCAL

"Shit," Jimmy muttered. The brake lights of the truck in front of him flared bright white through his night vision goggles. The driver's radio crackled with a hushed message in Daristani.

"Checkpoint ahead," the driver said.

"Insurgents," Jimmy answered.

"I am sure of that," the driver agreed. "What do we do?"

Jimmy keyed his own radio. "Bluff it or blow through?"

Hilton's reply came back almost instantly. "Bluff it first."

"Rog."

Jimmy would have played it differently, but Hilton rode in the command truck with Jazz, so it was their call. Still, Jimmy cracked open the breach of the 40mm grenade launcher and pressed his thumb against the back of the HE round in the chamber. With the shell firmly seated, he racked the launcher tube shut and leaned back in his seat, unbuckling his seatbelt.

The trucks all ground to a halt. Jimmy knew the driver of the lead truck was trying desperately to lie his way through the checkpoint. The Owls came up against illegal checkpoints before and rigorously trained in the procedure. Rule one was to never "break seal," or open your door. That would give an adversary the opportunity to pull the Owl out, or to shoot into the vehicle. If the dispute couldn't be settled through the bulletproof window—which couldn't be rolled down—the Owls would simply floor the pedal and ram through any barricade. The Owls piled into the truck beds would fire outwards from either side of the truck bed, creating suppressive fire. Those in the vehicle remained in place unless the vehicle was rendered immobile.

Jimmy couldn't hear the conversation at the front of the convoy. After what seemed like an eternity, he keyed his mic and asked, "What are we doing here?"

Hilton's voice replied, "Trying to convince these guys we stole all this equipment and murdered the Owl unit we took it from."

"How's that working out?"

"No shooting yet."

Before Jimmy could say anything else, one of the insurgents walked casually alongside the convoy, eyeballing each truck and the men huddled inside. The insurgent inspected the second truck. Then the third. Then he made his way back to Jimmy's.

"We may have a problem," Jimmy said.

"The inspector?"

"Yeah."

"Just don't talk."

Jimmy rode in the bed and would be made if inspected too closely. The insurgent called to the men in the truck bed. The gunner leaned casually on his PKM, bantering back and forth with the black-clad Al Badari fighter. Jimmy sat down on one of the wooden benches to hide his height, keeping his back to the insurgent. Even with a balaclava, his white nose and blue eyes would give him away in the dark.

The insurgent said something. The Owls glanced at Jimmy, who ignored their worried eyes, pretending he didn't hear the insurgent call out a second time. The insurgent reached up and slapped Jimmy hard on the back. Jimmy wrapped one hand around the grip of his pistol. The insurgent grabbed the back of Jimmy's plate carrier and tugged on it. Finally, Jimmy turned halfway in his seat.

The insurgent spoke to Jimmy in Daristani—which Jimmy didn't understand—but the frustration in his voice and authoritative gesturing with his AK was universally clear. Jimmy raised his chin and made an I-don't-know shrugging motion, left hand turned palm up. Not visible to the insurgent, his right hand quietly pressed the thumb release lever on his pistol holster.

The insurgent looked hard into Jimmy's face. Even in the dim glow of burning cars, Jimmy's metallic blue eyes were unmistakable. The insurgent made a high-pitched sound between a commanding shout and a warning shriek. Jimmy cut it short by snapping his Staccato out of the holster and dumping five rounds into the insurgent's face and chest from the seated position.

"Push through!" Jimmy said into his mic.

Guns in all four pickup trucks crackled to life simultaneously as the lead vehicle heaved forward. The armored trucks pushed through makeshift roadblocks with a lot of high revving and metallic grinding.

Jimmy holstered his pistol and raised the M4/M203 combo. Luckily, only a half-dozen insurgents stationed at the checkpoint, and they did not have heavy weapons or backup. Jimmy killed another one with his carbine as the last vehicle pushed through the roadblock. When they sped almost a full block away from the checkpoint, Jimmy fired his grenade launcher, lobbing a 40mm high explosive shell off the back of the truck toward the shattered roadblock. His round landed on an overturned vehicle.

First came the snappy crunch of the HE round detonating, followed closely by the hollow *whump* of secondary explosions as the shredded gas tank ignited. Even at near-highway speed, the fuel-air blast created a pressure wave that thumped Jimmy in the chest as if someone kicked his armor plate.

The convoy rounded a corner, weaving through a gauntlet of toppled push carts and scooters. Random gunfire cracked and popped on adjacent streets.

**VIKTOR
PRESIDENTIAL PALACE
TARKENT, DARISTAN
0044 HOURS, LOCAL**

Viktor perched on the edge of a cement parapet on the palace roof, legs dangling freely over the multi-story drop to the courtyard. He pulled a slow drag from the butt of his Apollo-Soyuz, exhaling through his nose. The city before him sprawled outward in every direction. Cars and buildings across the landscape burned dull orange like votive candles left unattended. Bright, white muzzle flashes of stuttering gunfire punctuated this soft glow, which dotted the entire cityscape.

He looked down between his feet. From this height, the shapes below might be mistaken for droves of homeless camped out on the Daristani government's front lawn. But the corpses of the presidential family and parliamentarians—many headless—could not be shooed away like vagrants in the morning. They needed to be burned.

To Viktor, this was both the best and worst part: the strewn bodies and burning cars; the organized and directed brutality of battle replaced with inept, ham-handed, raucous violence. While the streets filled with reveling insurgents high on bloodlust and humanity's basest inclinations, things at the palace remained so calm that it left Viktor with a heavy emptiness that pulled on him like a chain around his neck.

Viktor's age and experience diminished the satisfaction of conquer. In campaigns past, completion used to feel akin to finishing a gourmet dinner—filling, both physically and mentally, and calming to the point of lethargy. Now, victory on the battlefield felt more like an interrupted orgasm. The more intense the effort, the more singular the focus, the more jarring and agitating the disappointment became. Perhaps his palate changed over time, requiring violence less structured and more personal to reach fulfillment.

He took in the fire-speckled skyline with a different perspective. Maybe the unaccountable havoc below held something for him after all. He swung his legs over the parapet and hopped to his feet. Winding stone stairs led him from the rooftop to the ground floor, where one of his men literally bumped into him at the bottom of the stairwell.

"Sir," the younger man said in Russian. "For you."

Viktor took the drab green radio from the other man's hand, clicking the volume adjustment knob across the arc of small Cyrillic numbers. The voice on the other end delivered a report. Viktor asked him to clarify several times to ensure he did not misunderstand. Finally satisfied, he signed off the radio and handed it back to his younger compatriot.

"Get your gear, meet me out front," Viktor said.

The younger man hurried away, and Viktor went to his own room. He buckled on his nylon battle belt and matching plate carrier. The former came dotted with pouches for grenades and medical equipment, with his holstered Glock 17 pistol hanging off the right side. The carrier vest held spare magazines for both pistol and rifle, as well as his radio and a heavy dagger. Next, he strapped on his helmet with night-vision goggles flipped up over the brim.

Finally, he slung his short AK-105 rifle over one shoulder. Viktor preferred the smaller 5.45x39mm cartridge. It offered lighter recoiling, with a flatter trajectory and longer range than the older, heavier 7.62x39mm carried by Al Badari's fighters in their rickety AKM rifles. Instead, a Zenitco quad rail sheated his AK's twelve-inch barrel. This gave him plenty of space to mount the weapon light, infrared laser, and holographic optic that hung off his carbine. A compact suppressor threaded onto the muzzle. More than any other piece of equipment he carried, this served as Viktor's totem. It ccompanied him on multiple campaigns in Africa and southwest Asia, both as a soldier and now as a so-called consultant. He stole it from the military when he left active duty. It would only find a new home if it was pillaged off his corpse.

But that would not happen tonight.

Tonight, it would do more work for him—maybe some of the best work it had ever done—against his motherland's most notorious enemy for the past century.

HILTON PIERCE
CALLSIGN "ALLEY CAT"
RECCE TROOP - WINDSOR KRAFT STRATEGIES
TARKENT, DARISTAN
0102 HOURS, LOCAL

At the far end of the undeveloped dirt flat that served as their landing strip stood a cluster of half-constructed buildings that were—at one time—intended to house athletes. Six of the Owls spread out on foot, setting up a dispersed perimeter around the cluster of buildings. The trucks parked shoulder-to-shoulder, two facing north and two south, inside the bombed-out shell of half an apartment complex.

Hilton and Jimmy huddled close in front of the trucks, looking out an empty window frame into the night sky. Red and green tracers streaked back and forth across the dim silhouette of Tarkent's skyline.

"The good news is we're early," Jimmy said.

"The bad news?" Hilton asked.

"We're early."

Hilton smirked in the dark. Every minute sitting still as the city descended into anarchy increased their risk of being found. He knew the pilots would attempt a landing in the most harrowing conditions, but there were limits. Even the bravest pilots refused to descend into an active gunfight.

"Let's spread the perimeter out," Hilton said. "Tell the six on watch to spread out at hundred-meter intervals along the east side of the airfield. Hold the other four in reserve with heavy weapons. Those are your guys."

"What about you?" Jimmy asked.

Hilton reached into the bed of one of the pickup trucks. He heaved out a tan rifle with a long barrel seated into a chassis that looked like a sci-fi movie prop. He leaned the gun against the side of the truck. Reaching back into the bed, he shouldered a small backpack that clanked with the weight of loaded magazines.

"I'll be up top," Hilton said.

Without waiting for a reply, Hilton picked up the rifle and trudged up the three flights of stairs to the roof. He dropped the backpack on the ground, then lowered the rifle so that it stood upright on its buttstock, unfolding the legs of the bipod.

The B&T APR 338 served as one of Windsor Kraft's standard-issue sniper rifles, outfitted with a high-powered scope and clip-on night vision device. He laid the big rifle, chambered in the heavy .338 Lapua Magnum, on the edge of the roof and nestled down behind it, pivoting the gun back and forth on its bipod to check his field of fire.

He heard footsteps in the stairwell behind him as he slid the backpack full of mags next to his firing position. Jimmy's tall frame filled the darkness at the top of the steps. An RPG-7 launcher slung across his back, and he held an extra rocket in each hand.

"Figured you might want this too," Jimmy said.

Hilton gestured toward an empty spot of rooftop next to him. Jimmy placed the two rounds down on the ground. He shrugged off the launcher and laid it alongside.

"I'll call the GOC in twenty for an update," Hilton said.

"Sure thing," Jimmy said, turning around to return downstairs.

"Hey!" Hilton called. Jimmy looked over his shoulder. "We make it out of here, we spend Christmas at home this year."

"That's random," Jimmy said.

"Humor me," Hilton replied.

"Tell you what. I'll stay home for Christmas if you find a new therapist. Sleeping with you is hard enough by itself. Stop making Corrine pull double duty."

"It's only double duty for two minutes, once a week."

Jimmy laughed.

"Jim, if we make it through this, I'll spend Christmas with her parents," Hilton said.

"I'm gonna tell her you said that."

"See you on the plane," Hilton said, turning back to his rifle.

Jimmy disappeared down the stairwell.

VIKTOR
TARKENT, DARISTAN
0115 HOURS, LOCAL

Viktor slowed his truck to a halt at the four-way intersection. They stopped at every checkpoint they passed, asking for information about the Americans. None of them seemed to have heard about their comrades gunned down by a rogue Owl commando convoy. Most of them were high on hasheesh or simply drunk with the power of total victory. His young lieutenant clearly grew tired of the search.

"Sir," the younger man said. "Maybe they weren't actually Americans."

"You want to…what? Simply let them go?" Viktor said.

"Go where?" the younger man asked.

Viktor grabbed the younger man by his hair and smashed the side of his head into the passenger window. The man sat stunned in his seat, a splotch of blood on the glass by his head. After a minute, the man opened his mouth to speak, but Viktor grabbed his head again, this time smashing it into the window several times. The blood stain on the glass grew bigger. Tears streamed down the lieutenant's face.

He sniffled, wiping blood and tears from his upper lip as he stared out the windshield in silence. Finally, he whispered, "What if they have a plane?"

Viktor shook his head. "The airport has been taken over. There are no more planes there."

"What if it's somewhere else?"

"Where?"

The younger man shrugged.

Viktor clenched the steering wheel with both hands, his brow furrowed in thought. After several moments, he stepped out of the truck and jogged two blocks back to the last insurgent checkpoint they'd passed. Minutes later, he climbed back in the truck, his mood completely changed. He slapped his lieutenant on the shoulder playfully.

"Good work," Viktor said.

"I don't understand," the lieutenant said.

"You will," came Viktor's coy reply.

Suddenly, their rearview mirror lit up with the flare of approaching headlights. The lieutenant squinted into the mirror and saw four more trucks lining up behind them. All four pickups bristled with rifle barrels poking out the windows and each side of the truck beds. Viktor tapped his brakes twice. The truck behind him flicked its headlights twice in response. A smile twisted across Viktor's face as he let off the brake and put his truck into gear.

"There is only one other place," Viktor explained, "where they could land a plane."

"The Olympic Village," the lieutenant said.

"Yes," Viktor replied. "The Olympic Village."

HILTON PIERCE
CALLSIGN "ALLEY CAT"
RECCE TROOP – WINDSOR KRAFT STRATEGIES
TARKENT, DARISTAN
0137 HOURS, LOCAL

Holly picked up the satellite phone on the first ring.

"Operations," she said tersely.

"Holly, it's Hilton."

"How are you guys?"

"We're okay," Hilton said with robotic calm. "Pantheon is secure. What's our ETA on the flight?"

"Twenty-five minutes."

"Understood."

Holly wanted so badly to tell him about Corrine. That she knew he had stayed behind. That she was worried sick. That she loved him, even though Holly knew the two of them danced around that fact for months. She wanted to tell him that he better get his ass home to her.

Instead, she asked, "How are you guys on weapons and ammo?"

"We're good. NATO left behind enough gear to arm Al Badari for the next decade, but we put a dent in the stockpile. Where's Jack?"

"He stepped out. I'll tell him everything."

"Have you talked to Corrine?"

Holly swallowed hard and said, "She's fine."

"Is that what you told her about me?"

"We've got you covered back here. Finish the job," she said sternly.

"Wilco. Alley Cat out," Hilton replied, ending the phone call.

Hilton keyed the mic on his radio. "Wheels down two-five mikes."

"Copy, we're set down here," Jimmy replied.

The night vision mounted to Hilton's rifle flared bright green. He swung the big B&T to get a better look at the light source. Squeezing the talk button on his radio again, he warned the team, "Be advised, multi-vehicle convoy one-seven-zero meters east, closing slowly."

"Are they on a direct line?" Jimmy asked.

"Looks like they're weaving through cross-streets right now. They're definitely getting closer."

"I'll let the boys know."

Three floors below Hilton, Jimmy and Jazz huddled with the four Owls standing by as reinforcements. They waited armed to the teeth: PKMs, AKs with grenade launchers clamped beneath their barrels, and multiple RPG launchers.

The Hiluxes idled quietly, headlights and taillights masked off with hundred-mile-an-hour tape. Even the dashboard gauges had pieces of cardboard taped over them. The vehicles gave off no ambient light whatsoever. Jimmy didn't know how many sets of night vision coalition forces abandoned in their hasty retreat, but he assumed the number to be in the thousands. Al Badari's insurgents must have recovered some of them from hangars at the airport, or from the bodies of Daristani soldiers they killed along the way.

Up top, Hilton watched as the convoy of trucks crisscrossed through the side streets immediately adjacent to the east edge of the Olympic village. His earpiece crackled.

"What're they doing?" Jimmy said.

"Still weaving, but now they're doubling back on themselves," Hilton said.

"Maybe they're lost."

"No. They're searching."

"A methodical search? That's not really like Badari insurgents."

"No," Hilton said thoughtfully. "No, it isn't. But it is like whoever is helping them."

"Who's helping them?"

"Same guys who've been helping them this whole time."

The vehicles huddled up two blocks away behind a warehouse. Then, almost simultaneously, all five trucks turned their lights off.

"Here they come," Hilton said.

"How many?"

"Wait one."

Hilton continued to watch through the night-vision scope. All five trucks spit men out. He counted fourteen total milling around the vehicles. Two of them took charge. They stood taller and firmer than the rest, positioned in the center of the universal human horseshoe that happens when a team needs to receive instructions.

The pair were the only ones wearing night vision—a pair of dual-tube goggles atop ballistic helmets.

Hilton keyed his mic. "Head count is one-four bad guys, two with NVGs. Tell the sentries to get off the edge of the LZ, push one block east, and spread out into the last row of buildings and parked cars for cover. You and your guys stand fast."

"Rog," came Jimmy's clipped reply.

Hilton didn't need to explain the plan. Right now, the six sentries on their knees or bellies in mostly open terrain held the physical edge of the landing zone. Two guys wearing NVGs could easily spot them. Pushing them a block over allowed them to find better cover and stay out of sight while the insurgents approached. Then the sentries could turn their guns inward, shooting east-to-west across the open landing zone, with the western wall of Tarkent serving as a bulletproof backstop.

The building Hilton perched on sat at the north edge of the field, which meant Jimmy and his team downstairs already had a clean north-south line of fire. Once Al Badari's men started their sweep of the open ground, the LZ itself would become a perfect kill box for the Owls.

Time ticked by on the quiet rooftop, each second longer than the last. None of the Owls moved.

Some of the insurgents filed out of the parking lot, while others returned to their trucks and climbed into the respective driver seats. One of the two men in charge went back to his truck and pulled a rifle out of the pickup bed. Its long barrel and rectangular skeleton buttstock were unmistakable as an

SVD sniper rifle—the iconic Russian "Dragunov." "Bad guys on the move. Nine closing on foot. The rest are holding back. One reserve with an SVD," Hilton said.

"They're doing the same thing we're doing."

"Get the Owls moving. Now." Hilton said anxiously.

Jimmy didn't reply. Hilton understood the hold-up. Jimmy needed to brief the plan to Jazz, who had to translate into Daristani over the radio to his own men. The language barrier created lag time they didn't have. Finally, the Owls clambered to their feet and took off in a jog heading west.

The insurgents on foot moved single-file toward the airfield, their commander with NVGs at the front of the line. Hilton repositioned his rifle to put the crosshairs on that commander when his radio crackled to life again.

"Alley Cat, this is Paddy Wagon, your freq," came a voice.

Windsor Kraft used "Paddy Wagon" as the callsign for the Pilatus PC-24 jet launched from Dubai.

Hilton squeezed the PTT box clipped to his chest rig to answer the pilot. "Go for Alley Cat."

"We are one-zero mikes out. SITREP?"

On the street below, Owls still scrambled to find cover. The column of insurgents moved less than a hundred yards from them, closing at a cautious march. The point man's night vision goggles swept methodically left and right as he moved. Now Hilton could see his face. Even though his features were obscured by the goggles, Hilton could see the tight beard and shaggy, shoulder-length hair spilling out under his helmet. It was the Russian he'd seen at the palace.

"Paddy Wagon, LZ secure. Be advised we have hostiles inbound. Local commandos are closing to engage," Hilton said.

"Alley Cat, are you in contact?"

"Not yet."

"Hot landing is a no-go, Alley Cat."

"Keep me posted. Out."

Hilton squeezed the other button to talk to Jimmy, "Ten minutes to wheels down."

"Cuttin' it close," Jimmy said.

Hilton keyed his mic to answer but let off it when a piece of concrete two feet to his left burst into powder with the metallic zip of a ricocheted bullet. Hilton cursed himself and swung his rifle off the column to look for the sniper.

On the ground, a flurry of muzzle flashes erupted as two of the Owls opened fire on the insurgent column. The Russian barked commands, and the column broke into two groups, fanning to opposite sides of the street.

Hilton jerked the massive B&T back toward the warehouse, scanning the rooftop. The Dragunov's muzzle flickered again. Hilton heard the whip-like *snap* of the Russian slug flying past him. He pressed the B&T's match trigger. The .338 magnum launched with a thunderclap, the rifle bucking on its bipod as the stock smacked Hilton in the shoulder. He ripped the bolt handle back and slammed it forward to chamber a fresh round.

The Russian marksman pulled back off the edge of the warehouse roof, lining himself up behind a piece of corrugated sheet tin for concealment.

"Alley Cat, Paddy Wagon is on final descent. What's your status?"

Hilton ignored the pilot, focused on his counterpart on top of the warehouse. Hilton didn't know if the Russian had any secondary barricades behind that sheet of tin, but it was worth the gamble. Hilton lined up his crosshairs over the edge of the sheet and pressed the trigger again. The rifle bucked and roared another time. Hilton cranked the bolt back and forth, squinting through his scope for effect on target.

The SVD rifle laid flat on the ground next to a limp arm. Hilton couldn't see the rest of the shooter's body, but he wasn't moving.

"Hilton, they're here," Jimmy spoke in Hilton's ear this time.

Hilton pulled his head off the rifle and looked up. He saw the broad outline of the Pilatus with no lights on, inky black against the dim night sky.

Hilton dumped the big rifle to the ground and leapt to his feet. That's when he saw four sets of headlights flick on in the warehouse parking lot. The trucks maneuvered to line up inside the parking lot. He glanced down at the landing strip. Stray rounds from the firefight one block over skipped off the ground, kicking up puffs of dirt along the would-be runway.

Hilton grabbed the squawk box on his shoulder and smashed the button for the airplane's frequency. "Abort, abort, abort. Incoming rounds on the LZ."

A couple hundred feet off the ground, he watched the

plane's nose jerk hard into the sky for a nearly vertical ascent out of the firefight.

"Fuckin' warn us next time!" the pilot snapped.

"We are in direct contact, trying to suppress."

"Alley Cat, we are in violation of both sovereign airspace and presidential orders. You get one more pass. Then you're walking home."

"How much time?" Hilton asked.

"Ten minutes."

Hilton held up his wrist, tapping the backlight button on his watch: 01:50.

"Ten minutes," Hilton confirmed and ran down the stairs, taking three or four at a time. He panted hard by the time he got to Jimmy and the reserve team of Owls.

"Their trucks are moving," Hilton said.

"We can kill them," Jimmy replied confidently.

"I know, but if we kill them on the LZ, the plane can't land and we're dead anyway. We need to go to them. Fire up the VAMPIRE."

Jimmy ran to the truck with the rocket launcher on it.

Hilton turned to Jazz, gesturing to the three men standing behind him, and said, "We'll take care of the technicals. You guys finish the street fight."

Jazz turned toward his men, but Hilton grabbed the Owl commander's shoulder and said, "Get in the back of the truck. We'll drop you off on the way."

Jazeeri barked the orders to the other men. The four of them crammed into the pickup bed around the four-pack launcher and its laser guidance turret. Hilton ripped open the passenger side door and flipped the PVS-14 down over one eye. Jimmy already had his dual-tubes down. They drove by night vision.

"The warehouse is two blocks east, three south. The Owls jump out halfway there and catch the foot troops from behind," Hilton said.

Jimmy cranked the wheel hard, pulling the truck out onto the street before accelerating hard. The truck skidded as Jimmy hit the brakes.

Hilton pushed his door open, leaned out, and whispered, "Go, go, go!"

Jazeeri and his three-man team tumbled over the side of the truck bed onto the street and took off in a sprint.

Hilton leaned back in, letting forward momentum close his door as he powered up the VAMPIRE's control unit on the dash in front of him. The laser guidance system required Hilton to use the joystick on the control unit to hold the designator's crosshair over whatever he wanted to hit.

Jimmy hooked a hard right onto the street with the warehouse. The column of insurgent trucks pulled out of the parking lot, leaving only the taillights of the rearmost truck in Hilton's line of fire.

Hilton's thumb swiveled the small joystick until the red laser spot on the screen hovered right over the rear window of that last pickup. He took his thumb off the stick and smashed the fire button.

The first rocket flew over their heads with a metallic *whoosh*. The 70mm Hydra rocket covered the one-block distance in fractions of a second before its point-detonating warhead, loaded with 2.3 pounds of B-4 explosive, hit the back of the cab.

The insurgent Hilux blistered open in a mushroom of flame. Not moving the crosshair, Hilton pressed the fire button one more time. The second rocket sailed through the smoke and flame of the first explosion, smashing into the next truck in the column, the blast flipping it over on one side.

"The other two already rounded the corner," Jimmy said.

"Cut 'em off!" Hilton snapped.

Jimmy gunned the engine, turning down a parallel side street back toward the airstrip. They got close enough to the Owl firefight to hear the bristling symphony of gunfire from Jazz's team, which used the chaos to plant on a corner in the middle of the insurgent column. In their battle frenzy, the Owls were far less concerned with friendly fire than their American counterparts; Jazeeri's four-man assault team had opened fire in both directions.

Jimmy swung the truck hard left. The edge of the landing strip sat directly to their right, with the last row of buildings to their left. Of the two insurgent trucks left in the column from the warehouse, one already positioned in the middle of the LZ. The other pulled up on the edge, directly in front of them.

Hilton couldn't tell why the second truck paused, but he pressed the fire button anyway, sending the third rocket away at point-blank range—now measured in car lengths, not blocks. It was so close that the impact fuse didn't have enough distance to arm. Instead of exploding, the rocket punched through the side of the truck like a harpoon. The tail-fin assembly of the un-detonated rocket stuck out of the passenger side window of the pickup like a toothpick.

Hilton snatched his carbine out of the footwell and leapt from the truck. Jimmy yanked the shifter into park and bailed out on the opposite side.

Hilton ran half the distance between himself and the last remaining insurgent truck before slowing to a fluid walk. He shouldered the Cobalt and fired a steady stream of single rounds as he closed in. Jimmy fanned out to the side of him, raised his own rifle, and fired.

A flash erupted from the front of the truck as an RPG sailed between the two of them, detonating into the side of a building behind them. The driver crumpled into the dirt on the LZ.

Hilton slung the carbine over his shoulder and took off in a dead run. Jimmy caught up to the idling insurgent truck only steps behind him. Hilton hurled the empty RPG launcher into the back of the truck, crouching down and hooking his arms under the dead man's armpits.

"Move the truck. I got him," Hilton said.

Jimmy stepped past him and climbed into the truck. Their bullets had crackled the entire windshield into blue-white spiderwebs, so Jimmy hung his head out the driver's window to steer.

"Alley Cat, Paddy Wagon. We're out of time, boss," the pilot said.

Hilton dropped the corpse and pressed his talk button. "LZ is green. Bring it in."

The pilot's relief was audible on the other end. "Solid

copy, Alley Cat. We're inbound on final approach."

Hilton picked the body back up and dragged it to the edge of the field. Hurried footsteps came up from behind him. Jazz stood before him when he turned around.

"How bad is it?" Hilton asked.

"We have two dead, six more wounded. They will survive," Jazz said.

"Bad guys?"

"All dead."

"Even the Russian?"

"What Russian?" Jazz asked.

"Fuck," Hilton muttered. He held one hand up at shoulder height.

"Long hair, like this," Hilton said. Then he held both hands in front of his eyes, making them into circles like imaginary goggles. "Night vision, two tubes."

Jazz shook his head.

Hilton shouldn't have been surprised. Knowing they would be wholly routed by the Owls, Al Badari's advisor abandoned his men to fight another day.

Hilton flipped up his PVS-14 and wiped his face with both hands. Behind him, the whine of the PC-24's engine grew louder. The plane lowered slowly, its wheels kicking up a stream of dust as they touched the earth on the south end of the airstrip. The pilot threw both engines into hard reverse, slowing the plane just in time to pull a U-turn in front of the three-story building occupied minutes before.

Hilton turned on his heels and strode quickly toward the airplane. Jazz hustled to match his gait, Jimmy intersecting them on the way. They approached the Pilatus just as the side door lowered to meet them.

The pilot, dressed in cargo pants and an untucked dress shirt, leaned out of the open entryway and shouted, "Which one of you is Alley Cat?"

"Hilton Pierce," he replied, raising his hand.

"Rick Stahl."

Hilton smiled faintly. "Hey, Rick."

"We have zero time," Rick said curtly.

Hilton turned to Jazz and put his hand out. "For everything, Jazz."

Jazz shook the hand literally fell out of Hilton's handshake. In the same instant, Hilton heard the familiar glass-rod *snap* of bullets breaking the air around him.

Hilton splayed out on the ground, covering Jazz's body with his own as he jerked the night vision monocular down over his eye. The Owls fired indiscriminately into buildings across the street as Hilton swiveled his head back and forth, searching for a target.

Jimmy, on his stomach ten feet from Hilton, cursed under his breath. "I got nothing!"

"Ditto," Hilton muttered.

Behind them both, Rick Stahl's voice sounded controlled but emphatic. "We leave now, or not at all."

Hilton got up on one knee and ripped open the trauma kit on his chest rig. The medical supplies spilled out onto the ground next to Jazz. Hilton picked up the shears and cut away Jazz's plate carrier, then his shirt. He couldn't find an exit wound out the front, but a puddle of blood formed underneath Jazz's body.

Hilton heard the signature wet wheeze of tension pneumothorax—a sucking chest wound. He dropped the shears and pawed around on the ground until he found the chest seals. Jimmy's carbine finally came to life alongside all the AKs.

The PC's engines whined louder.

"Ten seconds!" Rick yelled.

Hilton rolled Jazz onto his side, wiped away as much blood as he could with the tail of the commander's cut-up shirt, and slapped the chest seal over the entry wound just as he felt Jimmy grab back of his shirt collar. Hilton swore as he let Jazz roll back into the dirt.

The plane edwas already moving by the time the door retracted. Inside the plane, both men unbuckled their gear, throwing it into a heap on the ground. They took their seats just in time for the G-force of a near-vertical takeoff press them into the cushions.

Both men pressed their faces against the porthole windows just in time to catch a glimpse of machine gun tracers streaking back and forth across the city, backlit by the glow of burning vehicles. Jimmy looked away, slamming his window shade down.

Hilton stayed glued to his porthole until the tracers were too far below him to see.

**HOLLY TOMASSI
OPERATIONS ASSISTANT
GLOBAL OPERATIONS CENTER - WINDSOR KRAFT STRATEGIES
CHESAPEAKE, VA
1804 HOURS, LOCAL**

The satellite phone in Jack's hand rang. He walked over to Holly, their shoulders touching, and put the call on speaker.

"Send it," Jack said firmly.

Hilton's voice came through crystal clear, with the steady thrum of engines in the background. "Sorry we're late. Got held up at the office."

Holly clasped a hand over her mouth. Jack wrapped his arm across her shoulders and pulled her tight.

Clearing his throat, Jack said, "The fuck've you been doing? I was beginning to think you applied for citizenship there."

"Yeah, well, you know Jimmy likes to party late. Someone had to look after him."

In the airplane, Jimmy rolled his eyes.

His tone softening, Jack asked, "Are you guys okay?"

"Yeah, we're fine."

"When you land, leave your gear on the plane. Rick has a company credit card. Have him book you rooms and connecting flights."

"We're gonna need food and clothes, too," Hilton said.

"You left your suitcases in Tarkent?"

"Wouldn't you know it."

"Send Holly your itineraries once you're booked. I'll be waiting at the airport for you both."

"See you tomorrow night."

"Out here," Jack said and tossed the phone onto a nearby desk.

Holly burst into tears. She collapsed into his chest with heaving, wracking sobs. He rubbed her upper back.

Face still buried in his shirt, she cried, "I thought we lost them!"

"Yeah, me, too. But you did it."

She pulled her face away from him, smearing the wetness away with both palms. "What did I do?"

Holding her gently by the shoulders, Jack smiled and said, "You did your job."

A thought sprouted in Holly's mind. She took a small step back from Jack and collected herself. "I need to go make a phone call."

Jack nodded.

Holly walked out of the GOC, heels clacking on the cement floor all the way to the elevator. When she got off the elevator, they clacked across the tile floor of the front lobby, then on the pavement of the sidewalk outside. She fished her phone out of her pocket and tapped Corrine's name. The call rang twice before Corrine answered. Holly knew she'd been crying.

"I'm sorry I hung up on you earlier, I just...," Corrine started to say.

"Corrine, he's out. He made it."

"Are you sure?"

"He just called from on-board the aircraft."

"Where are they?"

Holly cringed. "I'm sorry, I can't…"

"I understand. He's going somewhere safe? Is he flying back here?"

"Not directly, no. They need to stop somewhere first and change planes, but *that* place is completely safe. I promise. He should be back in the States tomorrow night sometime. I don't know exactly when."

"Holly, I can't thank you enough for everything you've done."

"Thank you."

"I'm sure you still have a lot to do. I have to try and convince the people here I give a shit about work right now."

"Good luck with that," Holly said.

"Don't bet on me. Talk to you soon," Corrine said before hanging up the phone.

Holly dropped the phone in her pocket and pulled out a pack of cigarettes. Her hands shook as she tapped a smoke out of the small box and pressed it between pursed lips. She needed both hands to work the lighter. The first, heavy drag burned up a quarter of the entire cigarette. Still holding the pack in her hands, and the smoke in her lungs, Holly closed her eyes and tilted her face toward the afternoon sun. ,Light from the setting sun warmed her face as she slowly blew smoke out of her nose.

JACK YOUNG
DULLES, VIRGINIA
2242 HOURS LOCAL

Jack watched in the rearview mirror as Hilton tossed his bags into the back of the all-black Land Rover. Hilton slammed the rear hatch closed, walked around the side of the Rover, and folded himself into the passenger's seat next to Jack.

Slamming the door hard, Hilton said, "Anywhere but another goddamn airport."

Jack smirked. "I can do that."

They rode in silence for the first ten minutes. No radio. No small talk. Just the gravity of recently written history hanging over the top of them. Hilton watched the urban sprawl of northern Virginia race by them at highway speeds.

"All these Beltway people," Hilton said. "They're all going to forget about this in six months."

"We'll be lucky to get that long out of them," Jack said grimly.

Still staring blankly out his window, Hilton asked, "What now?"

Jack didn't answer until, a minute later, Hilton turned in his seat to face the older man. Jack glanced over to meet his gaze before darting his eyes back to the road. Finally, he replied, "I've been thinking about that. For a lot longer than the past week."

Hilton stared hard at Jack's silhouette behind the

steering wheel.

"Come back to work for me in Operational Compliance," Jack said.

"OCP?" Hilton asked rhetorically. "I told you I wanted out of that black-bag shit."

"And I got you out. You've been rotating in and out of Daristan for a couple of years. Besides, I think the program might be expanding."

Hilton cocked an eyebrow and said, "Regrettably, you have my attention."

Jack cleared his throat, setting his best Power Point briefing voice. "The mission of OCP is to apply the company's asymmetric, problem-solving resources with discretion and prejudice to the most complex operational issues facing our deployed personnel. As you know, we've historically been focused on high risk, low signature, contingencies to protect our own people."

Hilton shrugged in concession as he filled in the blanks. "Right. What if another team of guys gets trapped inside a failed nation-state? Or we wind up in a whistleblower situation on a government contract we're servicing? Or one of our own is abducted in a foreign country during an operation?"

"Exactly!" Jack said. "Contractors protecting other contractors."

"I know you're trying to lead me to something else, but it's been a long couple days."

"What about counter-PMC warfare?"

Hilton leaned back in his seat and squinted. "What are you talking about?"

"How embedded was this Arkangel outfit with Al Badari's takeover?"

"Al Badari had a personal advisor. I saw him, face-to-face, when they took the palace. Then again at the fallback LZ."

This time Jack raised his brow. "He found you guys at the final pick-up?"

"The plane flew into a hot LZ. It was Al Badari's men, but this advisor was leading them."

"What'd the guy look like?"

"Straight-up Cold War villain," Hilton said. "Shoulder-length hair, bushy moustache, scar on his face. Hollow cheeks, ice-blue eyes."

"How close did you get?"

"Had him in my crosshairs. Literally."

Validating his own idea, Jack explained. "It's coming, Hilton. Contractor-versus-contractor. No referees. No hiding behind grunts in uniform. I'm not talking about tripping and falling onto these guys like you did in Daristan. I'm talking about negotiating a contract to target them directly. Map and neutralize their leadership. Disrupt their support networks. Cripple their ongoing operations. We'll get money and authorization from Capitol Hill. After that, it will be full-blown, privatized warfare."

"Just like they're doing."

"It's only a matter of time. And not much time. When it happens, it'll be our problem. Not the American people's, and not the US military's."

Hilton remained quiet.

Jack expounded further. "OCP is going to be more than a broom closet. Windsor Kraft Strategies will continue to serve pre-negotiated contracts with specific clients. But OCP will run without a leash, using money routed through offshore slush funds and vaguely chartered private foundations."

"That's ambitious," Hilton said, clearly incredulous.

"What little we know about Arkangel indicates they're already doing most of this, and they're not afraid to blur the lines between a private company and outsourced state policy. Our side is about to take the gloves off, so long as we keep our hands under the table."

"Poetic," Hilton said with a smirk.

Jack ignored the jab. "I'm going to need a lead shooter. Someone who can work in the gray. Who knows what we're up against."

Hilton faced back toward the passenger window and let out a sigh. Jack tried to comfort him by saying, "We don't have to talk about it now."

"Let's head back to the office. I can debrief tonight on these guys."

Jack shook his head. "Hilton, it's ten o'clock at night. Nobody is there."

"Call someone in. One of the intel guys. An eastern Europe specialist."

"You need to unplug for a day. I'm not bringing you to the office."

"Nobody wants to go home to an empty apartment," Hilton said.

"You want to stay with me?"

Hilton dug his cell phone out of his pants pocket. Staring at the black screen, he told Jack, "Take me to Newport News."

**JIMMY TOOMS
CALLSIGN "JAMESON"
CHESAPEAKE, VIRGINIA
2330 HOURS LOCAL**

Jimmy stood at the end of the walkway, staring hard at the front door of the townhome. He already picked up his bags and walked away from it twice. Each time, he'd only gotten a few steps before he turned around and came back. Anybody peering out their windows at night would have noticed his weird behavior.

He needed to make a decision.

He walked up to the door, placed his bags down, and knocked just hard enough. Moments passed and, growing anxious, he knocked again. The sounds of a deadbolt being thrown rewarded him, followed by the scraping of weather stripping. The door eased inward. A slender woman in a loose t-shirt and baggy sweatpants, her brunette hair in a messy bun, looked more than mildly irritated.

"Jim? What the hell are you doing?"

He looked down at his boots, forcing his eyes off her body. "Hey, Em…"

"It's almost midnight," she said curtly. "We talked about this. You can't just show up whenever…"

Jimmy picked his head up, eyes glassed over with tears he fought to hold in place.

Emily's demeanor softened. "Jimmy, what's going on?"

He blinked, and a pair of tears raced down his face, clinging to his beard like dewdrops on blades of grass.

"I swear to Christ, Em, I haven't had a drink in months. It's just been…" He blew out a slow breath. "…I had a rough couple days at the office, and I just wanted to see Lizzy. I'm sorry."

"Where were you this time?" she asked.

"Daristan."

Her eyes widened. Like most Americans, she watched the disastrous collapse of the world's protracted campaign in Daristan in real-time on TV and social media.

"When did you get back?" Emily asked.

"I came straight here from the airport."

"Oh, Jimmy…"

Breaking her own rules about physical affection between them, she stepped into the night and gave her ex-husband the tightest, most sincere squeeze either of them traded in years. A single, yelping sob escaped from Jimmy before he clenched his teeth, pulled her tighter, and swallowed the knot in this throat.

Emily pulled away from him just enough to look him in the eyes. "I'll go wake Lizzy up."

For the first time in six years, Jimmy Tooms didn't give a flying fuck about Daristan.

CORRINE MACKENZIE
NEWPORT NEWS, VIRGINIA
0006 HOURS LOCAL

Jack dropped Hilton off in front of Corrine's house. If it'd been up to her, she'd have run down the front walk and thrown herself into him, sobbing and kissing his face. But Corrine knew Hilton didn't like what he called "Hollywood reunions".

Instead, she stood on her front porch in the dark, waiting with vibrating stillness until he climbed the front steps with more effort than it should have taken. His battered. three-day pack hanging off one shoulder, he slipped both arms around her and sank the entire weight of the war against her.

She also knew the best thing for him on his first night back was quiet. She wanted so badly to catch him up, fill him in on hospital drama, and ask how he felt to be home. That only caused him to retreat inside the walls of his mind, offering one-word answers and pre-programmed grunts of agreement or feigned interest.

Instead, they'd sat at her kitchenette table listening to 1940s love songs and drinking Four Branches Bourbon out of cut crystal tumblers she only used with him. He loved the classics—Vaughn Monroe, Tommy Dorsey, Glenn Miller. Before Hilton came into her life, Corrine never cared for vintage music. But it so keenly completed his dystopian existence; sipping cocktails and taking in the orchestra crooners with a pistol at his side.

Fifteen minutes into his comfortable silence, she asked, "Are you home yet?"

"Almost," he said quietly. Then he looked up from his glass, met her eyes, and smiled as he let out a slow breath. She smiled back, blinking tears out of her eyes.

"I'm okay," he said. "It was just…this was a long one."

Corrine looked down at her glass, sniffling as she said, "Holly told me you missed the last flight out."

"She told you that?" Hilton asked incredulously.

"Not at first. There was a big deal on the news when the last military flight landed in Germany. When I didn't hear from you, I kind of put two and two together. She just confirmed it."

The flood of relief that came with his smile—his acknowledgement that he was, indeed, here in the present with her—pushed her therapeutic instincts out of hiding.

"Do you want to talk about it?" she asked.

His smile fell, and she recoiled slightly in her chair.

"We're both off the clock," he said sternly.

She shook her head, self-chastising. "I didn't mean it like that."

Hilton reached across the table, taking her hand.

"*I'm* sorry," he said. "I wasn't alone. It was me and one other guy. We both made it. He's already home."

Corrine wiped her eyes with the back of her free hand. "I'm thankful for that."

"We had some locals. They were supposed to come with us. Some didn't make it. The others refused to leave."

Knowing nothing she could say would fill the void, Corrine just squeezed his hand. He squeezed back. She leaned down to the table and gave his fingers a bourbon-wet kiss, brushing her cheek against his scarred knuckles.

In that moment, he was finally—fully—home.

Hilton drained his glass and stood up, pulling her to her feet. Corrine gulped down the rest of her drink. They kissed at the kitchen table for what felt like hours. Then came the quiet walk up the stairs, hurried desperate lovemaking, a long shower, and another round—slower this time—before they fell asleep in a tangle of limbs and bedsheets.

Her sleepy eyes drew to the pistol and phone on her nightstand. The phone buzzed, and her heart rate quickened. Jack's name, with a text message icon, lit up the screen for a few seconds.

Corrine looked up at Hilton's face, still slack with the stillness of sleep. Hilton would be hers until he saw it but, perhaps, not for long after he did.

She placed her head back on his shoulder. Minutes later, she dozed off again to the steady beat of morning rain on the window.

EPILOGUE

25 KM OUTSIDE OF NHAHRULLAH, DARISTAN
1200 HOURS, LOCAL
SIX MONTHS LATER

A year after the exodus of coalition forces from Daristan, life returned to the closest thing either side could call normal. The American people were, by-and-large, relieved to be free of yet another protracted counterinsurgency they couldn't explain in a country they couldn't find on a map. The administration in place at that time declared it a relief for the nation's warfighters, with no mention of Windsor Kraft in front of the press.

Hundreds, maybe thousands, of Daristani-Americans and loyal Daristani nationals remained stuck in a country that systematically hunted them down. Al Badari's ongoing marathon of public executions and political imprisonments never got a second of airplay in Western media.

Daristan still existed as a sovereign nation, albeit under the rule of autocratic Sharia law. They established and maintained diplomatic relations with a select number of countries who had chosen to avoid the NATO-driven campaign there. In particular, the Badari government relied heavily on the assistance of east European advisors from the Russia-based private military firm they now knew as PMC Arkangel.

The leadership of Arkangel rostered supposedly retired officers from Russia's GRU—its military counterintelligence wing, responsible for covert operations on foreign soil. Arkangel worked with the Iranian Quds Force, the Libyan military, and the Assad regime in Syria.

In recent years, Arkangel operatives had been sighted amidst coups and uprisings throughout Africa and South America, helping warlords and plutocrats topple democratic regimes in exchange for funding and geopolitical leverage. By the time foreign intelligence agencies could confirm their involvement, they'd already vanished.

But all that could change.

Two men laid in a rocky alcove a hundred meters from the edge of a single strip of unimproved road that ran endlessly into the desert in either direction. Far in the distance, a rooster tail of dust rose into the afternoon sky. High, wispy clouds streaked haphazardly across the blue canvas above them, but the weather looked otherwise crystal clear. The leading edge of the dust trail moved closer to their position.

"Are your men ready?" one man asked.

The other nodded, his face still pressed to the spotting scope perched on a short tripod between them.

The first man dipped his head, speaking quietly into a satellite radio laid out next to him.

A convoy of four, white Toyota Land Cruisers sped into view, the dust trail following them like a specter floating above the last truck.

The man on the spotting scope squeezed his partner's arm. The partner spoke once more into his radio before placing the handset down in the dirt and glancing skyward. Just as the line of trucks passed directly in front of their position, the first one exploded.

Before the blast cloud fully formed, ten more men came up out of the dirt. They threw off their dusty, brown blankets and sprinted toward the road. A pair of two-man machine gun teams dove back into the dirt, firing long bursts from their PKMs as the rest continued to advance. At the front-edge of the bum rush, four more men dove forward and opened fire as the first two teams picked up their belt-feds and ran to catch up.

The fire teams leap-frogged like this across the hundred-meter stretch of no-man's-land, keeping a constant chatter of machine gun fire aimed at the remaining three vehicles.

When the lead fire team came less than twenty meters from the road, a glint of light streaked through the bright sky and smashed into the rear truck. In movies, vehicles always flipped over or tumbled into the air when hit by missiles. This one didn't.

Instead, the roof smashed into the ground like it'd been hit by Thor's hammer. The windows and doors on either side exploded from the impact of a kinetic kill warhead. Unlike the explosive warheads of legacy drone missiles like the Hellfire, kinetic kill models rely on the raw impact energy of an incredibly dense, solid projectile hitting its target at near-hypersonic speed. This minimizes both the visual signature and collateral risk of surgical strikes.

The ten-man platoon closed on the remaining two trucks, ripping open the doors and firing start-and-stop bursts from their AKs into each vehicle. Seconds later, they dragged out the one man left alive and kicked him into the roadside dirt. Two of the commandos hauled him to his feet, punched him hard in the face and spun him to face the two men in the alcove.

The spotter squinted through his lens. "It's him."

He passed the scope to his partner. The partner looked hard into the scope for several seconds, taking in the bloody face of Ansar Al Badari. Both men stood up and hurried across the hundred-plus meters to the convoy.

When they reached the edge of the road, the partner poked his head into each vehicle. The bodies inside, most still buckled into their seats, showed a mix of Daristanis and Russians. He pulled a small, digital camera from his pocket and took pictures of each face and uniform jacket front. He looked hard at each white face. The long-haired man with the scar on his face was not among them. Then he looked down at the camera, scrolling through the photos he took, zooming in on one just to be sure. Whomever he saw at the palace gates last year was not among the dead.

Tucking the camera back into his cargo pocket, he said, "Check all the Russians for ID."

The spotter barked clipped orders in Daristani, and several men hauled light-skinned corpses out of each vehicle, rifling through their pockets. They laid out the IDs they found in a string on the ground. The partner took photos of each, while the commandos pushed Al Badari to the front of his vehicle. Two men sat him down, spread his arms out, and zip-cuffed him to the Land Cruiser's bumper. A third set up a video camera on a tripod pointed directly at him.

Pocketing his camera again, the partner looked at his spotter. "I need to leave."

"Mister Hilton, you should take him with you. Put him on trial. The world needs justice."

Hilton let out a long sigh, shaking his head sadly. "Jazz, the world doesn't care anymore. They gave up on us. This is the closest thing to justice we're going to get, but I can't be here to see it."

Jaziri put a hand on Hilton's shoulder. "I understand, Hilton. Thank you."

"What happens after this?" Hilton asked.

Jaziri's face set firm with conviction. "I have more men in Tarkent, waiting for my orders. We will finish this fight. Then you can come back and have chai with me once again."

Hilton didn't know if they would be successful, but he did know he'd never be back. "I look forward to it, Jazz."

The two men hugged roughly, holding it for longer than either one expected. Deep down, Jazz knew all the same things Hilton did. When they pulled apart, Jazz drew a long, curved dagger from the studded leather sheath on his belt. With his free hand, he gently patted Hilton's cheek, then touched his own heart, and spoke in Arabic instead of Daristani.

"Alsafar bi'aman, muharib Amriki. Shukran."

This translated to, "Travel safe, American warrior. Thank you."

Hilton nodded and turned away. He walked back to the alcove, picked up the satellite radio, and strode down a gentle slope, where he peeled the camouflage netting off his Hilux. Large cans of fuel and water were bolted to either side of the truck. Several hours' drive laid ahead of him to the border with Daristan's closest neighbor, where an MI-17 helicopter waited with a Windsor Kraft air crew. He buckled up behind the wheel and slammed the driver's door with one hand, turning the ignition with the other.

A battered AK, with EOtech sight and cheap vertical grip, rested on the passenger seat next to him. A bandoleer of magazines hung from the headrest.

He placed the satellite radio on the seat next to his kit and picked up the handset. "Mongoose, Alley Cat, Oscar Mike."

In other words, "on the move."

The drone pilot's Texas twang came back through the handset. "I have eyes on. Mongoose, out."

Hilton's company-issued burner phone came pre-loaded with a playlist of music for the trip. He tapped the screen a few times, turned the volume all the way up, and dropped his phone into the cup holder. The sad harmonica riffs of Ryan Bingham's "The Poet" mingled with the high, diesel whine of his Hilux rolling off into the desert. If he recalled correctly, Mr. Bingham was also from Texas.

Hilton smiled to himself. Mongoose would approve.

ACKNOWLEDGMENTS

First and foremost, I want to acknowledge Jim Schlender and the team at Caribou Media Group for giving me the opportunity to bring my work to an audience beyond my friends, family, and colleagues. On that note, I'd also like to thank those same loved ones who continue to show nothing but immense outpourings of support, encouragement, constructive criticism, and thoughtful suggestions. Ben Sobieck's editorial work added a layer of finesse to both the grammar and narrative that I'm not sure I'd have entirely figured out on my own.

Perhaps biased by my own background and entertainment preferences, the accurate portrayal of battlefield hardware is important to me. Every vehicle, aircraft, piece of ordnance or tactical gear used by both Windsor Kraft Strategies and PMC Arkangel is real. While I've had years of experience as both an end user and evaluator to get my hands on most of this stuff, some brands went above and beyond to support the Windsor Kraft universe by loaning out gear, working with me on particular modifications, or allowing me a peek behind the curtain for products that weren't even on the market at time of writing, but will be by the time you read this, or shortly thereafter. In particular I'd like to thank:

- Buck Pierson and the leadership team at Staccato
- Kristen Gooding and her team at 5.11

- Aaron Quinn and Gabe Cabrera at Cobalt Kinetics
- John Bailey at EOTECH
- Travis Haley and the team at Haley Strategic Partners
- Andrew Wright and team at Surefire
- Jeff Quan at LAS Concealment
- Scott Lascelles and Ed Murphy at Colonel Blades (Stay tuned to the Colonel Blades website for the release of the Contingency Dagger mentioned in the story, which we are actively collaborating on at time of writing.)
- Chris Mudgett and Nate Gerhart at B&T USA (I'd also like to acknowledge that Nate currently holds the world record for reading the entire draft manuscript of *Close and Destroy*, coming in sub-72 hours, cover to cover. If that isn't a writer's best compliment, I don' t know what is!)

I'd like to extend deepest gratitude to some fellow professionals in the Special Operations and Intelligence communities—men who built their legacies in a world I was blessed to touch the tangent of, if only for a brief period. First and foremost among them, my friend and brother-in-arms, Ric Prado. Ric was one of the first "industry professionals" to look at the first few chapters and offer some immediate encouragement. It's somewhat serendipitous that, since then, Ric has become an ambassador for 4 Branches Bourbon, who I'd also like to thank here. Mike Trott, Rick Franco, RJ Casey and Harold Underdown all offered words of encouragement and the use of 4 Branches in a brief but meaningful cameo. Rick, I hope I honored the VMI legacy appropriately.

Finally, I'd like to personally thank both Eric Poole of *Guns & Ammo* and Iain Harrison of *RECOIL*. I would not be a professional writer in any sense without their initial faith in a then-untested junior Captain from the Cavalry who had been reading gun magazines since high school and couldn't possibly have fathomed making a legitimate career out of content creation in the firearms and tactical space.

If you're still reading at this point, I'd like to thank you, too. Content exists in a void without an audience who enjoys and connects to it. I look forward to the opportunity to interact with as many of you as possible, and continue to bring you more adventures from the world of Windsor Kraft.

A graduate of the U.S. Merchant Marine Academy at Kings Point, Tom Marshall spent more than a decade as a professional writer and content creator in the firearms and tactical markets. After several years as a staff editor at RECOIL Magazine, Tom moved into his current position as Director of Communications for Staccato. Before his writing career started, he served as a Cavalry Officer in the U.S. Army, managed security at a Bureau of Prisons community corrections facility, and worked as a private military contractor providing force protection services to American intelligence officers serving overseas. He deployed to Iraq for a year, and to Afghanistan 13 times in four years, as well as having worked in or traveled through nearly two-dozen other countries. When he's not behind a keyboard or a gun, Tom can usually be found within arm's reach of a cigar, a glass of bourbon, or a dog. Find him on Instagram at @tom.marshall.author and learn more about the world of Windsor Kraft at @windsorkraft on Instagram.